A Girl Like Moi

·

The fashion-forward adventures of Imogene

Written by
Lisa Barham

Illustrated by
Sujean Rim

SIMON PULSE
New York   London   Toronto   Sydney

A Girl Like Moi

The fashion-forward adventures of Imogene

For Mom & Dad

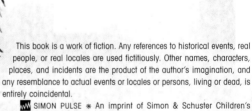

SIMON PULSE ✳ An imprint of Simon & Schuster Children's Publishing Division ✳ 1230 Avenue of the Americas, New York, NY 10020 ✳ Copyright © 2006 by Lisa Barham. ✳ All rights reserved, including the right of reproduction in whole or in part in any form. ✳ SIMON PULSE and colophon are registered trademarks of Simon & Schuster, Inc. ✳ Designed by Karin Paprocki ✳ The text of this book was set in Cochin ✳ Manufactured in the United States of America ✳ First Simon Pulse edition December 2006 ✳ 10 9 8 7 6 5 4 3 2
Library of Congress Control Number 2006922369
ISBN-13: 978-1-4169-1443-3 ✳ ISBN-10: 1-4169-1443-9

acknowledgements

I owe a debt of thanks to Valentina Zhou, for her inspiration and her long-distance translations. My heartfelt thanks to Frank Spina, who I unmercifully hounded with questions, and who was always graciously there with the answers. I would also like to wholeheartedly thank Andrea Pappenheimer for her unwavering support and friendship. Thank you Sheri Koones, Sarah Littman, Cindy Masters, and Leigh Rudd Simpson.

With sincerest gratitude and respect to my editor, Bethany Buck, for her enthusiasm, wit, and generous support, not to mention her laser-sharp editing.

Thank you Jen Bergstrom, Orly Sigal, Katie McConnaughey, Caroline Abbey, Lila Haber, and Karin Paprocki for her incredible book design, and everyone at Simon & Schuster who have all been fantastic to work with.

My thanks to the amazingly talented Sujean Rim, for her delicious art.

With deepest appreciation and thanks to my agent, Jodi Reamer, who, through her clear vision and creative insight made happen the fate of a girl such as I.

I could never have written this book without the steadfast support, consistent feedback, and sound judgment of my husband, Tom, whose eagle eyes (and lots of early mornings and late nights) made this book infinitely more readable.

Last, but surely not least, thank you to my son, Jack, who has made my every dream a reality.

prologue: *I, Imogene*

One thing about Greenwich girls is they're completely backward. I mean, to my knowledge this is the only town in the world where girls actually wear their Dior silk flowered sandals to school in winter (snow boots are *sooo* middle class), and fur coats through summer. Don't get me wrong—if I owned that superscrummy J. Mendel mink capelet Tinsley Vogelzang wore to school yesterday, I'd wear it in June too. (Of course, having a full-time driver with 24/7 climate control at her fingertips helps.)

The other thing about Greenwich girls is that they're *super*-spiritual. In fact, my school, Greenwich Country Academy, is higher consciousness to the zillionth power. Although, you absolutely wouldn't believe how much economic energy it takes to create an *aura* for oneself these days. One misstep can be utterly fatal. I mean, you wouldn't think so (and please don't repeat this to anyone), but it's not easy for a girl such as I. You see, a girl such as I is expected to be a trendsetter. If I'm not wearing the latest and greatest, I'm *not* the latest and greatest. I'm invisible: an amorphous non-being from a planet somewhere else in the universe — certainly not the one you and I inhabit. Lately, it's been especially challenging to keep up with one season, let alone four! We all know reputation is everything, and since I seem to be on everyone's see-and-be-seen-with list (due to the fact that I write the widely read "Daily Obsession" column for my school newspaper), it's my absolute sworn duty to uphold mine. Reputation, that is. I mean, people look up to me. What would they say if (heaven forbid) I walked into tenth-grade European History wearing an L.L.Bean Gore-Tex vest over my plaid uniform — with last season's Marni bag? (Perish the thought!) Hey, no problem for Kelly Winthrop — she's the captain of the lacrosse team. But for me? Well, I shudder to think about it.

But, who am I really? Well, lately I've been wondering that myself. On a physical level, some people say I remind them of a young Jackie O. Not that I listen to what some people say, mind you. But those same people to whom I do not listen also say I've got a certain *je ne sais quoi*, which — if you don't speak French — means that I simply sparkle!

I like to think of myself as a seeker. I mean, I know there's more to life than material things. Unfortunately, as of late my search for metaphysical truth has been strictly confined to shopping. (I guess more than three outfit changes a day isn't exactly a sign of inner peace, is it?) But while I was busy upholding my fashion-forward reputation, I guess I got a teensy bit carried away. I mean if there's one word you could use to describe me it's OBSESSIVE.

Like any obsession, my fashion fixation started innocently enough—a bit of Juicy Couture here, a little Miu Miu there, and of course, the occasional accessory. But it didn't stop at that. Next came the bi-weekly mani-pedis, the Japanese thermal reconditioning treatments, the deep cellular facials, the faux glows, and naturally, my Saturday morning teen Pilates class (the best for abs). And well, how could I deny Toy—my precious new French bulldog puppy—that little Burberry Nova Check trench? I mean it's the absolute cutest. Besides, without his trench he'd catch his death of a cold riding around on the back of my scooter all day.

Like I said, I may have gotten a smidge carried away. But I can't say it's entirely my fault. Because truth be known, acquiring, spending, splurging, indulging, frittering, and squandering must be in my genes, because like most of my fellow GCA (Greenwich Country Academy) classmates, I come from a long line of ancestors who did all of the above while employing the services of such people as chauffeurs, masseuses, maître d's, concierges, cobblers, maids, valets, couturiers, decorators, nannies, cooks, seamstresses, secretaries, room service attendants, bartenders, caterers, stylists, tennis pros, psychoanalysts, and a slew of others too numerous to mention. However, by the time I came along, those halcyon days were a thing of the past. Today, at *chez moi*, while everything on the surface may *look* right to the naked eye, beneath it all the foundation of my family's fortune, figuratively speaking, is a tad cracked.

You see, at some point in the early twentieth century, my great-grandfather, a large and somewhat looming figure judging from the portrait that hangs over our mantel, left France and brought his little family to the States with the intention of buying a little property, building a house on it, and settling down. Which in fact he did. I mean, he did buy some property (about fifty acres of lush farmland smack dab in the middle of Greenwich) and he did build a house on it (the size of a baronial chateau on steroids).

Anyway, just down the road from his house he built several smaller houses on the property, all of which were passed down to my grandparents and—almost—to my mother. The last and smallest house my grandfather built was the gardener's cottage, which was terribly charming. Larger than most would expect something called a cottage to be, it is now brimming with lovely family heirlooms, overstuffed chintz-covered furni-

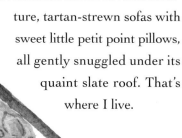

ture, tartan-strewn sofas with sweet little petit point pillows, all gently snuggled under its quaint slate roof. That's where I live.

My point is this: Even though my house is charming and roomy and all that, and through the eyes of most of the world would be considered quite lavish, by Greenwich standards we are practically homeless.

The rest of the property (you remember: fifty acres, huge baronial chateau) was donated to the founders of my school — tax deduction, hello! — which eventually became the first all-girls school in Connecticut. Oddly enough, what was formerly my grandmother's sewing room is now my chemistry class.

Needless to say, the founding fathers of my family — Mom's side, anyway — were quite affluent. Make that loaded! And, as far as I know, still are — which means by all rights, I should be too.

But you see, Dad was an artist to the core, and he was more than somewhat out of Mom's set. My grandfather, being very old-fashioned (or so I'm told, since I've never met the man), strongly disapproved of her choice. Not just because my dad was a painter, and completely creative, but because he didn't have the *pedigree* Mom had. And she had *beaucoup* pedigree.

Anyway, long story short, she married him. Don't get me wrong, I love my dad — he's amazingly sweet and hugely talented, and like I said, nothing if not creative. And he's always there for me. But that's sort of why I'm a *should have*. (See later.)

Well, the cottage was the first (and last) gift from my mom's parents to my parents. They completely disowned her after the wedding. So with her allowance, a small trust fund from her debutante days, and the money my dad makes from his art, we live modestly. This, I might add, has resulted in me having a tad of secondhand embarrassment for my parents due to a lack of any major outward signs of substantiality (aka wealth). I mean we still take vacations and everything—summers only. As opposed to most of my friends who winter in the Greek Islands or Ischia or St. Barths or ski in Courchevel or Aspen or some other completely fabulous place over spring break. And so while everyone else is off cruising the Mediterranean, I'm cruising the channel guide for reruns of *Project Runway*.

I guess the best way to look at things is to view life in Greenwich as a tale of two cities, comprised of the haves—A-list Super Socialites—ASS for short—who are social butterflies over the age of 19, and A-list Super Social-ettes—ASS-ettes for short—who are social butterflies under age 19. And the *have-nots*, who, for the record, will not be mentioned here. Then there's a third category comprised entirely of a minority of one. Which is *moi*: the *should have*: old money rich, cash poor. Not that I have anything against Greenwich or A-list Super Social-ettes or anything. I mean, some of my best friends *are* ASS-ettes! But I, for one, have *always* prided myself on being a shade outside of the standard ASS-ette thing. I mean, an ASS-ette doesn't worry about getting good grades, or about her future, or about much of anything else for that matter, because, unlike a girl such as *moi*, her future is set . . . *and she knows it!*

Fortunately, I had no desire to follow in anyone's footsteps—ASS-ette or otherwise. Which is where Evie, my very best friend in the entire universe, comes in. You see, for most of our lives, Evie and I had dreamed of a life outside the mainstream, of blazing new trails. In other words, we were ambitious. And even though Evie didn't share the same financial issues as me, at least I had a partner in crime—so to speak.

Which brings me back to where I started, and the burning question: So what is an ambitious, trail-blazing girl such as *moi* with a reputation relief fund on the verge of bankruptcy to do?

Well, up to now I had three secret weapons:

1) *The twins.* Babysitting the Andersen twins the last three years has been a great gig! At 3:00 Chester, the family driver, picks me up at school, twins in car (Maybachs are so comfy!). We swing up to North Street, where Chester drops us at the Ivan Lendl Tennis Center. Ivan grabs the kids. While they do tennis, I get to work. I promptly check my Sidekick for the daily deluge of e-mail for my fashion column, mostly from my network of private school stringers (thank you Friendster). I return e-mails, IM Evie, and, of course, get my homework done. Then we dash back to the Andersens', where I help the twins with their homework. When Friday rolls around, Elsa (the cook) hands me an engraved Smythson envelope containing my salary. Chester takes me home and all is well with the

world. Now, $150 a week may sound like a lot of money, but believe me, I earned every penny of it. I mean, the Andersens got more than mere babysitting services. Mrs. Andersen would have had the twins in Lacoste all year if it hadn't been for me turning her on to Fred Perry. In Greenwich you always have to stay at least one step ahead of the curve (or in this case, the *serve*). She was so grateful, she gave me a $2,000 Christmas bonus last year (which completely boosted my holiday spirit)!

2) *Estate sales* and preemptive raiding of GCA charity gift shop. I mean, this season's heavenly python Fendi bag? At $20 it's totally unreal! I mean, in Greenwich, vintage takes on a whole new meaning. As an unspoken rule, no A-list Super Socialite (ASS), or A-list Super Socialette worth her weight in Gucci would be caught dead wearing anything more than three times. (Given my current financial status, my personal "use-by" date runs a tad longer.) So finding a good sale is like winning all the toys in a toy store. I mean, just yesterday, I couldn't believe my luck. How often do you find 150 yards of Christian LaCroix hand embroidered chiffon draped, gathered, and ruched to perfection? Well I had to have it. You never know when you'll need a ball gown at the last minute. And if you're as deep a thinker as *moi*, it stands to reason that if you're going to be on the best-dressed list someday, you have to start looking the part today. I mean, it's only logical that what I buy today will be vintage in 10 years. And Lord knows what things will cost in 10 years. So if you think

about it, I'm actually getting a designer wardrobe tomorrow at today's bargain basement prices.

3) *Evie.* My third and ultimate secret weapon in the battle of the budget was my very best and sweetest girl-friend, Evie. We have this whole system down. It's called shop and return. Once a month we take the train into the city to shop the stores. Jeffrey, Barneys; Soho, Upper East Side, Lower East Side. Me for my fashion column, and Evie for her clothing collection. We sketch, photograph, and buy samples. Then we scurry back home, where Evie copies the pattern, sews it up, and voilà, instant Prada!

So up until now everything was just hunky dory. But alas, things change. First, Mr. Andersen was suddenly transferred back to Switzerland *avec les twins*, so my fashion fund went *pffffft*.

Second, let's face it, estate sales are not as hush-hush as they used to be. I mean everyone's into them now—yes (gasp!) even A-list Super Socialettes. And third, as for Evie stitching up Prada knockoffs *pour moi*, let's just say her father had other ideas for her which took up all her free time. Namely, a job at McDonald's. And as her best friend, I couldn't possibly let her take that after-school

job without me. Ergo, Evie and I put our heads together and figured out how we could make the most of a not-so-great situation. In other words, we had a plan. A big plan. Looking back though, the problem with us was that we just couldn't leave well enough alone. As serendipity would have it, that turned out to be a good thing because that's when fate came along and changed everything.

Heart,

Imogene!

chapter one

Plan A

date: JUNE 2ND

mood: ACCOMPLISHED

Bee called to tell me that my "can't-live-without" Corto Moltedo shoe order came in. $566 later, I must make a note to curb my accomplishments.

"C iao tutti!" (that's Italian for "hey y'all") I called to Toy while wobbling across our driveway that was covered by a billion pebbles. "Come on baby. What a big boy!" He ran to me, happily wagging his barely-there tail.

Toy came with my shiny new Vespa Granturismo (thanks Aunt Tamara!) at Christmas—or should I say Kissmas, because that's what Hugo and I were doing on the annual school ski trip. I mean when you're stuck at the top of the mountain with the absolute cutest boy from your neighboring boys school—well, put it this way, skiing wasn't all we practiced.

But that's ancient history.

Toy panted excitedly, his little tongue hanging to one side. Lucky for me, Toy loves going for rides. Aunt Tamara had a special car seat made for him that straps to the luggage rack and doubles as a carrying case when we're through riding. I could tell he was smiling. I mean, he is unequivocally the absolute cutest. And as an extra bonus, he's black, so he matches every outfit I own!

I reached into my bag for a doggie treat for Toy.

"Et pour moi, un petit four." I absolutely have *the* most wicked sweet tooth on the planet, next to Evie's that is, and *je t'adore* completely petit fours! Especially from France, particularly from Paris, and specifically from Pierre Herme, the eating of which is, I mean, a completely religious experience.

Evie and I had our Paris vacation planned from our first day until the last. My aunt Tamara has a sweet little pied-à-terre there. I mean, I've dreamed of France even before I knew it existed, and for the last 365 days, it was all I could think about. Of course our first stop would be Pierre Herme for petit fours galore, then we'll hop skip and jump over to the Jardin de Tuilleries, since there's no better spot for boy watching and feeling *soooo* French. And then because it's a mere stone's throw away, on to the Louvre and that infamous

Pyramide. And of course who could forget the Eiffel Tower, which is beyond *bon*, and then cafés, cafés, cafés, walks along the Seine, sculpture gardens, fountains, flowers in bloom, but best of all we'll go *shopping*! I could not wait!

With that lovely image in mind, I slung my "Queen of Couture" bag diagonally across my shoulder and dabbed a bit of Diorissimo behind Toy's ears while savoring the last lingering thought cloud of Paris.

"Uh-oh, where's your baby?" I asked Toy, who never goes anywhere without his blue bunny plush toy, Booboo. He picked Booboo up in his mouth. "Okay, are we ready, Toy?" I said, turning the key while trying to remember what to do once I got it started.

"All right then, is it clutch, shift, twist, clutch, gas? Or is it twist and go, or go and twist?" I sighed. Toy barked. He wanted to get moving. Frankly, just starting my Vespa gives me flashbacks. Which is exactly what happened.

Suddenly I'm smack dab in the middle of my first DMV road test. Dad is on the sidelines, alternately cheering and biting his fingernails. The tester is shouting instructions.

"Clutch, CLUTCH! Clutch first! Now shift. . . . NO! DO NOT BRAKE! Left turn signal. I said left!"

I mean, tense was an understatement. Long story short, I failed, despite the many hours Dad had spent coaching me. So he consoled us both by taking me out for a soda just like when I was little, when Sunday was *our* day, when just Dad and I would go to Lenny's Sweet Shop. It was an old fashioned drug store, with a soda fountain, a long counter, and stools that I'd twirl around and around on. We'd arrive, and everyone would say hi to us. When I was a kid, it seemed like we knew everyone in Greenwich. In those days Dad had an old Chevy convertible, which he kept it in mint condition. I thought it was the coolest. He'd open the door for me, and I felt like his most prized possession (I still do). He sold it a couple of years ago to a collector during one of his "slow" periods. I don't think he wanted to, but when you're an artist, life can be like that.

Anyway, over soda Dad said, "When you fall off the Vespa, you've got to get back on and ride." So with Dad's encouragement, I took the test again, and voilà—four figure eights, two four-way stops, a left turn signal, and a three-point turn later, I passed!

I checked the digital clock flashing on the dashboard. It was already 6:30 and as usual, I was late.

"Let's see, key, release brake, gas. That's it!"

Walking into Evie's bedroom was like walking into an ultramodern Japanese cartoon. Everything, from the bright red, lip-shaped sofa, the oversize, canary yellow Pikachu plush pillows, the fuchsia paper-cutout butterfly lamps, and the origami-inspired folding desk, to the enormous glittering silver disco ball dangling from the ceiling (a remnant of her bat mitzvah), was a not-so-subconscious nod to her bicultural heritage.

I found Evie sitting on the floor in the middle of her room in her usual state of flux, which is to say, half buried under a pile of fabric swatches and clothes. She peered out from a tangled bird's nest of pink highlighted hair that flowed to the top of her below-the-hip ultra-distressed Joey jeans. Her iPod speakers pounded out the Beastie Boys.

"Hey girlene!" she shrieked, standing up to double-kiss hello. Unlike the few freckles sprinkled across my nose and cheeks, Evie's freckles covered her from head to toe. A swag of muslin was draped toga-style around her pleasingly plump body, highlighting the cutest floral silk Sabbia Rosa bra. She was a sight.

"Check these out!" she cried, showing off her new white summer Moon Boots.

"Well, I guess it's official," I told her. "You really are a space cadet."

"Cute, right?" she said, picking up the Gummi Bears that had fallen from her lap. Evie is a major nostalgia-candy freak. At any given moment, one may find an assortment of Abba-Zaba bars, Sugar Daddys, Chunkys, and Good & Plentys scattered about her room, but her fave are Gummi Bears. Proust had his madeleines, I have my petit fours, and Evie has her Gummi Bears.

I dropped my bag on a pile of magazines and lifted Toy and Booboo out of the carrier and searched for a clear spot to sit down. Every square foot of her room (and there were lots of square feet) was covered with fabric samples, patterns, paintings, and hand-inked

design sketches. As long as I've known Evie, she's been cutting, shirring, ruching, silk screening, laminating, tea dying, tie-dying, dip-dying, slashing, ripping, twisting, layering, and beading her T-shirts and anything else she could get her hands on. She wears things rolled up, rolled down, backward, sideways, inside out, upside down, half on, half off. Grommets, rivets, embroidery, appliqués, pins, clips, buttons, and beads are just a few of her preferred embellishments. However pillowcases were her preferred medium. A quick snip here (head and armholes), an embellishment there, and voilà, instant Evie de la Couture.

Unfortunately, not everyone was enamored with Evie's talent. Her kindergarten classmates said she dressed like a freak. And, well, I admit it—I was one of those kids. That was until the school play: *Our Friends from the Garden*, a lighthearted romp about friendly, healthy vegetables. You know the one. Anyway, I got into a huge fight with my teacher about the carrot-and-brussels-sprout scene because she insisted that the carrot be made out of polyester. Everyone knows you can't mix a brussels sprout with a carrot anyway. The colors clash. Well, Evie, in one billionth of a nanosecond solved it completely, suggesting that the teacher replace those icky carrots with beets and volunteering some red crepe de chine she happened to have. Genius! So long story short, two things happened that day: We became best friends forever and have been plotting global style domination ever since.

Evie pointed at two dress forms in the corner. "These uniforms are going to be sooooo to die for!"

Enter the McDonald's Makeover Scheme, otherwise known as Plan A. This was the plan that was going to permanently change my finances and free Evie from her dad's illusions about her future in his restaurant business.

It all started the day Evie's dad got her the job at McDonald's. I mean she only took the job to make him happy, because Lord knows it's not like she needs the money or anything. And we decided right away that I would join her for moral support. Anyway, in the midst of slinging burgers and frying fries, we hit on a way to generously unleash our chicness on the world. And it was right there under our noses. We decided to do a complete makeover of McDonald's. Menus, décor, and most importantly, uniforms. This way Evie and I could demonstrate our overwhelming aptitude in, like, a real-world scenario. I could show off my style skills, Evie's dad would finally acknowledge her brilliant talent for fashion design, and our manager, Mr. Murray, would reap all the benefits—especially since his management review was coming up. So, we'd planned the whole thing for tomorrow, like the very the day of his review! Like a total surprise!

"Let me seeeeee!" I said, as I excitedly peeled the microscopically short new McDonald's uniform jacket off one of Evie's forms.

"I silk-screened the pattern by hand. What do you think?" she asked.

"*C'est tout ce que j'aime.*" (French translation? "Lovin' it!")

"This one's for Frieda," she said, wrestling to get it on. "It's a bit tight, but . . . well you get the idea. Right, Im?"

"Right," I said, pulling out a mini notebook from my bag.

"I brought the guest list. Everybody who's anybody is going to be there tomorrow."

My cell phone rang.

"*Oui*?" It was Dominique Day, who in the true spirit of GCA sisterhood had agreed to help with the décor along with a small coterie of her fellow DIYers. Dominique recently attained a community service merit badge in fret-free entertaining (specifically—advance party space makeovers). "Dominique says everything's set," I whispered to Evie. Then back to Dominique. "No, no, no, the trees go next to the booths—not around the tables," I explained, running through a few last-minute options. "For the flower arrangements, I think the hydrangeas with viburnium berries sound incredible and Dominique, please make sure you have enough bamboo to cover the windows too, not just the walls. And also, don't forget the cherry blossom stencils for the floors. We can do that in the morning, before opening, okay? Good. Bye, bye. . . . Air kiss, kiss to you too!" I said, clicking off.

"Everything's falling into place so perfectly." I was beyond excited.

I mean, if there were one word you could use to define us, it would be "resourceful." From years of living in Greenwich (like our whole lives), we were naturally overflowing with names of stylists, publicists, interior designers, stationers, party planners, florists, DJs ad nauseum to the the millionth power. So all we had to do was gather our old Filofaxes, search our old Treos, delve into our ancient Palm Pilots, rummage through our diaries, and before you could say "Gala Opening," we had the whole thing planned.

"Is Takeshi ready?"

"Yup. The menu's set. He loved your idea about the toro tartare, and he said to tell you that per your request, he's substituting lobster ceviche for the sea urchin pate. I mean ouch, you're so right about the litigious aspects of those potentially killer sea urchin quills."

"It's so sweet of Takeshi to do this on his only day off. Are you sure your father won't be mad that we hijacked his chef? Or about the money?"

"No way. After all, he's always wanted to get me into the restaurant business. I'm just showing a little initiative. He'll respect that."

"Great."

"Besides, that's what credit cards are for. He'll write it off as a business expense like he always does."

"Evie, it's really happening. I mean our future begins, like tomorrow! I mean, with your design genius . . ."

"And your styling genius."

"Not to mention tons, tons, tons of free press we'll get — well, how can we lose?"

"Best of all my father will finally take me seriously and let me apply to design school next year."

"And with the consulting bonus we're sure to get from McDonald's . . ."

"For sure."

"I'll be able to pay off my AmEx card right away. Before my parents find out. They'll probably even raise my spending limit,"

"Just in time for Paris!!!!!!"

"This is going to be the best summer ever!!!"

"Eeeeeeeeeeeeeeeeeeeeeeeeeee!!!!!!" we said, hands locked, jumping up and down and screaming with excitement just like we were five years old all over again.

Evie's housekeeper arrived with a tray of Chinese food.

"Thank you Fay Li," Evie gushed as the housekeeper left, closing the door behind her. "Dig in." Evie grabbed a spare rib from the Chaine d'Ancre Blue Hermès platter. "I really shouldn't be eating this," she said, pulling out a piece of food stuck in between her Invisalign braces. (Teeth fixed. Humiliation not included.)

I rummaged under some fabric for the TV remote and flipped it on.

"Thank God for *Full Frontal Fashion.*"

"I know," said Evie, slurping up more than a mouthful of lo mein.

"It really fills the void in between monthly magazine deliveries," I added sagely.

"And when all that's on TCM is a Doris Day movie." Evie's seen every Doris Day movie ever made at least three zillion times. "Oh, look!" Evie squealed. "They're replaying the Proenza Schouler show."

Proenza Schouler? I mean, at first I thought they were one person who came here from like, Cheko-slovakia or something, but it turned out they were TWO guys. Well, personally, they are utter genius but what kind of name is that for a fashion company? (And don't ask me how to pronounce it—it's a miracle I can even spell it! I mean, just when I was getting used to Badgley Mishka.)

"*Hellll-o*! That is *sooo* fly!" Evie said as the models hit the runway.

"It's super-fly!" I responded enthusiastically.

"It's insane!" she countered.

"It's hot!"

"It's *haute*!"

"It's happening!"

"It's hip-hop!"

"It's Courchevel!"

"It's more Cortina!"

"Couture is *sooo* where it's at!"

"Want it!"

"Need it!"

"*J'adoring* it!"

"I'm screaming!!"

"*Oooh girleeenaaaaa*, look!" Evie mumbled excitedly through her lo mein. "I want that hair! Whoever did the hair is a god . . . a HAIRGOD!" she continued, sloshing down gulps of diet Sunkist Soda while her fast moving chopsticks dribbled dumpling sauce down the front of her toga. At this point she could use a hair god, I thought, peering at her slightly fried, partially-corn-rowed, over-processed, brightly colored extensions.

"I think that's the 'new girl' everyone keeps talking about," Evie said. "Caprice something. She's absolutely *gorgissima*. I mean look at her, she's flawless. That honey skin, those bee-stung lips. Do you think they're real?" She frowned, her eyes glued to the 50-inch plasma screen. "That body deserves its own MTV show."

Here it comes. I mean, every girl I know has a touch of model envy—it's utterly rampant. Evie was no exception.

"I think I've been suffering from a false sense of adorableness," she sighed between spoonfuls of yang chow fried rice.

This is her pattern: We watch the shows, we scan the magazines. And five minutes later, Evie totally self-destructs.

"I was on my way home yesterday and just when I was thinking I was a total babe in my new Dsquared tee. I mean, I was totally channeling Jessica Simpson during the height of her cuteness. Then I caught my reflection in the bakery window and realized that I was a complete and utter *Glamour* don't."

"You're crazy!" I lied. The truth? Evie had issues with something very close to her heart, which was her stomach. Evie is a yoyo dieter for sure, and I could see that extra five pounds she'd put on right there around her middle, despite her crazy orange eDiet. I mean, how anyone could live on carrots, Sunkist diet soda, and Cheez Doodles for two weeks is beyond me.

"Oh really?" Evie grimaced. "I know the real reason Miss Simpson made me do those extra crunches in gym today. She thinks I'm putting on weight." I didn't want to tell her because I'd hate for her to worry, but of late, my secret to weight control was stress. It's a proven calorie burner—right up there with crushing.

In the midst of consoling Evie, my cell rang again and like a dope, I answered it.

"Hello Imogene, this is Miss Stevens from American Express."

Damn! Mental note: Next incoming call—utilize caller ID!

My head immediately started pounding; she had a way of calling at the most inconvenient times.

"Hello? Hello?" I said, recovering. "Is anybody there? Whoever this is, I can't hear you," I said, pretending to be out of range.

"I know you can hear me, Imogene," Miss Stevens said patiently. "We still have not received the payment you promised to send by—"

"Hel-loooooooooo, Mom? Is that you? I'm in a tunnel. Hello? Mom? Helloooooooooooo? Is anyone there?" I ripped the wrapper off a fortune cookie and crumpled it near the mouthpiece.

"All right Imogene, we can talk later," Miss Stevens gave in. "Please do try to make this payment. It's for your own good."

"Helloooooooooo?"

"We've known each other a long time, and I really would hate to report this to the credit agencies. Why don't you call me when you get out of 'the tunnel'—you know my number."

"Sorry Mom. I'll call you later." Click. Miss Stevens was gone.

"Ohmigod," I moaned, collapsing against a giant Pikachu.

"If my mother finds out about this, I'm going to be grounded for life."

Seriously, I really needed my head examined. Formerly at times like this, I'd call Mercedes (my therapist), but unfortunately, due to recent budget cuts, my shrink fund shrank. Maybe she'll take me back as a charity case.

Evie smiled at me sympathetically. "Did you miss a payment again?"

"Yup." It was my turn to be depressed.

"Don't worry girlene—it's all going to work out fabulously. One day, when we're the toast of the fashion world, we'll look back at this and laugh." She zeroed in on the fortune cookie in my hand. "Are you going to eat that? Here, I'll read your fortune," she said with a loud crunch. "'Chances are present to make huge personal gains.'" She turned the fortune over and continued, "'Learn Chinese: Spring Roll = *Chun Juan*.' Cool."

Fate Happens

d a t e: JUNE 3RD

m o o d: MCMANIC

*It's a jungle out there. Leopard, jaguar, zebra, giraffe, pony, cheetah. . . .
I mean, I've heard it said that the only thing that separates us from
the animal kingdom is our ability to accessorize. The thing of it is,
with all those choices, how's a girl such as I expected to make up her
mind?*

They came, they ate, we conquered. Well, at least that's
the way it seemed at first. On Thursday night, after
three months of planning, about 400 of Greenwich
society's crème de la crème converged on McDonald's with
the common folk to witness the launch of the official first
prototype of the New McDonald's.

"Oh my God, I can't believe it," exclaimed Fifi Mellinger,
whose voice floated over the sea of blond pony-tailed soccer

moms, ASS-ettes, and their prominent moms. She had just tasted the prior-to-now top secret hors d'oeuvres, which were filled with special sauce, lettuce, cheese, pickle, onions on a sesame-seed foccaccia.

"It's absolutely fabulous!" she exclaimed to her group who concurred, munching like a pack of sugar rushing, wide-eyed four-year-olds let loose inside a candy store.

Here it was, the day Evie and I worked so hard for and believe me, it was exactly as we imagined, only more so. If it weren't for the Golden Arches *outside*, you'd never know you were *inside* McDonald's at all. I mean, the menu was totally divine. I was salivating from the aroma of Takeshi's creations wafting from the kitchen. Behind me, gorgeous flowers, natural river rocks, bamboo walls, and cherry trees were stunning, creating a mood much like a Japanese meditation garden, minus the meditation. And gauging from the size of the crowd, it was the hottest ticket of the season. Truth be known, it was an absolute zoo!

"I got two trays of Mini McRawburgers comin' at you," shouted Assistant Manager Ernest over the row of whirring blenders filled with tropical fruit smoothies.

"We need more McCrabcakes, stat!" hollered Frieda, the resident octogenarian, as she heaved an enormous, lacquered tray onto the counter. "They're flying off the platters faster than you can say non-hydrogenated oil!"

"Excuse me, but . . . can you take my order now?" a deep voice muttered impatiently from behind a large Greenwich Lawn Care T-shirt. "I've been here fifteen minutes already!"

My cell phone rang—again.

"*Un moment, s'il vous plaît,*" I told my customer, smiling politely while attending to my phone. It was like the millionth caller asking for directions. I mean, what happened to good old-fashioned global positioning devices? "Okay, you're not far," I said. "Make a left on the Post Road, it's right across from the Ferrari dealer. *Ciao.*"

Having finished my *communiqué*, I looked my customer in the eye.

"Num-ber-four-and-Su-per-size-it!" he grunted, super-aggravated.

"Oh, that is so totally wrong for your type," I responded thoughtfully. "I'll bet you're an A positive . . . or possibly a type O."

"Whaddya mean I'm a typo?"

"Not typo. Type Ohhh."

"Ohhhh?"

"You don't know your own blood type?"

"No. But whatever it is, it's hungry."

"Well, just to be on the safe side I would suggest the number two Tuna Tartare meal—Iced Green Tea Smoothie included. And if you want my advice, I'd skip the fries. Go for the side of edamame instead."

"Edda who?"

"Trust me, it's you. See?" I pointed to the menu behind my head, admiring the beautiful calligraphied sign Roberto provided. "It's right there." His lips moved slightly as he slowly scanned the new canvas menu, tastefully draped over the old one.

While he perused the menu, Frieda returned with another empty tray.

"Will somebody get me a hairpin?!" she demanded, blowing a wisp of gray hair out of her eyes. "This blasted hat keeps falling off!"

Actually, it was a visor imprinted with Evie's tastefully abstracted Golden Arches logo re-do. I mean, the new McDonald's uniforms were to die for. Instead of the shapeless acrylic two-piece jobs that were so last millennium, Evie's uniforms consisted of four pieces: the visor, a pair of butt-skimming short-shorts, a bustier, and a skimpy, short-sleeve, portrait-collar jacket. It was absolute perfection. The new colors were a tribute to Lilly Pulitzer: pink lemonade, sunshine yellow, spring green, and white. Evie really knows her market. The logo was patterned overall into the stiff cotton pique. The new uniform was crisp, clean, and most importantly, super chic.

After receiving said hairpin from *moi*, Frieda leaned forward and propelled herself back into the party in her pink Prada patent leather ankle boots (thank you Grossman's of Greenwich!). Though not giving her the traction of her usual purple Keds high-tops, the boots did add at least three, albeit very unstable, inches to her petite stature. As she staggered past the front door, a loud commotion broke out.

"Hey, who's in charge here?!" barked an agitated Katie Couric look-alike pushing her way through the door. A halo of glaring white light from a video camera crew suddenly illuminated the entire room. It was like a UFO had landed, but instead of spacemen, what appeared to be a bodyguard, a producer, and—helllooooo—a very hunky cameraman followed in her wake.

"Do you know who I am? I demand you let me through immediately!" the faux Couric sneered indignantly to our door guy, Brian. (Ex-boyfriends can be very handy.) Poor Brian obviously couldn't find her name on the guest list.

"Outta my way!" she bellowed, plowing past him with the strength of a full back. "Let me through, I say!" she insisted. "Don't you know who I am?" *Ohmigod*, I thought. She doesn't even know who she is. I was genuinely concerned.

"That poor deranged woman," a nearby soccer mom added. Clearly I was not alone in my concern. I waved her over, past the highlighted mob, while frantically motioning Evie to join me.

"Yoo-hoo, over here!"

"Are you in charge?" faux Couric asked in her best, serious reporter voice. I scanned the room for Ernest, who was nowhere to be found.

"I guess"—I said, looking around in vain for a glimpse of Ernest—"I am."

"Good. Missy Farthington, Connecticut Eyewitness News," she said, extending her hand. "Get a shot of her, George," she barked at the hunky cameraman. "Is it true that after fifty years, McDonald's is debuting a new look—right here in Greenwich?"

"Well . . ."

"And"—she gasped—"a new menu?"

"I . . ."

"Who came up with the idea?" She shoved a Channel 412

microphone in my face and snatched a mini McRawburger from Frieda's tray. She was extremely dexterous. "And who designed the uniforms? They're . . . they're . . . mmm . . . YUMMY!"

"Yes, the uniforms are yummy, aren't they?"

"Not the uniforms! This . . . this . . ."

"McRawburger?"

"McRawburger! Wow!"

For a journalist, her vocabulary was somewhat limited. I yanked Evie into the spotlight and gave George the cameraman a big smile.

"This is Evie. She's the genius behind the uniforms." Evie blushed, trying to sidestep out of camera range, but I held her fast.

"Imogene, don't you know the camera puts on ten pounds . . . ," she hissed in my ear.

"Say hi, Evie," I said, ignoring her.

"Hi."

"When we first started working here," I explained, "it was clear this place was due for a major makeover." There's nothing the public likes more than a makeover, I mused. "I mean, a re-branding effort was long overdue, don't you agree?"

"Absolutely!" Missy chimed in, clearly having a limited vocabulary kind of day.

"Our market research indicated"—at this point I leaned in close to camera and spoke in hushed tones, implying top-secret, insider information—"that what the modern McDonald's customer really wants are gorgeous clothes, healthy and delicious food, and divine decor!"

"Amazing!" Missy beamed, munching her third McRaw-burger. "And who is doing this fabulous food?"

"Oh! That would be Takeshi Moritomo."

"Not the Takeshi Moritomo from Heshi in New York!"

"The same," I responded proudly, with a wink to Evie.

"I've been trying to get a reservation there for months," Missy murmured as a cloud of unhappiness passed briefly over her otherwise perfect features. "What's he doing here?"

"Oh, he's on loan to us. . . ."

"On loan?!"

"Oh, why don't you tell her about Takeshi, Evie."

"Uh, well . . . you see, my father owns this restaurant and . . ."

Evie is going to absolutely murderlize me later because, as everyone who's anyone knows (aka *moi*), Evie suffers the worst secondhand embarrassment when it comes to anything about her well-known father and his world-famous restaurants.

"Heshi? Your father owns Heshi??!!"

"Well . . ."

"Heshi Nakamoto is your father?!"

I could see where this was going. You see, as I was saying, Evie's father is like this really big restaurateur—New York, Tokyo, Los Angeles, that sort of thing. And everybody just dies for a reservation. Unfortunately, there's usually a six-month waiting list.

"Jimmy," Missy snapped at her producer, who was busy stuffing McHand-rolls in his face. "We've got a scoop here. This thing is big, big, BIG. It's national! No, it's international!

Call the studio; get a full crew over here—pronto! Move over Diane Sawyer, I'll be promoted to prime time for this one." Missy shoved me out of the way and was all over Evie like the LVs on her monogrammed Vuitton backpack. "Tell me, Ivy?"

"Evie."

"Of course. When did your father decide to partner with McDonald's?"

"Well, he didn't exactly. . . ."

"WHAT IS GOING ON HERE?!" the voice of the manager, Mr. Murray, bellowed over the din. Missy barked at Jimmy again. She was good at that.

"Jimmy, shut that guy up!"

Jimmy practically leaped on him. "Sir. Please keep your voice down. We're trying to conduct an interview—"

"What interview? Who are you people?!"

"We're with Channel Four Hundred and Twelve News." A look of complete panic swept over Mr. Murray.

"Have we been robbed?! Are we on fire?!

Missy spun around. Camera lights followed, blinding Mr. Murray.

"Look shorty, do you mind! I'm in the middle of a news story!"

"Story?" He squinted. "What story?! Who are you?!"

Missy's eyes narrowed. "You don't know who I am?"

I could tell by the look on her face that she'd had another lapse of memory.

"You don't know who you are?" Mr. Murray was completely confused now. It was clearly time for me to jump in.

"Oh, hi Mr. Murray!" I smiled.

"Who is this person?" snapped Missy. I slipped on my Chanel sunglasses before the camera spun back toward me.

"This is —"

"*I'm* the manager here!" Mr. Murray snarled. "And I want —"

"Manager?!" Missy glared at me, her eyes widening. "I thought you were the manager!" A blue-ish vein was beginning to pulse along Mr. Murray's forehead.

"You?! Manager?! Where's Ernest?!"

"Who's Ernest?!" A similar vein in a similar location began throbbing on Missy.

"Ernest is the assistant manager," I said calmly.

"He's in the back flipping the foie gras," Evie chimed in. Mr. Murray's mouth began moving, but no words came out.

Finally he belched in Evie's direction. "Foie gras?" He looked her up and down. "And what the hell are you wearing?!"

"Isn't it delish?" I smiled. Mr. Murray turned to me, the vein on his forehead now a shade closer to aubergine. (That's French for purple.)

"Where are your uniforms?!"

I know that change is a difficult thing for some people. Clearly, Mr. Murray was one such person. So it was just a matter of showing him how life-affirming change could be. After all, he should be getting that big promotion he's been talking about for the last three weeks any minute now. At least in theory.

"It's all part of the *new* McDonald's," I beamed. "Me and Evie didn't want to spoil the surprise! We knew you'd love it! I mean, you have to admit the old McDonald's was a tad . . . 'Old McDonald.'"

"We're runnin' low on the lobster ceviche at sample station two!" Frieda shouted into the kitchen.

"Lobster??? Lobster!!!!! What lobster? What samples? YOU'RE GIVING THE FOOD AWAY????"

"We're not giving the food away. We're sampling it." I said. "So that our customers—your customers—can experience the new menu."

"WHAT NEW MENU?!"

I was beginning to feel sorry for Mr. Murray. I mean, it looked as if his white collar and brown tie had tightened significantly around his neck. The vein on his forehead had gone neon.

"Oh, Miss, can I get another edamame?" The lawn-care guy was back.

"Sure!"

"It was really good. I'll tell my friends. . . ."

"Who's Edda?" Mr. Murray looked faint.

"Don't go there," I cautioned. Mr. Murray's face was ashen. I mean, he really looked ill.

"Mr. Murray, maybe you should have a green tea smoothie. They're very revitalizing."

He squared off in front of Evie and me, breathing heavily, clearly stressed. "Do you know what day it is?" I began to worry that whatever it was that caused Missy Farthington to forget her name, Mr. Murray had caught it. It must be contagious! I took a step back.

Evie followed.

"It's Friday, Mr. Murray."

"I know it's Friday," he seethed. "Do you remember what happens on Friday?"

"Shabbat?" Evie said.

"I warned you two. I told you both that today was an especially important day for me. The regional manager will be here in five minutes, and look what you've done!" he cried (literally).

"I can safely say that I am definitely positive that I'm picking up a somewhat negative vibe around here and that someone is unhappy with our upgrades." Evie had hit the nail on the head and I jumped in.

"That's precisely it, Mr. Murray. Our market research indicates that being twenty-six miles from the heart of the world's fashion center, you needed to upgrade your style to reflect the needs of the evolving marketplace. I mean, how else are we going to attract new customers? And new customers mean more money, and more money means promotion. Imagine what the regional manager will say about what we've done. You've done."

"Sir," squeaked Ernest bravely, appearing out of nowhere. "I checked the sales sheet, and our figures for today show sales up forty-five percent more than this day last year."

Mr. Murray stared at Ernest.

"Take that stupid hat off," Mr. Murray insisted.

"*Chapeau*," explained Ernest.

"Actually, it's a visor," Evie corrected.

"What?" asked Mr. Murray incredulously.

"It's a *chapeau*-visor," I mumbled.

"Ernest, get these two flakes out of here! And when you're done with that, FIRE YOURSELF!!!!" Overcome with anger, Mr. Murray proceeded to put an end to the Gala Opening.

"That's it!!! Everyone out, party over!!!" Mr. Murray announced. He then proceeded to storm through the room in a major huff, shutting down the DJ booth and shoving all the customers out the door.

"Well that's gratitude for you," said Evie, snatching the last piece of McSashimi off Frieda's tray. "But I'm not worried, because, thanks to our PR genius, in about one hour, we'll be all over the news and on every blog within three thousand miles of Greenwich." I couldn't believe her voice was so upbeat after what just happened. "We'll be famous!" she continued as Mr. Murray bolted the door shut behind us.

As usual, when I got home, Mom was sitting in the kitchen at the French marble-topped island staring at our perpetually-on, portable JVC while rummaging through her weatherproof Martha Stewart Faux Bois Garden Tote Bag, which matched her Faux Bois Garden Boots. All A-list Super Socialites, and especially Ex-A-list Super Socialites like Mom, are Martha Stewart devotees. I mean, Mom actually cried when she went to jail! Like Martha, Mom absolutely adores gardening. Unfortunately, despite her best efforts, Mom has a black thumb. Our once proper English garden was now, well, let's just call it "ecologically friendly." Dad and I just pretend it's lovely. After all, if it weren't for denial, we'd all be insane.

Mom pulled out a bottle of spearmint extract—a clear indication of an impending ulcer flare-up. Though why a 38-year-old woman would use spearmint extract to tame an ulcer was beyond me.

So I decided right now wouldn't be the best time to tell her about McDonald's. Not that I had to, because the familiar voice of Missy Farthington was, to my complete annoyance, blaring from Mom's TV and doing a very thorough job of informing her for me. I crept into the foyer as the voice of Mr. Murray ranted and raved about the destruction of an American icon.

Clearly "out of sight, out of mind" would be the best strategy at a time like this, so I made for the stairway, hoping to avoid—

"Imogene!" Mom called out. She was using the Tone, the one that made me feel like I was three years old again and had just colored in all the flower motifs in her cream on cream French damask wallpaper (to this day referred to only on the rarest of occasions as The Incident). I mean, what else does a three-year-old do with a brand-new box of 64 Crayola Crayons? Especially a three-year-old such as I, born with overactive creative genes vibrating at maximum intensity.

"Imogene, come down here this instant!" Translation: Go directly to the living room, do not pass go. That's where our "family discussions" always took place. By the time I dragged myself downstairs, she was already in her spot on one of the overstuffed sofas. The decor was a combination of traditional family heirlooms mixed with Dad's sculptures and paintings. Years ago, in deference to Dad, Mom replaced her tasteful collection of Edward Lear mid-19th century parrot illustrations with Dad's huge and somewhat odd paintings. Odd because most of the time, we couldn't make out what they were. If you squinted, you might think that they looked like carnivorous monsters with cone-shaped heads and huge fang-like teeth dripping with blood — or huge flowers. Beautiful, though somewhat jarring. To say Freud would have a field day is an understatement. So I guess that really proves Mom did marry him for love, because anyone who could swap those gorgeous parrots out for Dad's paintings, ruling out insanity, must be completely in the grip of the real thing.

"This can't be right," Mom said, her brow furrowed, lips tightly pursed. "Please tell me this isn't right," Mom persevered. I didn't have a clue what she was talking about. Or what she was holding in her hand.

"As if the McDonald's debacle wasn't enough for one day, and I assure you it is, I just received a call from a lovely woman named Miss Stevens who faxed me this." She waved a piece of paper in my direction. Suddenly all I could hear was a whooshing sound in my head. I closed my eyes and took a deep breath. I couldn't bring myself to open them, because then I'd have to look at my credit card bill with that miserable little box at the bottom right-hand corner, where I'd see a figure just north of my annual GCA tuition, sans financial aid discount.

"You remember Miss Stevens, don't you?" Mom asked sarcastically. "She's your American Express account representative," she said, switching to her I'm-going-to-stay-calm-no-matter-what voice. "Apparently you know each other quite well." Only on rare occasions was I speechless. This was one of them.

"How could you have been so irresponsible? You know that card is for emergencies only!"

"They were emergencies, Mom,"

"Really?"

"Fashion emergencies!" As soon as it slipped out of my mouth, I regretted it; thankfully she ignored the comment.

"Look Imogene, I am perfectly aware of how vulnerable you girls are today to material temptations, but this is way beyond comprehension. It's completely outrageous! What sixteen-year-old spends this kind of money in just a few weeks?"

"But Mom, I needed some things . . . clothes and things."

"Didn't you ever hear of the Gap? What's wrong with the Gap?"

Unlike her garden, I knew her ulcer was now in full bloom. "You must realize how reckless this was! When were you going to tell us? When they carted you off to prison?"

"Mom, aren't you being a tad dramatic?" I tried diffusing the situation. "They don't have debtor's prison anymore."

"Well, what if they did?! What would you do then?!"

Mercedes, the shrink I could no longer afford, would say that I'm still struggling with some "inner conflict." It's true, I'm more than a little angry sometimes. I mean if Mom hadn't married Dad, I wouldn't be in this mess. And I wouldn't need an after-school job to make ends meet. We'd be like all the other Greenwich families, and life would be a lot less complicated. Although I guess that's a stupid argument, because I mean, if there was no "them," there would be no me.

"When you wanted a cell phone, we said you'd have to babysit or take some sort of after-school job in order to pay for it. We felt you were up to having that much responsibility. And you were. And we were very proud of you. Because of that and since you did so well in your financial management course at school, we felt that you were ready to have one credit card, with the understanding that you would completely manage your own expenses. We didn't expect you to go on a binge with it."

"But, I—"

"Well, you are not getting off the hook this time."

"What do you mean?"

"You don't think your father and are I are going to pay this, do you?" Before I could reply in the affirmative, she said, "I've worked out a payment arrangement with Miss Stevens, who has generously agreed to a slightly lower minimum monthly payment. By my calculations you will be done paying off the balance in two years. And if you stick to it, your credit record will remain clear. Of course this means no more charges on the account at least through the summer."

I didn't like where this was going.

"Summer?! But I'll be in—"

"And you can forget about your trip to Paris!"

"WHAT?!" I shook my head. She couldn't have said what I thought she said.

"You heard me, no Paris!"

"Are you joking?! You can't cancel my trip to Paris! I've been looking forward to it all year. No, all my life!!!" Okay, pass the spearmint extract, quick.

"Maybe you'll learn a lesson and finally begin to grow up."

"Mom, pleeeezzzzze," I said, in my best three-year-old whine. "I'm too young to grow up."

"Furthermore, I've contacted Nini Langhorne's office and enrolled you in the GCA summer intern program. They have a few openings left and Nini has agreed to be your parent advisor."

"You called Nini?!" I said, extremely embarrassed. Maybe if I swallow her whole bottle, my brain won't remember any of this when I wake up tomorrow morning and it will all have been a bad dream. "I mean, what is this? I don't get a say in my own life? I don't need a *parent advisor*."

"Obviously, you do!"

"Next you'll be marrying me off to the highest bidder!"

"What a good idea!"

There's that sarcasm again.

"We'll use the money to pay off your credit card . . . assuming anyone would want you."

"Ha, ha, very funny." I hate sarcasm.

"Here's what you are going to do." Mom was in full control now. "Miss Stevens has recommended debt counseling and I've agreed."

"Debt counseling?!"

"Please don't repeat everything I say."

I almost repeated that.

"If we told you once, we told you a thousand times: There

are no free rides in life. You are sixteen years old now. Old enough to know right from wrong."

We already covered this.

"But since you can't seem to manage that, we've taken the matter into our own hands. Once a week you're going to attend a meeting of . . . well, for fiscally challenged people."

Oh God. I was sinking fast.

"Got it?"

Post-traumatic stress syndrome was beginning to kick in. All I could do was stand there with my mouth open. "Imogene, you are going to learn the meaning of responsibility if it kills you."

"Does Dad know?" I asked, praying he didn't.

"Of course he knows," she continued, "and he's very upset."

Dad has always been sensitive when it comes to me. I mean, usually, of the two parents, it's the mother who cries when their child takes her first step, loses her baby teeth, gets the lead in the school play, etc. But in my case it was always Dad.

"And don't disturb him. He's in his studio, finishing the Hartmann commission."

As I skulked into my bedroom, Toy jumped up from his bed to greet me. His little legs and oversize ears made him look half dog, half bat. He was carrying his threadbare Booboo. I knew he wanted to play. Unfortunately, I was feeling about as flat as my size 8 pink Repetto ballet slippers. (Not to go off on a tangent or anything, but just so you know, pink were for polite Greenwich girls like I; black were for bohemian East Village rebel types. Of course, Evie's were black.)

"Oh, Toy," I cried, picking him up for a cuddle. He licked the tears from my face. "Where was my big strong guard dog when I needed him, huh?" I said. Around his neck was an antique Hermès silk scarf that I'd tied into a loose pompom. Another gift from Aunt Tamara. She found it at the Marché aux Puces in Paris—the best flea market on Earth.

Which completely reminds me, I'd better e-mail her to cancel Toy's fitting at Le Bon Marché. How did things get so screwed up? I tried contemplating a shiny, happy designer label parallel universe. It didn't work. Rather than dwelling on my dim future, I decided to finish my column, because whatever the opposite of *joie de vivre* is, it was setting in fast. Dumping the contents of my backpack, I plopped down on my bed and jacking the Cyber-shot into my gorgeous Titanium PowerBook, I got to work. As GCA's cultural chronicler and all-around cool hunter, I consider it my responsibility—make that my sworn and unalienable duty—to provide guidance and clarity to those individuals who are a tad confused and/or otherwise befuddled by the myriad of choices that plague modern girls. So, working fast, I laid out all the photos in iPhoto. Thankfully I had snapped enough pictures to more than cover my column for this last issue before summer vacation. It would only take another few minutes to uplink everything to the GCA website. I reviewed it one last time.

Hey all!

AS SUMMER STARTS, LIKE, ANY MINUTE NOW, IT'S time to blow the dust off your shekels, which I'm sure won't be a problem thanks to your cash-infused trust funds, and update your look. Why not begin by getting rid of that old stuff from last season. Remember, when you were the too, too chic ingenue channeling a young Grace Kelly? Right down to the pleated skirt and printed round-toe pumps? (Thank you Miuccia Prada.) Well—newsflash—as much as we loved them then, they are soooooo OVER! That said, here's my current list of must haves:

- Do you believe in God-dess? I'm a recent convert. Try sexy and drapey for night and for day as well.
- A Goddess needs gold—sandals that is! I choose Gucci.
- The gold bag to match my sandals. Ouch! (Real metal!) So <u>moderne</u>. So streamlined.
- And some Indian jewels. Mmmm! Mumbai!
- Mmmm! Makeup. No makeup. Neutral is a natural, so go for that golden, just-back-from-Jaipur look.

And, let's not forget color: White is the new black. . . . Orange is the new red. . . . Pale yellow is the new powder blue. . . . Twenty-two karat is the new gold. . . . Brown is the new neutral. Pinks rock, greens go everywhere, and flowers rule!!! And of course, the black AmEx Centurion card is the new platinum!!!

<u>Mon Dieu</u>, I almost forgot beauty tips:

- Ta-tas are toast! The new silhouette requires a more modest figure. Big bonus: no more conjuring up those tiresome old explanations for why your bra size suddenly increased three sizes over the summer.
- Forget poor old Dr. Atkins—Color-Coding is the key to good health. Blueberries, blackberries, and raspberries have amazing antioxidants, which prevent aging. And while we're on the subject . . .
- To keep your chin from sagging by the time you're 18, touch your nose with your tongue 50 times a day.

Now for your e-mail questions:

DEAR IMOGENE,

The influx of greens and blues in this season's clothing makes me feel as if I'm back on Capri or yachting around one of our Greek islands, and I'm feeling absolutely giddy enough to spend my entire trust fund all at once. My mom says green looks best on blondes with dark or olive skintones—unfortunately my complexion is fair. Seeing you're such a color authority, which color is right for my skin tone? And lastly, how do you suggest I spend my money? Do you have a charity of choice?

Sincerely,

FLUSTERED PHILANTHROPETTE

DEAR FLUSTERED,

I detect a tremor of parent distrust. To answer your question, your mom is probably lying to you. Yes it's true, shades of blue and green are popping up all over the place. But watch out, styled incorrectly, green can leave you looking green-around-the-gills, and feeling seasick, queasy, nauseous, jealous, and just plain ill, no matter what your complexion. As far as your unfortunate super-abundance of cash, let me remind you in plain English that charity begins at home. To that end, I am presently accepting personal styling appointments and have reserved a private consultation for you at my in-house atelier. Cash only, but in an emergency I will accept cash cards to the following: Jeffrey, Bergdorfs, Prada, Chanel, and/or Barneys.

Well that's all for now. Wishing you all a wonderful summer. <u>Tanti baci a tutti</u>!! (Which if you have to ask, means "kisses y'all"!!)

Heart,

Imogene!

I lit a black Diptyque candle (a remnant from an extremely short-lived Goth phase). For the first time ever, my column felt flat. The effervescence was just was not there, which was starting to really freak me out. So I decided to do the only logical thing: sulk. Which for me meant indulging my sweet tooth with the last of the Pierre Hermé petit fours while watching *Breakfast at Tiffany's* —my instant antidote (second only to lip gloss) for what I call "the gloomies."

"I know I have it here someplace," I said out loud, scouring the shelves behind my bed while Toy bolted under it. "Rats!"

Note to self: Next Netflix order—*Breakfast at Tiffany's*.

That does it! Flinging open the double French doors, I stepped into my walk-in closet—my refuge—where I kept all the things that had meant something special to me at one time or another. I went for my never-fail, guaranteed-to-make-me-happy-and-forget-everything things that I've had since preschool—my Hello Kitty collection. I pulled it all down off the triple deep shelves: T-shirts, change purses, pins, watches, hair clips, jewelry, stationery, hats, wallets, key cases, even my Hello Kitty suitcase. Instead of the usual rush of soothing nostalgia, I felt only a slight uptick on the happy scale.

I continued rummaging further through everything else in my closet—the clothes, the shoes, the bags. Finally I pulled out my old scrapbooks. (Yes, geeky as it sounds, I scrapbook.) I sank down on the thick pistachio green pile carpet to lose myself in the images from my past.

There were pictures of me, Aunt Tamara, and Mom and

Dad in front of Big Ben wearing Union Jack T-shirts. There was Mom in her garden, Dad coaching my 4th-grade lacrosse team. Wow, me and Dad snorkeling; me holding up giant starfish on a beach in Eleuthra; Mom and Dad, dressed up as Cruella de Vil and Lord Byron for Halloween; Dad in his studio—his clothes covered in paint, and with an old paint brush pinched between his upper lip and his nose like some crazy moustache, which made me laugh. Then I turned over an old picture of my parents. It was faded and a little fuzzy, but I could tell they were standing in front of our house. Mom looked so young and pretty. She was smiling gently at the baby that she held snugly in her arms. Dad was smiling too. They both looked so proud and happy. Suddenly all I wanted to do was go back in time and be that baby again.

I picked up the last picture on the floor—it was a picture of the 1950s ribbon and lace floor-length gown and bolero jacket that Aunt Tamara and I found in a London thrift shop last summer. I brought it back for Evie. She surprised me with her own version of it, naming it Audrey (she names all of her dresses, mostly after old film stars), a gift for me to wear this summer in Paris. But I guess I won't be wearing it after all.

The tears were unrelenting now.

Finally I slammed the closet door and, rushing to my bed, started throwing everything from my bed back into my backpack when I felt my cell phone vibrate. It was Evie. "OHMIGOD." I totally forgot to call her!

"Where've you been, I've been dialing your cell phone like crazy!" she said, not letting me get a word in edgewise. "The worst possible thing you could ever imagine happened to me when I got home. Promise you won't freak out. For one thing, I'm not going to Paris with you this summer!" She burst out crying. "Can you imagine that? Paris—the center of the universe," she said through hiccuppy sobs. "The birthplace of haute couture, the land of Lagerfeld, the last bastion of civility on the planet . . . and I'm not going!"

She was inconsolable and I began to feel crummy all over again. "I mean, no visit with Aunt Tamara, no LaCroix, no Louvre, no Ladurée! No Ritz, no Eiffel Tower, no Left Bank, no Lenotre raspberry tarts! And no stinky cheese! Paris—the only place left on Earth where cheese is good and gyms are bad!"

"It's all completely and utterly *tragique*!" her quavering voice sputtered. "My dad finally snapped." I could almost see the tears streaming down her freckly face. "He's making me work at the restaurant in New York with him— FOR THE ENTIRE SUMMER! All I ever wanted to be was a designer. He's got that stubborn Japanese father disease and there's nothing I can do about it. I think he's always resented the fact that he doesn't have a son to carry on the family business. But now, well—he totally jumped off the deep end, and my chances of going to design school are over. My *life* is over. O.V.E.R.!"

"Well, that makes two of us, because I'm not going to Paris either. Not only because of today. It turns out Miss Stevens and my mom had a long talk. She even faxed her my credit card account statement!"

"Oh no, what did your mom say?" she asked, still sniffling.

"Two words," I said. "Nini Langhorne."

"Nini Langhorne? What about Nini Langhorne?"

"She's my new parent advisor."

"What?" she said, emphasizing the *t*.

"For my internship."

"What internship?"

"The one Nini is going to help me find. As of now, I am officially enrolled in the GCA Summer Intern Program."

"Imogene, the only GCA internships are like working for the library, checking in books and unsticking the gum from under the study tables and things like that. If you don't believe me, just look what happened to Sima Smithers."

Even though it hadn't yet begun, I couldn't wait for summer to end.

chapter three

Life BH

date: JUNE 11TH

mood: CARPE DIEM—

which, in case you don't know, is Latin for "take advantage of every opportunity that fate sends your way because you never know when the next one will come along."

I mean I look at my life in two chapters: Life BH (before Hautelaw) and life AH (after Hautelaw). Anyway, I guess all the charity thrift shop shopping I'd done in my life must have earned me some extra karma points, because I was about to hit the jackpot.

It was 10:45 Saturday morning and between us, I was really beginning to wonder if I'd end up like Sima Smithers, interning at the Greenwich Health Department. All day long, Sima looks at ticks. Ticks on dogs, ticks on cats, ticks on birds, ticks on kids, ticks on ticks. I mean, looking at ticks all day long would drive a girl such as I completely bonkers and I'd probably develop a few of my own.

Or maybe I'd end up like Michelle Sutz, who is doing her internship at the Greenwich Town Hall and has undertaken the daunting task of sending out 175,000 beach cards with pertinent information like where to put the parking sticker on your car. But her boss doesn't want her to spend her whole entire internship stuffing envelopes, because Tuesday is filing day and that's when Michelle gets to alphabetize the change of address forms. Strictly nervous-breakdown time. I mean, the stress would drive me straight into a straightjacket. (With no label. Can you imagine?)

Well, it seemed like everyone in the GCA Intern Program had found an internship. I on the other hand, had not. Of course, it's a given that ASS-ettes don't concern themselves with such matters. Being the daughters of deposed royalty, shipping magnates, and Wall Street tycoons, they've always had *arranged* internships. Their destinies, like their Super Social mothers before them, lay in the elite corridors of money, fame, and power. Oh, and in case you were wondering, A-list Super Social-ettes don't spend summers cruising the Mediterranean anymore. In modern ASS-ette circles, that kind of thing is totally *démodé* (meaning over, and entirely five minutes ago). ASS-ettes are working girls now. I mean, it's the absolute trendiest.

FYI, the A-list Super Social Internships were broken down as follows:

- **Sotheby's**—notorious for hiring ASS-ettes due to the fact that it's a built-in direct pipeline to their A-list Super Social parents.
- **Literary agencies**—which require that you actually read.
- **Office of a US Congressman**—completely fine, but . . .
- **Office of a US Senator**—considerably better.
- **Private banks and hedge funds**—don't stink either.
- **Magazine internship**—I shall say no more.

Oh, and before I forget, just in case you're wondering how to spot an authentic ASS-ette, here are a few clues:

- The colors may vary, the silhouette might change, but the labels? Never. Look for **Dior**, Chanel, Valentino, **Prada**, Bulgari, and Cartier.
- They live within a 25-mile radius of **Bergdorf's**.
- Their boroughs of choice are: Manhattan, the Upper East Side, Greenwich, and the Hamptons.
- While they cannot darn socks, sew buttons, or open vacuum-sealed jars, they rarely have problems with **champagne corks**, digital hotel keys, or **caviar tins**.
- They don't wear Wonderbras. Stilettos and

silicone afford enough personal enhancement for their taste, thank you.

- They follow the **Golden Rule**. That is, accumulate it.
- They suffer from amnesia (when it comes to manners).
- They enjoy the great outdoors, especially from the front seat of an **Astin Martin DB9** convertible, but they never pitch tents.

Well, never mind them. They'll all eventually graduate and ultimately marry powerful, multi-billionaire corporate raiders and have fashion collections, jewelry lines, television shows, charities, and tabloid scandals of their own.

By June first, the A-list Super Social-ette girls were completely snatched up. But, well, no one snatched me up, because the type of company I'd be interested in didn't do any snatching. On reflection, I may well have been clinically depressed. However, it only took a thirty-second call from Evie to restore my mental balance. It happened right there on Greenwich Avenue just as I stepped into Scoop for the third time that day. I mean, I almost lost consciousness, and not because the Temperley dress I'd been jonesing for had finally gone on sale.

She was so out of breath I could hardly understand her. "Girlene, listen to me! You've got to call Nini. Quick, fast, and in a hurry!"

"What are you talking about?"

"I just left school . . ."

"What were you doing at school on a Saturday?"

"I had to drop off my research paper—listen to me, 'cause I've gotta go in a second. I just passed the intern job board and saw the posting."

"What posting?"

"There's a new intern posting on the board that is perfect for you!!! And, it's in New York. We can both be there this summer! Me working for my dad, and you working for this fab company. . . . Girlena it's so you!!!" she screamed. "It's writing! And spotting trends! Just like your column!"

"OHMIGOD! What else did it say?!"

"It's at a fashion forecasting company called *HAUTE-LAW*! And it's a *paid* internship. Hurry, Im, and call Nini. Tell her you want an interview immediately, before someone else gets it. I have to go; my dad's waiting for me in the car. Call Nini now!!!"

I hung up, reeling. Ohmigod, I should have asked her to take it off the board before someone else saw it!

Well, needless to say, I called Nini immediately, but she was out (A-list Super Socialites always are). I left a message. I was sure she'd call me back after hearing my offer to walk her dog for life, iron her countless Porthault linen sheets, trim her 160-yard English hedge, dust her 7,000-bottle imported-from-Umbria wine cellar, and polish her extensive James Robinson silver collection—*for life*.

A mere ten minutes had elapsed since Evie's phone call, but by the time I reached school the doors were locked. I just had to get that posting before someone else saw it first. So I zipped home at maximum speed and ran up to my room, jabbing redial on my cell. This time Nini's housekeeper answered, only to inform me that Nini wasn't due back until late Sunday night.

Rats. I decided to be proactive and send a note to Hautelaw after Google-ing them like crazy. And not to go off on a tangent or anything, but at this juncture, in case you didn't know, the word *haute* in French is pronounced "out" (especially if you happen to be Canadian). Although it's really anything but, because it means "the ultimate" as in what Haute Couture is. So all in all, even though Hautelaw is pronounced "outlaw," it's so totally clever that it's completely *in*!

I found out everything I possibly could about them. I researched backgrounds and read anything and everything I could find. It seemed that everyone who is anyone — from Dolce & Gabbana to Ralph Lauren, from Christian Dior to Versace to Prada—had one thing in common: HAUTELAW.

The more I learned about Hautelaw, the more I realized Evie was right: I belonged there, because a girl such as I has style by the bucket loads. I always knew on a molecular level, deep inside, instinctively, that I was destined to make a name for myself in fashion. The place at which I was going to do that was *the* hottest fashion forecasting company in the world, Hautelaw. Unfortunately, one thing stood in the way. The weekend. So after two days of massive obsession, numerous e-mails, phone messages, research, hope, and prayers, my passion went on life support. By Monday morning, I was a psychotic mess. It was six a.m. when Jimmy, the school custodian, arrived with the keys. I had been there since five. I have to admit I didn't 100 percent believe the posting, even after Evie read it to me. I had to see it with my own eyes, because secretly I felt that anything that great and still available was as improbable as stumbling across a fully let out Fendi Fur in the middle of the Target coat department.

But there it was, just as Evie said, pinned to the bulletin board next to the teachers' lounge, squished between the Greenwich Hospital posting and the one for Greenwich Library tour guides:

Very Last Minute Summer Intern Additions

Although 99.9% of our young ladies participating in the GCA Internship Program have already been placed, here are a few last-minute additions:

Greenwich Library: Special Projects Coordinator. Duties include: coordinating guided tours, photocopying, and sorting returns. Expert knowledge of Dewey Decimal System a MUST.

Hautelaw, Inc.: Exclusive international, New York fashion forecasting firm is looking for bright, intelligent, enthusiastic, fashion-forward individual for FULL-TIME paid summer internship. In-depth fashion knowledge and writing skills a plus.

Greenwich Hospital: Needle recycling program. Entry Level intern. FULL-TIME. No experience necessary. LOCATION: Greenwich. SALARY: 0. Requirements: none. Latex gloves provided.

All candidates MUST be 16 years of age by June 1st. If interested, please call Mrs. Nini Langhorne: 203-555-1111 before June 7th.

I ripped it off the bulletin board and shoved it in my pocket fast, and once again phoned Nini.

Everything A-list Super-Socialites plan, think about, and do is for charity—in fact, they are completely full of it. Charity, that is. You could even say they were saviors of a sort, because their charities were usually things like Save Greenwich, Save the Sound, Save Greenwich Library, Save Greenwich Hospital, Save Our Schools. Unfortunately, for all the new saviors making their way up the ranks, the only charities left to champion were diseases. And Lord knows, all the good diseases were taken. But for those still available, the unspoken rule of thumb is: If you can pronounce it, you can have it.

The reigning queen of all A-list Super Socialite saviors was Nini Langhorne. My family's connection to Nini goes way back. She and Mom were best friends throughout their GCA years, until Mom met Dad, that is, and you know what happened there. Nini on the other hand went on to marry George Langhorne III, heir to the Langhorne Hotel fortune. When it was time for me to start school, Mom was insistent that I carry on the GCA tradition, even though we no longer had the disposable income to send me there. Enter the benevolent alumni association, headed by—guess who—Nini, who has seen fit to provide me with financial aid throughout my academic career at GCA, where I'm quite a novelty, because you see, they now have a real live charity case at very close range, which makes them quite pleased.

Well, I know I balked at first, but now that Nini was my assigned parent advisor, I felt at least I had a chance at a decent internship—meaning Hautelaw. As I lay in bed placing the cucumber slices over my eyes, I vowed to convince Nini at all costs that the Hautelaw they're looking for is I, Imogene.

"NINI!" I shouted, flooring it, as the shiny black Range Rover flew up the back-country road, passing me *and* the 160 yards of trimmed-to-perfection prize-winning continuous Juniper hedge. I followed her into the imported, Belgian block, walled courtyard.

"Nini!" I shouted again, not taking my eyes off of her as she emerged from said Range Rover. Behind her stood an enormous French Normandy starter castle. In the distance one could barely make out a well-hidden tennis court, a six-car garage with a shuttered, ivy-covered guest cottage above, and an enchanting ivy-covered pool house, which sat in front of the still-as-glass fifty-foot-long swimming pool.

Nini slammed the car door just as I squeezed the hand brakes (Yay! I was finally getting the hang of it), and she returned my greeting, deftly sidestepping my front wheel, though nearly tripping into the one of the potted topiaries that lined the path leading to an arched interior court-yard.

"Nini, I have to speak with you—it's a matter of life and death!" I said, flipping down the Vespa kickstand fast and scurrying to keep in step with her.

"Imogene, how nice to see you dear," she said, reposition-ing the cream-colored TSE cardigan just so, over her shoul-ders, and endeavoring not to appear annoyed as she marched toward the house. "But I'm sorry, I can't talk now."

"But Nini—"

The medley of diamonds, blond highlighted hair, cash-mere, and stilettos that was Nini shushed me, stopping cold to answer the Swarovski Crystal covered cell phone as it chimed "Oh What a Beautiful Morning."

"But, I—"

"Shh, Imogene, please," she hissed in a sharp whisper, covering the mouthpiece. "It's my pre-interview segment producer from *The Today Show*."

It had been all over the papers and gossip columns: Nini was in pre-production with a major television net-work to host her own reality TV show, which was to be shot in New York, Greenwich, and the Hamptons late this summer. In the series, entitled *The Champagne Life*, Nini will introduce a group of unpolished people to her A-list Super Socialite world of good grooming, cultural events, and exclusivity. One lucky contender will end up with a new job, wardrobe, and car, a rent-free year in an exclusive Park Avenue penthouse, and of course a complimentary consultation at the Silver Hill Clinic if, by the season finale, it is deemed necessary.

"In life each of us is dealt a hand of cards," Nini intoned to the producer, who was no doubt listening raptly on the other end. "This is my chance to help a few young people change their lives," she said, sauntering slowly toward the front door. "It's all about empowerment. And for me it's such good karma."

Huh? I mean, who needs karma when you're renovating your Irish castle and maintaining at least three homes on two continents and your personal net worth is more than the GNP of a small Western European country. I mean, really!

Nini whispered to me in between sound bites that she couldn't talk just then and I got the distinct feeling, as she slammed the front door, that she was trying to get rid of me. But I was relentless. I mean, if there were one word you could use to describe me, it would be "RELENTLESS." (Did I say that already?)

When Nini finally opened her front door again (my finger was actually getting numb from pressing the doorbell), she said, somewhat exasperatedly, "Listen Imogene, the network is throwing a little party for me at Soho House tonight, and if it's really that important to you, we can talk there."

OMG. Well, like, I almost freaked.

"I mean, Soho House? Ohmigod!"

Well, just so you know, platinum cards are *sooooooooooo* five minutes ago. The latest and greatest card of choice is the private club card. (It's absolutely the new black!) And the private-est of private clubs was Soho House.

"Yes, Imogene, Soho House—I'm afraid that's the only time I can spare. We can talk about your goals then. Ask your mom if that's all right with her."

"I'm sure Mom won't mind, Nini. I'll see you tonight!" I said, dashing back to my scooter.

"Imogene," Nini called me back, extending a card with teeny embossed gold script, "you'll need an invitation to get in."

"Oh yes, thank you," I said. "That would help."

Mom at first said no, then after much begging, yes. And she *just had* to call Nini to verify she'd be taking me home (how embarrassing). Much outfit anxiety, a major wardrobe confab with Evie, and an emergency last-minute mani later, I was ready to go. Heels, handbag, cell phone, lip gloss: check! Mom handed me an extra twenty-dollar bill and we hopped in the old Jeep (more embarrassment), and a few minutes later she saw me off at the station—or rather, insisted on waiting with me until the 5:40 train arrived. After a hyper-impatient journey into the City on the slowest local train ever, I dashed to the cab stand outside Grand Central, hopped into the second cab after cutting off a bunch of tourists who didn't seem to be paying much attention anyway, and at precisely 6:35 p.m.,

I found myself at Soho House, ready to discuss my destiny with Nini.

D on't look now, but isn't that Kirsten Dunst over there?" I asked the white-gloved waiter as I skoshed a glass of sparkling water from his immaculately lacquered tray. I absolutely adore freebies, especially these days.

"Like I could care," he murmured, and huffed away.

Said celebrity was at the far end of the room holding a camera phone at arm's length and photographing herself. Which usually means one of three things: 1: Mobile shopping, i.e., while trying on clothes in one's fave retail establishment, unaccompanied by one's best friend, one clicks self-pix, sends via e-mail to one's best friend, and awaits best friend's response. 2: Major self-love. Or (perhaps I was witnessing the birth of a new trend) 3. Stars cashing in on their own celebrity by snapping and selling their own pictures. I decided to confab with Evie.

I dialed her number while I scanned the hall for Nini. Soho House was divine. Green crystal chandeliers gave the room a warm, intimate feeling. In the corner, an enormous Chesterfield sofa was crammed with a bunch of deeply tanned, heavily bejeweled, heavily be-bosomed vintage glitterati—clearly Beverly Hills escapees. Waiting for Evie to pick up, I gazed out the huge picture window, which had the best view of lower Manhattan I'd ever seen. The city lights twinkled brightly and mixed with the reflection of the party inside, with my image superimposed over the whole thing. At that moment everything seemed possible.

Affirmation to self: I am about to embark on my mythical journey.

Tonight, I stop starring in my own personal version of *Survivor*. In fact, tonight my whole life is about to change!

Evie finally picked up. Yay!

"Hey you, what's going on?" I asked.

"Hey girlena! Are you there? Is Soho House *SoooHo-happening*?"

"Ohmigod! Beyond! For one thing, the room is jammed with the most inutterably chic people," I said between sips. It was true. Small cliques of A-list Super Social types mingled with model types, who hung out with famous-looking mogul types, who occupied the only other seating in the room—probably the VIP section. "I absolutely love New York!" I said.

Another waiter buzzed by and I snatched an interesting little *amuse-bouche*. Clearly quick reflexes were required to obtain proper sustenance.

"It was a nightmare getting in, though," I continued. "I mean, they even scanned my fingerprints."

"Wow," Evie sighed.

"I wish you were here. The place is just swarming with celebrities. I mean, you know me, not that I'm into that or anything. But I just saw that what's-her-name, from *The OC*, and Kirsten Dunst, who was like three feet away from me! It was unbelievable . . . and, ooohhmigod, you're not going to believe who just walked in the door. . . ."

"Who?"

"Donatella."

"Donatella Versace?" shrieked Evie

"The same!" I shrieked back quietly. "She's sparkling brighter than a Christmas tree!" I mean there must be at least a thousand mega-watt-mega-karats dripping off of the famous fashion mega-star. (PS: Now I know why she's in such good shape because who needs a gym when you're hauling your own portable ice palace around all day long.)

"Listen girlene," Evie's frenzy started to rise, "you have to make Nini give you that job. Besides the fact that it's so totally you, it could do more for your social status than a season's worth of air kisses from the Hilton sisters!"

I was getting psyched—*again*. "Evie, sweetie, I have to go," I said, lunging for the same white-gloved waiter as before. "I'll call you back right after, okay?"

"Okay. Don't forget. Break a leg, girlena!"

"Thanks. Luvya!" I clicked off just as a waiter appeared and held out an offering.

"What's that?" I asked pointing. I could tell that he resisted rolling his eyes.

"Tiger shrimp salad with chili paste, pickled cucumber, and lime leaves," he sighed. "Would you care to try it?"

"No thanks." Lime leaves are so last season. I opted instead for the beet tatin with marlin carpaccio.

By 7:15, I was getting a tad concerned about Nini's whereabouts, not to mention the fact that milling around the room all alone was beginning to affect my smile, which is not a good thing when a girl's destiny is at stake. So when the sea of people momentarily parted, I dove for the suddenly free table nearby. Just as I sat down I felt a tap on my right shoulder.

"Do you mind?"

I turned around to find her looming menacingly—one hand on her hip, the other running a French manicured finger back and forth through a 22K gold horse-bit link necklace. Though she could be my age, developmentally, I could tell we were poles apart. With her big blond hair (think a young Pamela Anderson), wraparound Gucci sunglasses (hello, the sun set, like two hours ago), Gucci horse-bit print dress, and roach-killer stilettos, she hovered above me, power personified. She was accompanied by, I presume, her *nontourage*—two underdressed friends, who were seemingly joined at the hip. One was channeling Lindsay Lohan for sure, while the other, judging by her snarling Chihuahua and vacant stare, was a Paris Hilton wannabee.

"Hello?" she said in a tone that demanded immediate attention. She slapped her bag onto the table directly in front of me. "This table is reserved."

"Are you talking to me?" I asked.

"Well, duh," she said with an avalanche of attitude. "I'm not in the habit of talking to people I don't want to know, but just this once"—she looked me over disdainfully—"I'll make an exception."

Well, I couldn't help thinking that Soho House (which, by the way, is not, I repeat, *not* in Soho) had really lowered its standards.

"Yeah," said the redhead in an English accent that sounded a trifle more Manchester than Mayfair.

"You go girl!" affirmed the Paris Hilton wannabe.

"I don't think any of these tables are reserved," I said politely, hoping Nini would show up and rescue me.

"Look Dorothy, you're *not* in Kansas anymore," said the blonde, "so why don't you just do as I say and take a hike. This is my table!" She pointed a long, French-manicured nail tip in another direction.

I could tell she was about to have a complete hissy fit, which was the last thing I wanted to be part of at this par- ticular moment—especially with Nini out there somewhere and my destiny still up for grabs. I stood up to leave when another perfectly manicured hand pushed me back down into the chair.

"Is this person bothering you?" a deep, velvety voice with a decidedly New York–meets–Puerto Rico accent broke in. I stared at first in awe, then in disbelief, because OMG, it was Caprice, that model Evie and I saw on *Full Frontal Fashion.*

"Well, I . . . ," I said, not knowing what to say. My knight in shining sequins turned her gaze to the blonde.

"Begone, you hideous witch, before someone drops a house on you!"

How did I get trapped in a scene from *The Wizard of Oz*?

"*Mira,*" she trilled at my blonde assailant, completely ignoring the other two, "if you're looking for free food, the trough is over there." Caprice snapped her head toward the kitchen. The blonde narrowed her eyes for a split second then recovered, smiling as if nothing had happened.

"Oh, Caprice," she oozed, "don't get your extra large knickers in a knot." She smirked.

In person, Caprice's figure was a lot curvier than it seemed on TV. Clearly, the focal point of her otherwise perfect model-thin physique was her derriere. I mean, there was no getting around it. Literally. It had a vibe completely unto itself.

"It speaks!" Caprice returned the smile, choosing to ignore the insult. "Perhaps we can teach it to do a trick. Like disappear." She waved her hand dismissively at the fiend.

"You have the most delightful sense of humor," she replied. "It must be something native to Bronx girls."

"What's amusing, Brooke, is that girls from the Upper East Side think they own the entire city." So the fiend had a name.

Note to self: In future, avoid this Brooke person at all costs.

The two stared each other down for what seemed like forever.

"Okay Caprice, luckily for you and Dorothy here, our friend is holding court at another table, right girls?"

"Right. Completely," the wannabes affirmed.

"You can keep this one—it's in Siberia anyway," she gloated.

"Yeah," echoed the wannabes. "Totally!"

"But *you* haven't seen the last of me," Brooke said, eyes squarely on me. "I have a long memory, and if I ever see you again, I won't be quite so accommodating." She slinked away, leaving me to process the current events.

I couldn't help wondering why Caprice came to my rescue that way. She sat down and I just gawked at her. Evie was right, she's gorgeous! Preternaturally gorgeous! I felt like I was staring into the face of a goddess. She stared back for what felt like an eternity with the darkest doe-like brown eyes I'd ever seen. Tossing her gloriously shiny black hair over her shoulder, Caprice signaled to a nearby waiter.

"I can't believe you let her talk to you like that," she finally said.

"Oh, well, I . . ."

The waiter appeared with a tray full of goodies, which Caprice perused at her leisure as he stood by adoringly.

"She has a lot of nerve. I've seen her do that at other clubs—her and her ridiculous Wolfe Pack friends. I just couldn't let her get away with it this time."

"What's a Wolfe Pack?"

"Just a bunch of girls who hang with Candy Wolfe and think they're better than everyone else, that's all. Actually, I'm surprised they ventured out without their lead dog. . . . Anyway, I hope you don't mind that I did that—you looked like you needed a friend," she said, piling a ton of shrimp onto a tiny plate. She smiled back at the enraptured waiter and dismissed him with a gentle wave of her hand. "Besides, you remind me of my little sister."

"Really?" I said, beyond flattered.

"Yeah. I really miss her sometimes. She's still in Puerto Rico." Caprice's expression turned sad, and I thought it best not to ask any questions, so I said, "Well, I think I just made my first enemy. Great way to begin a new life."

"Oh, don't worry about her. She's just full of hot air. Are you new to New York?"

"Kind of. With any luck I'll be doing an internship here for the summer. What about you? Are you from New York?"

"Oh yeah. The Bronx," she said, throwing her neck back to devour a piece of shrimp, "via Puerto Rico."

"Did I just see you in the Proenzzz . . ." (I'm clearly still having a problem with that one.) "The Oscar de la Renta fashion show?"

"Oh, that was a few months ago. Yeah, Oscar's real good about giving young Latinas a break, but I haven't exactly broken through yet. To say I have an unusual figure for a model is an understatement, in case you haven't noticed. But I'll get there one of these days."

I noticed her yummy gold charm bracelet and to fill the conversational void said, "I love your bracelet."

"Thanks, I got it at a sample sale last year. Actually, I'm going up there again Friday—the designer is a friend of mine. Why don't you meet me—I'll introduce you. It'll be fun."

"Really? I'd love that!"

"I've got some appointments in the morning, but I'm free after twelve o'clock. Here's my number," she said, pulling out a cute little Kate's Paperie minipad and matching pen. Models are so cool—they always have things like that in their bags.

"Okay, great!"

"Oh, what's your name, by the way?"

"Imogene."

"I'm Caprice.

"I know."

"Nice to meet you, Imogene." She stood to go.

"Nice to meet you, too," I said, spotting Nini at last. I waved and she headed over, drink in one hand, cell phone in the other.

"Imogene, I've been looking everywhere for you."

"Hi Nini," I said in the sweetest voice imaginable.

"Listen, Imogene," Caprice said. "I gotta run now — it's my rule to be in bed by midnight before a morning of 'go-sees.' A girl's got to get her beauty rest, you know." Caprice giggled. "See you Friday!"

"Bye Caprice . . . and thanks."

"Don't mention it."

Nini sat down and said, "I don't know if you're quite right for the Hautelaw internship dear."

I froze. I mean, I really didn't expect her to say that. No one has ever thought I wasn't right for something before, especially when it came to fashion. Clearly she needed to be convinced.

"Of course I'm right for this Nini," I said. "I am absolutely the most right person for this! I have a very passionate personality. And I feel one should really follow their passion. And I don't feel any passion whatsoever for any internships other than Hautelaw," I continued enthusiastically as she nibbled at her paté, pondering my words. "I mean if there's one word that defines me, I would say it's 'PASSIONATE'!"

"Got it," said Nini, finishing off her chocolate martini. "Well dear, your 'Daily Obsession' column *is* adorable. It's fresh and young and I think your perspective would be of some interest to my friend Spring Sommer. And of course your recent McDonald's work was quite . . . innovative."

"Thank you."

"But this internship requires a level of maturity. And commitment."

"I'm committed. For sure, I'm committed." Well, at that point, they could have had me committed, for all the anxiety this conversation was causing.

"When you go out into the work force as a GCA intern, you are a reflection of your entire school."

"Yes, Nini, I know."

"This particular internship is full-time and the hours can be long. So a commute is out of the question. Do you have a place to stay in the city?"

"Of course, that's all taken care of," I lied.

Note to self: coordinate apartment confab with Evie.

"Well it's lucky for you that Spring Sommer is such a close friend of mine. That position has already been filled by a more senior gal, but because they've recently moved from London, I know they could use a bit of extra help, and Spring has agreed to make a spot for you—*if* she likes you, that is. Things might be a bit disorderly for a while, but I'm sure you will have no trouble fitting right in. I've arranged the interview for eleven o'clock tomorrow morning. Does that work for you?"

Every girl in the GCA Intern Program gets an interview day. "It's perfect!" I shrieked.

"That's fine, dear."

Then Nini, in all her Cartier-double-strand-necklace

(with pearls the size of golf balls) splendor, proceded to give me instructions on how to dress and behave during my interview. "The dress code is relatively reserved, but definitely fashion-forward. Chanel, Lanvin, Balenciaga, Zac Posen, or any top designer, all get the green light. As for shoes, Jimmy Choos always delight, as do Manolos. As far as manner goes, chewing gum is a definite no-no, as are hair brushing, tooth picking, nail biting, lip glossing, message texting, and cell phone answering. Acceptable topics of conversation—for this particular interview—are: Atlantis, transcendental meditation, UFOs, handwriting analysis, longevity, reincarnation, recent advances in time travel, and hunks. Non-acceptable topics of conversation: basket weaving, bunions, musk melon farming, new cures for acid reflux disease, the life cycle of chickens, philatelics, verb conjugation, the subatomic structure of rubber bands, and car mechanics—unless in direct relation to hunks. Any questions?"

"Uh . . ."

"Good. Now, your internship requirements for school are as follows: You must keep a time sheet and a journal to document your experiences." I was about to ask her about the journal when we were interrupted by the squeal of one of Nini's fast approaching acquaintances.

"Nini! Nini Langhorne! I haven't seen you in an age, and oh my what you've been up to . . ."

"Kitty, darling . . ." Nini and Kitty air kissed hello. It's a little known fact outside of her set, but Nini actually invented air kissing.

"Imogene, sweetie, would you excuse us, I just need five

minutes." She paused in midthought, plunged her hand inside her purse, handed me the ticket, and said, "On second thought, be a dear and have the valet pull up the car. We'll discuss your future in more depth on the way home."

I squeezed my way through the crowded dance floor and was standing near the door waiting for an opening, when I felt a searing pain in my foot. When the offender stepped off my shoe, I guess I went a hair bonkers. You'd think after all those *Sex and the City* reruns, people would have more respect for a girl's shoes. They only cost the absolute earth!

"I'm so sorry," acknowledged the desperado, who was definitely channeling Enrique Iglesias. I peered in anger, first at him, then in the direction of my feet.

Great, I thought, scanning for damage, I'll only be dining with "The Colonel" a year to pay for them! Fortunately, the damage was minimal.

"Please forgive me. Did I hurt you? I am sorry," he said, seemingly sincere, while homing in for a closer look.

"It's not my foot, or my feet. . . . It's my new shoes." I mean, how annoying.

"I would be honored to repair them," he said in earnest with a detectable accent. His brownish black hair was somewhat disheveled, as if he'd just thrown the long sleeve faded Gap T-shirt over his head without checking the mirror after. I noticed that the color of his shirt matched his deep Adriatic blue eyes perfectly.

"I guess they're fine," I murmured. Then he said something truly amazing, and I quote:

"I should have been more careful. Corto Moltedo, right?"

He knew about shoes! How can that be? Well, I guess his accent was from Mars, because what Earth boy ever recognized the designer of a girl's shoe?

"They're beautiful," he smiled, "as are you." Whoa, I was totally off balance now.

"Did you know that *chun juan* means "spring roll" in Chinese?" Ohmigod, did that just come out of my mouth? Could I say anything more stupid? I popped a melon-flavored Aqua Mint in my mouth to keep it occupied.

I mean, it's no excuse that going to an all-girls school gives little opportunity to interact with boys—unless you count the annual Spring Fling, co-sponsored by our all-boys sister school. But that, like all co-ed school events, was heavily chaperoned and the boys usually stayed with the boys and the girls with the girls.

"So what are you doing here?" I finally managed to say.

"I'm here with a friend," he said, smiling from ear to ear.

"Hmm." I studied his knee-weakening dimples. To be perfectly honest, while my heart was supposed to be on hiatus, my hormones were working themselves into overdrive. Lately, and this is strictly hush-hush, despite everything else that was going on in my life, boys had definitely become a distraction for me. And while we're on the subject, the constant bombardment of hormones on the prefrontal cortex of my brain wasn't helping my conversation skills much either.

"It sounds like you know a thing or two about fashion."

"I love fashion. Although when I'm home, I rarely have a

chance to leave the factory, but I'm crazy to see it on people,"
he said.

"Oh—you're a factory worker?" Great. Just my luck to
have a potential new crush on some poor factory worker,
albeit a well-informed one on the fashion front. I mean, as if
I have time for that kind of distraction right now.

"Yes, I help my family out by working in the factory
when I have time off from school."

I decided to put all that aside, and concentrate on his
accent which was totally blowing my mind. I mean an accent
really ups the desirability quotient. Ask any girl.

"Oh, that is soooo cute."

"What's cute?"

"Well, your accent of course . . . I mean . . . not that—"

"You are making fun of me."

Oops, there go my conversation skills again.

"No, no. It's just that I was just wondering where you're
from. Are you from Spain?" I asked, popping another melon-
flavored Aqua Mint in my mouth, just in case.

"No, but close," he said, tauntingly.

"Hmm," I said directly to the now-famous dimples. "Oh,
you mean like Portugal?"

"No, no, no. Eeee-taly," he corrected me gently.

"Ooooooooh. Eetaly, I just *j'adore* Eetaly. Are you just
vacationing here?" I asked, fishing.

"Umm, not exactly. . . . I'm actually taking accelerated
high school courses so I can start college here in the fall,"
he said, reaching over my shoulder to rest his glass on the
bookshelf behind me. He was so close I could smell his

accent, which was completely intoxicating. Here's what else I think he told me, though I barely paid attention to his words: He's starting college in the fall; he likes house music and plays soccer with his friends; and whenever he goes back to Italy, he watches his soccer team almost every Sunday. He also likes cooking, as, he says, do all Italian guys; and finally, Italians prefer their girlfriends be tall and slim and well dressed. Like me, of course.

"Oh, how interesting," I said inhaling him. A gold necklace dangled free from inside his shirt. It had some writing on it.

"What does this mean?" I asked, lightly touching his necklace.

"This?" He smiled, holding out the chain for a better look. "Roughly translated in English, it means something like . . . 'live, laugh, love.'"

"Oh, how completely corny!" I teased, rolling my eyes. He laughed.

"And what's this?"

"This?" I asked, rolling my right hand over the Cartier "love" bracelet Aunt Tamara gave me when I graduated middle school.

"No, this," he said, pulling gently on the red string, which I've worn around my left wrist for the last two years. Kabbalists say the string protects us from the evil eye. It also helps remind one to refrain from negative thoughts, which, I can attest, is working brilliantly.

"It's my protection."

"Protection? What do you need protection from?"

Well, it crossed my mind that what girls such as I need protection from are boys like him, who look as if they've broken the hearts of a million girls like *moi*.

"It's just something I've worn for a while now," I said, hoping to de-emphasize the red string thing for the moment.

"So, when class are you in at what do you go to school?" he asked in charmingly fractured English. The question didn't make any sense to me, but I was grateful that he took my hint to change the subject. I took a moment and reached down to rummage blindly through my bag for my lip gloss and sneak a peek at the message window on my cell phone, a talent we multitaskers have absolutely perfected.

"Can you hold this?" I asked him, handing him my cell phone while attempting to locate my missing-in-action lip gloss.

"Do you always do that?"

"What?" I said, smearing on a glob of Addict. "The lip gloss?" I suppose I was a bit nervous. That's generally the second reason I find myself reaching for my lip gloss. Okay, so I'm lying. I admit it — I'm crushing.

"No, I mean change the subject," he continued.

"Do you live in New York?" I said, changing the subject. "I mean when you're not —"

But smack in mid-sentence, out of nowhere, he kissed me, just like that! Time stopped and I felt firsthand the raw power of galaxies colliding. My soul had left the building and traveled to an eternal realm beyond time and space. And the aforementioned heart I'd forgotten about for so long suddenly reminded me it was still there. It was the kind of kiss that made you want to keep kissing forever. It was a kiss that I secretly hoped would happen one day—different from anything I'd ever known.

We paused to take a breath. My heart was pounding so hard that I wondered if he could hear it. And then it hit me like a bolt of lightening: It's official, I am no longer in love with Orlando Bloom! I felt like I was either going to laugh out loud, or cry when we stopped for another momentary breath. Lungs refilled, we resumed, and had my life ended then and there, it would have ended in a state of perfect bliss. But alas, a far off voice brought me jarringly back to reality.

"Making friends so soon, Imogene?" she asked as my soul re-entered my body. But that voice was now recognizable as . . .

Ohmigod, how totally embarrassing! Nini! I pushed myself away from him, trying to look as cool as possible. She eyed the boy carefully.

"Hello. Have we been introduced?"

"Uh, Nini Langhorne, this is my friend . . . uhhhh . . ." *I DIDN'T EVEN KNOW HIS NAME!!!*

"Paolo," he said smoothly. "*Enchanté*, Madame Langhorne."

"A pleasure," she said, turning toward me with raised eyebrows.

"Well Imogene, I expected the car to be ready to go by now, but obviously you've been distracted," she said, reaching expectantly for the garage ticket in my hand. I was flustered beyond belief!

"We have to go, Paolo . . . ," I stammered as Nini held my elbow and torpedoed us through the crowd and into the warm night air of my brand-new life. He tried to follow, but the path closed fast behind us. I turned around for one last glance, but we were moving too fast and he was out of sight.

The entire way up FDR Drive, while Nini was droning on about how exhausted she was from the interviews she gave and how much her eyes stung from all those flashbulbs, I couldn't help smiling out loud. But I was feeling both sad and happy, and the danger sirens were blaring. I mean crushing is one thing, but this was a tad stronger. It was probably for the best that I'd never see him again. I mean I don't believe in love at first sight. In fact I don't believe in love. But something happened the minute I laid eyes on him. Like some kind of weird chemical reaction went off inside me.

I made a mental note. I am without fail sticking to my plan. I will under no circumstance: 1. worship, 2. adore, 3. obsess over, 4. crush on, 5. forsake meals for, 6. be distracted by, 7. lose sleep over, or 8. find irresistible anyone — especially him.

I dug into my bag to text Evie while Nini talked on. I needed an escape hatch desperately, and then it hit me — OMG! I left my phone at Soho House . . . with him!

chapter four

Plan B

date: JUNE 21ST

mood: RED

I used every drop of willpower in me to resist wearing my red patent-leather Lanvin bag until September, but I felt so sorry for it all alone in the closet, I just had to let it out.

S o today was the day of my fate-altering interview. I'd found a nice, quiet two-seater on the 10:10 Metro-North express to Grand Central—which wasn't exactly express, I noted each time the train doors opened to pick up passengers between Port Chester and 125th Street. Anyway, I decided that writing in my journal was a helpful process for dulling the ache that tapped at my heart. Unfortunately, though, my concentration wasn't concentrated. All I could think about was him—and how I was going to get my phone back.

I mean, how on earth is any normal sixteen-year-old, red- (or in some cases blue-) blooded American girl expected to live without a cell phone? Calling it was no use, because all it did was ring. He probably tossed it in his sock drawer or something. My Sidekick was useless, because Evie was spending the day with her father in the restaurant and he never tolerated interruptions.

I tried again to refocus my mind on my journal. Well actually, the journal requirement of my internship fitted perfectly with my agenda, since I planned to have a very big life, starting any minute now, and it would be completely horrible if this gloriously fabulous life went unrecorded. I began to think, what if I was writing a book about *moi*? Yes! It took less than a nanosecond to begin, and about one minute after that to fall asleep. Apparently a night at the Soho Club, a kiss from an Enrique Iglesias look-alike, and the anticipation of a life-altering interview had robbed me of a good night's sleep, and I made up for it on the train.

awoke as my train pulled in to platform 24, which is my favorite platform because you only have to walk two steps and you're right in the middle of Grand Central Terminal. A good omen, I thought. I entered the main hall and cast my attention on the emerging trend stories in the crowd milling through the Great Hall, as revealed by following the stream of thoughts bubbling inside my brain:

Yummmmmmmm. "Trench Connection." That new Chanel trench is so delish. Bye, bye, Burberry! Yup . . .

hmmm. Like, "Totally Waisted" by a Gucci purple Lizard Belt; so D.O. "Bohemian Rhapsody." Talk to me Roberto Cavalli, talk to me! Fashion flash: The hippie is back! Hmmm, actually, I don't think it ever left.

As for my own fashion statement this morning, I had taken Nini's interview-wear advice to heart and was dressed head to toe in a red Lanvin ribbon-tied jacket and voluminous skirt. (Thank you GCA charity thrift shop.) I usually didn't do head to toe—too fashion victim-y! But the enormous import of today's potentially life-altering event called for drastic measures. The toe part of head to toe was an issue, because without the right shoe you were dead, and let's face it, with this outfit the shoes had to be the matching red Lanvin ankle straps—the shoe of the season. After all, you don't get a second chance to make a first impression. Unfortunately, they had sold out faster than you could say "waiting list," which is where Bee came in.

Bee was in my homeroom, and the whole sophomore class was buzzing about the news that she'd recently snagged one of the most coveted internships in the GCA Intern Program, which was being Jeffrey's (as in the owner of Jeffrey) assistant. I mean, it's common knowledge that the shoe department at Jeffrey is beyond, beyond! When I called her yesterday to beg her for the Lanvins, she was very accommodating, snagging them from the shoe department on her way home.

Note: Please pause here to rewind the tape to Bee's bedroom, earlier this morning.

"Perfect," I said, trying to suppress my wincing facial muscles while cramming my size 8 foot into a pair of size 6 and 1/2's—the last pair left on the planet.

"Are you sure they feel okay?" Bee asked, studying me as I hobbled around her bedroom.

"I only need them for a couple of hours. Besides, I'll take a cab. I won't be walking."

"Suit yourself. I'll tape the bottoms. And please, Imogene, please make sure they come back in the same perfect condition you're getting them in."

"Don't sweat it, honey Bee. I have it all under control."

Affirmation: A thousand-mile journey begins with one step.

Fast forward to present.

After the long communications blackout, my Sidekick finally vibrated and Evie popped up on my IM.

FashngawdS: Girlena! Called u all morning. Some strange guy told me u left yr phone w/him/has it n wants to return to u...what's up with that?? He sounds xtremely kUt!
Imogenius1: Did he leave a #?
FashngawdS: B4 i forget - parents letting me stay at the Tribeca apt - restaurant hours 2 long n they don't want me commuting.

Imogenius1: Wow…

FashngawdS: Sed u could stay in the
xtra bedroom if yr parents say ok!!

Imogenius1: Eeeeeeeeeeeeeeeeee!!!
I'll call u after my interview. About
my phone

FashngawdS: Code red (Dad's on
the prowl) - TTFN :(

Ugh! I hate when she just clicks off like that! Especially at a time like this. And how will I ever get my phone back, I thought, nearly colliding with a frenzied commuter. I'll think about that later. For now I've got to think of a way to get Mom to let me live in the city for the summer.

Note to self: Chat with Dad after dinner.

I checked my feet for signs of swelling and moved toward the 42nd Street exit. I'll be across town in 10 minutes, I smiled to myself, while slipping through the door and into the street, carefully tottering over to the taxi stand.

"Hey, what do you think you're doing?" a deep voice next to me growled. I looked up at a large official-like person, whose wrinkled shirt was stretched between buttonholes. "Waiting for a cab," I replied. "Do my feet look swollen to you?"

"Do mine?" he replied, moving closer.

"No, not really." I frowned, studying his dilapidated Doc Martens.

"How 'bout theirs?" he asked, cocking his head toward the crowd behind him. I looked over at the long line that I'd passed on my way out of Grand Central. They loomed silently, craning their necks, glaring at me.

"That's right girly, there's the line," an annoyed commuter pointed out.

"Line?" I asked, astonished. It still wasn't registering.

"Don't you read the papers, sweetheart?" croaked an old woman who looked as though she could turn dangerous at any second. "Transit strike!"

"What?" I felt myself getting warm as more than a trickle of panic began to rise.

"Yeah girly. Transit strike. Only a few hacks runnin' today." He grinned.

"And no buses!" cackled the old woman.

Without thinking, I leaped into 42nd Street traffic. Horns blared, cars swerved, tires screeched, and people hollered obscenities—lots of them. It was time to switch to Plan B: walk.

"Stay calm, you'll make it." I hyperventilated while crossing the street toward Fifth Avenue. You've done this a million times. Just not wearing a borrowed pair of $600 shoes that were too tight and had to be returned without a mark on them, I mused, heading west as fast as my throbbing feet would carry me. I tried to remember a mantra for pain management. Despite that, and the fear that I might be a tad late, I kept one happy thought on the front burner of my brain. In ten minutes I'd be sitting in front of the most powerful woman in the fashion industry.

❄   ❄   ❄

By the time I hit Seventh Avenue I was so busy reciting "ohm, ohm, ohm" that I didn't notice a high-heeled girl's worst nightmare, the dreaded subway grating.

"Ohm, ohm, Ohmmmmm-migod!" I screeched as one heel slipped into the steel grid, snapping it off and propelling me forward into a hot dog cart. My hands slid across the nickel-plated counter, picking up buns, ketchup packets, and spare change as the cart began to roll forward, dragging me and its owner with it. He was a small man, wearing a grimy apron and thick glasses, and he was screaming.

"Vhat you are doing?!" he cried as we barreled down Seventh Avenue together, with the cart picking up momentum. I slammed both feet down to stop, but the one heel was gone and the other quickly followed suit. My feet shot out from under me and I found myself falling backward, grabbing the side of the cart as best I could, skidding on heel-less heels. The hot dog man managed to get in front of the cart and splay himself across it, screaming wildly, "Stop! My veenies! My veenies!"

"YOUR WHAT?! Help!" I screamed in between "ohms" as we flew past a policeman and headed straight for a pair of rolling clothing racks.

"Pull over!" hollered the policeman, running alongside the cart. I threw all my weight to the left, trying to steer between the oncoming racks.

"Watch out!" I yelled as we whizzed between the racks, perfectly averting the collision, but unfortunately picking off the policeman with a loud "Oooff!"

87

We barreled through traffic across 41st, clipping a bike messenger and slamming into the curb. "This cannot be happening, this is not happening," was all my psyche could relate. I closed my eyes as I flew through the air, landing face first on a table laden with merchandise, which proceeded to collapse, leaving me buried under a plethora of counterfeit Fendi bags.

What a mess. My perfect plan was ruined and my career as a glamorous fashion-forecasting intern was *pffft*! My incredible life, which was to have begun today, passed before my eyes in a nanosecond—a ruined shambles. "How could this have happened?" I wondered, completely out of it. A crowd gathered around me and stared in mass disbelief, catching a momentary entertainment break while waiting for the light to change. The hot dog man was now arguing with the wounded police officer, imploring him to arrest the miscreant (that would be me) who had caused this catastrophe.

"Let me see your vendor's license!" the police officer demanded angrily. It was the last thing I heard, because everything else faded into a blurry haze. I felt as if I was losing my precarious grip on consciousness, when out of nowhere, a hand reached down out of the chaos.

"Are you all right?" a concerned voice asked. I looked up into the face of the second-most gorgeous, well-dressed man I'd ever seen in my life. I died, and this was heaven and he was the angel that brought me there. His custom tailored white shirt was wide open at the collar, giving a hint of a trim, toned physique. His tan face glowed. This was NOT your nut-brown Coney Island Beach Club variety tan, nor was it your Tara Reid orange spray-on type, nor your golden, see-ya-in-Palm-Beach-and-bring-your-Michael-Kors-caftans kind of tan. His was a subtle, warm, rosy glow that emanated from within. His eyes were a deep Mediterranean blue and his classic Roman nose gave him an air of aristocracy. His glossy, rich blue-black hair was longish and casually combed, and his deep blue Ozwald Boateng pants were pressed to perfection.

"Let me help you," he offered, extending his hand once more. Total mortification set in as I came back to reality. I tried pulling myself together as best I could, straightened my soiled $1,200-had-I-paid-retail skirt, and brushed off the ripped and heel-less Lanvin pumps. I was trembling worse than Britney Spears's Chihuahua. As much as I would have liked to get to know this gorgeous Roman god-angel, I had a dire situation on my hands that prevented any such possibility.

Engage brain now! My wobbly brain commanded itself as the stranger helped me to my feet

"Do you have the time?" I asked, struggling with my words. He glanced at a most divine Chaumet watch.

"It's five after twelve." His voice was soft, but masculine.

"Uh, thank you. . . . I'm late. Thank you so much," I warbled, hobbling into 550 Seventh Avenue.

Walking through the front doors of Hautelaw was like walking into Oz. Although my ruby slippers were a tad unrecognizable, I immedi-ately felt at home.

The heavy double frosted-glass doors were adorned with ornately scripted letters spelling out the word HAUTELAW. The decor inside was awe-inspiring. The deep-plum plush carpeting, so cushiony under my tired feet, was set off by walls covered entirely in glazed, embossed leather the color of vanilla cream. Matching kid leather banquettes looked as soft as my Chanel pochette. The mood lighting was adjusted so that everything sparkled and glowed. Even the air temperature was perfect, and I distinctly perceived the faintest citrusy scent of lemon verbena, which stood in stark contrast to whatever I was reeking of which was, on reflection, a vile combo of sweat, dirt, and hot dogs.

I was so relieved to be off the street, though I had the feeling that it was just a trade-off for another kind of lunacy. Everything inside Hautelaw headquarters was a blur. Fashionistas rushed hither and yon as I made my way toward the reception desk. Everyone seemed to be checking messages and simultaneously answering phones. Impromptu meetings sprung up out of nowhere: creative director types, photographers, designers, colorists, art directors, salespeople, and editors met, chatted, and then went back to whatever it is they do. The vibe was unreal and I decided right then and there that Hautelaw just had to be my day-to-day existence for the next three months!

As I approached the large wraparound reception desk, I caught a whiff of musk.

"Hi," I whispered feebly to the hunky male receptionist. "I'm here to see Spring Sommer." Without so much as a word, he directed me to have a seat, and I sank into a chair in the corner as out of sight as possible, which of course was impossible because I was like an *eeeew* magnet, attracting all kinds of disdainful stares. Maybe they figured that mustard stains and broken heels were some sort of new look, I thought, picking up what appeared to be one of Hautelaw's recent publications. The cover read "Hautelaw—Spring/Summer Street Trends." Their logo and tag line were stamped along the bottom of each page as folllows: "Hautelaw—The Last Word in Fashion . . . First!"

As if on cue an inner set of double doors burst open from what I assumed was the conference room. A well-groomed man strode across the foyer toward the front door followed by a stream of associates and what appeared to be Hautelaw employees.

"I can assure you, Renzo," a woman around my mom's age was pleading, "we had those fabrics first. No one else could possibly have known about it."

"Spring, it's no use, I can get the same information from Winter Tan, but cheaper."

OMG that's Spring, as in Spring Sommer, the head of Hautelaw, I thought, patting down my skirt and jiggling my swollen feet back into my once gorgeous loaner shoes. Renzo went on. "She's been trying to get me as a client for years and frankly, Spring, it's time for a change."

"Renzo, please, I'm asking you, as an old friend, to reconsider. I *will* get to the bottom of this."

"I'm sorry Spring, but it's too late." With that he was gone.

"Deborah," Spring said to a sweet-looking girl who was

obviously her assistant. "How did Winter get that information out before we did? Someone has got to be leaking it, but who?"

"I don't know. But it isn't just us. Winter has been siphoning off everyone's clients left and right."

Without a glance in my direction, Spring Sommer disappeared. A moment later Deborah stuck her head out.

"Imogene?"

"Yes," I said awkwardly, "here I am."

"Spring will see you now."

It's great to be back in New York City," Spring Sommer drawled in her best East Coast Brahmin as she stood up to shake my hand, teetering on black MBT cellulite-burning sneakers as she ushered me into a nearby seat. Her voice was husky, doubtless from years of chain-smoking, gauging from the low hanging nicotine smog that filled the makeshift conference room and the fact that she was attempting to light a second with the currently lit one. On most of the tables and in every corner of the room were masses of flowers and plants with untouched notes sticking out of them, obviously from well-wishers. Boxes stacked in every corner spoke of the recent move, though the creamy walls were already covered with framed high-style fashion layouts, movie one-sheets, cosmetic ads, head shots, and magazine covers of Spring. French *Vogue, Harper's Bazaar, Cosmopolitan*, you name it, she had been on the covers of them all. But the photos didn't do her justice. Her cheekbones were higher, her skin more luminous. She was taller and far more beautiful.

Her style was rather unique: vintage off-the-shoulder Kamali *Flash Dance* sweatsuit and baby-blue terry-cloth Puma headband. Clearly, she was going for après-treadmill. And she sparkled. Literally. Her cheeks glistened pink and green with what looked like Playskool glitter.

Aside from flowers, the new carpet, and paint smell, I detected a subtle but distinct background note of *eau de chien*. Sprawled out on the plush carpet lay two wheezing and unmistakably overfed pugs—one black, one tan.

"New York is really where it's all happening. London is so over, don't you think?" she said.

"Oh for sure," I agreed. I was still quite out of breath. My heart was pumping, my feet were throbbing, and I was desperately trying to compose myself.

"You look so familiar to me," Spring said. "Have we met somewhere before? I'll think of it, don't tell me!" she continued, not waiting for an answer. "Imogene, Imogene, where have I heard that name before," she pondered. "Imogene, OH YES! *The e-mailer!*" She paused for what seemed like minutes, a taut smile pasted to her face. "Well, we finally meet. I must admit, at first I was flabbergasted, then somewhat alarmed, but after a while, I became quite impressed with your persistence. After your last e-mail . . . thirteen, right? Well, that was my omen. Thirteen is a very important Kabbalah number. It's right here in my *Kabbalah Decoder Handbook*." Spring began leafing through it for the meaning of thirteen. "It means . . ." Spring's eyes scanned its pages as she continued talking. "Well, whatever it means," she said, giving up her search, "I knew I just had to meet you . . . though I must say, I was advised by some not to do so. But sitting here with you, why you don't look dangerous at all. A little . . . messy, but, well. . . . You should have told me in your correspondence that Nini was your mentor. Nini and I go way back. And Nini gave you such a spectacular recommendation. Do you live in New York?"

"No. Yes, I'm staying at a friend's apartment for the summer."

"Fabulous." After some more chitchat and gossip, she got down to the hardcore interview, executed at warp speed with an endless barrage of relevant questions: the kind that a six-year-old would ask while pretending to play office.

"What shampoo do you use? . . . What's your favorite color? . . . Least favorite color? . . . Who is your favorite designer? . . . Where do you shop? . . . Fit or flared? . . . Diamonds or pearls? . . . Vanilla or chocolate? . . . Ketchup or mustard? . . . Fries or mashed? . . . Coke or Pepsi? . . ."

But what really counted at the end of the day was my horoscope.

"What's your sign Imogene?" Spring asked, jettisoning thin streams of Benson & Hedges 100s smoke through her flaring aquiline nostrils. "I'm an Aries, you know."

"Oh, so am I." My heart raced

"Really? What's your d.o.b.?"

"March 28th."

"OHMIGOD! The same as mine!" trilled Spring.

Suddenly, every subatomic particle in my body was vibrating faster. This was unreal. It was an unequivocal match—a veritable Vulcan mind meld. *Sistahs!* I screamed to myself.

After another twenty minutes of comparing personality traits, Spring was ready to move on.

"By the way dear, I love your flats. It looks like tattered is making a comeback. And gauging by your *ensemble*," she said in the French way, "deconstruction looks like an emerging theme as well. . . . Hmm, now that I think about it, your look is so fresh and new, I see a trend on the horizon. What do you call it?" she asked sincerely, contemplating my Lanvin shambles.

"This?" I stammered in disbelief, looking down at my pathetic, once gorgeous rags.

Deliberating further, she said, "'Ragamuffin chic' might work. Then again, 'poor little rich girl' has a certain ring to it," she said, chewing on the tip of her pencil.

I was witnessing my very first trend conceptualization and I was both bewildered and excited.

"Hmmm, I just can't decide. Oh well, I'll make a note," she said, scribbling on a yellow legal pad, "and discuss with Mick. In fact, I can't wait for him to meet you; I know he'll simply adore you!" As if on cue, a shadow crossed the entrance to Spring's office. Spring called out, "Mick? Is that you dear? I'd like you to meet someone. Can you come in here please? Thank you, my dahling."

"He stepped out, Spring," came a voice from the shadows of the connecting office door. "Is there something *I* can help you with?" said the young woman who was about my age, as she stepped into the office. She was completely clad in serious Azzedine Alaia black leather, and ohmigod! It can't be! IT IS! *The supreme witch from Soho House!*

"Brooke, I'd like you to meet Imogene, the newest addition to our summer intern program."

"Interesting statement." Brooke eyeballed my once-perfectly-chic-ensemble-cum-tattered-bunch-of-rags. Didn't she recognize me? I mean, it was only just last night!

"I have high hopes for Imogene, who I believe will no doubt be a considerable asset to our little family."

"But Spring, I didn't know we needed anyone else this summer. I would have happily suggested Fern or Romaine, had I known you . . . ," she said, trying to keep her equilibrium intact.

"Brooke was a first year intern last summer." Spring went right on talking, turning in my direction. "And happily she's back with us again as our senior intern this year." Brooke glowed. "If all goes well, she may someday be our editor in chief." At this, Spring winked at Brooke.

BLECH!!!

"Right dear?"

"Right, Spring," she said, flashing her best game-show smile.

"I have no doubt that with a little guidance you can accomplish great things here too, Imogene . . . just like Brooke." Spring winked again. DOUBLE BLECH!!!

"Thank you, Spring. It was such a pleasure working with you last year, I simply couldn't pass up the opportunity to do it again." If she were any more unctuous, my face would have broken out.

"My old, er, rather, my dear friend Nini Langhorne is Imogene's parent faculty advisor at my alma mater, Greenwich Country Academy," Spring extolled. "And Imogene's our little Eliza Doolittle for the summer. So we must be outstanding role models for our Imogene, mustn't we?" Spring rambled on. "You know, Imogene, Nini and I were thought to be the brightest stars on the GCA horizon. We and another dear friend were called the Les Trois Coquettes. We were absolutely inseparable. That is until our dear friend, well . . . I heard later that she'd married someone from out of town. What I would give to relive those glorious days," she trailed off nostalgically. "Now, if you need anything—anything at all—Brooke's the one to talk to. Though hopefully we'll have you working with Mick on some great projects, Brooke is the one you'll be reporting to each day."

OMG, I thought, momentarily freaking. I mean, this is some very heavy karma.

"Brooke darling, be a dear and show Imogene around the office, won't you? We must get her up to speed quickly. The way things have been going around here lately, we need all the help we can get."

"Of course, Spring," Brooke said with a wax smile. She led the way through the door.

"Um, Spring, does that mean . . . ," I began sheepishly,

"Oh and Imogene," Spring called, "you're hired. I'll see you next Monday, dahling."

"Oh, thank you Spring. You won't be disappointed!" I took

a deep breath, and my legs wobbled as I stood up to leave. Then I suddenly remembered that I'd brought along a sample of my street trend photomontages to show to Spring.

"Spring, I forgot to give you a sample of my work," I said, whipping them out of the Mylar protective sheath and handing the stack to Spring.

"Hmm, really. . . . When did you . . . ? Exciting . . . I can see you really have quite an eye. . . . How refreshing. How with-it . . ."

With the unexpected positive reinforcement, I said, "They're from a series . . . I had more, but unfortunately they're on my cell phone and I didn't have time to download them."

"Oh I'd love to see more! They're brilliant. We're always looking for fresh talent my dear. Ooooh, I'm beyond tickled! Just leave everything with Brooke and I'll take a closer peek this afternoon," she bubbled. "Ta, dahling!!!"

As I followed Brooke down the narrow hallway, she mumbled something that sounded suspiciously like "This is either one of Spring's mercy hirings, or she's having another acid flashback."

"I'm sorry?" I said, not believing what I just heard.

Brooke suddenly stopped and faced me. Clearly, she was straining to be polite. "Look, Dorothy —"

So she did remember! "Imogene," I corrected her.

"Whatever," she heaved. "Listen, I guess we got off on the wrong foot last night. Why don't we wipe the slate clean and start all over. Last night was such a nightmare.

I'd just broken up with my boyfriend and I must admit, I was a tad bonkers."

"Oh, that's okay," I lied, not knowing what to say, but thinking it was necessary to get along with this person. Maybe Brooke wasn't all that bad. I mean, I should have more sympathy for what she's going through. Maybe underneath it all, she's a really good person. Although I had a hunch that underneath it all, there was no underneath it all.

Affirmation: Fake it until you make it.

After the brief tour, Brooke showed me my office, which was directly behind the reception area and looked like a small supply closet. It contained the requisite office *accoutrements*: one minidesk, on which sat one luminous white iMac, one Artimede Museum of Modern Art desk lamp, one phone answering pad, one pen, and one phone. That was all the desk had room for. Just beyond my makeshift office was the kitchen. I resolved to remind myself everyday not to faint because it's beyond a dream, even if it means I would be sharing my summer with a copier, fax machine, a few million reams of paper, regulation office supplies, a coffee maker, and a refrigerator full of Diet Coke, which I would soon discover was the 24-hour-a-day drink of choice for the fashion flock.

"Have a seat," she faux smiled. "Okay, Imelda," she said, leaning against the copier with one hand on her hip.

"Imogene."

"Let's get one thing straight," she said icily. "*I* am the senior intern here and a hair away from becoming assistant editor in chief. *You* are a junior intern. You report to me.

Not Spring. Not Mick. Not anyone else. Me and me alone! From now on, if you have anything for Spring to look at, including your sweet little cell phone pictures, it goes through me first—got that?"

"Got it," I said, feeling my stature shrinking by the second. I suspected that anytime anyone got near Spring, Brooke's internal radar system would sound off, intercepting any and all trespassers.

"Good. I'm glad we understand each other." I searched her face for clues that our chat was coming to a close. She turned toward the door and I followed, like a dutiful underling, when in sauntered a wisp of a man.

"Well hello, who do we have here?" he said playfully, English accent and all. He was quite an oxymoron, elfin in looks and stature, but dressed rather like a biker—leather jeans, vest, and tall black boots (very Village People).

"Hi," I said enthusiastically. Maybe they're not all as bad as her. Brooke, barely hiding her annoyance, made the introductions.

"Malcolm, meet Imogene, our *junior* summer intern. Imogene, Malcolm. Malcolm runs the art department. He and Ian, his assistant, design our books."

"And Brooke, well she's our Spring's little watchdog. We all must be careful what we say around her, mustn't we Brookie," he said, sarcastically upbeat. "Brooke is vying for a major promotion that she hopes will happen at the end of the summer. Play your cards right and you, too, can go places."

I liked him. He was funny and I hoped we'd be friends.

Brooke hustled me along, pretty much concluding my

introduction to Hautelaw. When we got to the front door Brooke said, "I'm so glad we had this little chat." She held the frosted-glass door open for me and added, "Oh, and a couple of other things I should mention. I like my lattes iced, skim milk, NEVER ever whole. And with a sprinkle of vanilla, hold the sugar. You will find things to be filed in the box behind my desk. Check it each morning, as I hate a messy file area. When the mail comes, bring it directly to me. I sort all of Spring's mail. Do not, and I repeat not, speak directly to Spring without seeing me first. Ta," she said whisking me out the door like some vile germ.

I was halfway down to the lobby when I realized, "OHMIGOD!", unintentionally startling everyone in the elevator, "I left my bag upstairs!"

Swinging back through the Hautelaw inscribed doors, I saw Brooke standing exactly where I'd left her, but this time, she was playing serious tonsil hockey with an unidentified man.

"Sorry, I left my bag in the conference room," I said, trying to sneak past without disturbing them. But I didn't have to go any farther, because Brooke had it in her hand, and they both turned around.

"Imogene . . . what a coincidence . . ."

It was . . . Paolo?! And I was having an out-of-body experience. What was he doing here? Kissing her?!

"How great to see you!" he gasped nervously. "Amazing! I've been trying to reach you all morning. Did your girlfriend tell you I called?" he asked, anxiously pushing Brooke away.

"You two know each other?" Brooke puffed, as if she couldn't believe we would.

We spoke in unison:

"Yes!" he said

"NO!" I said.

"I think you have something that belongs to me," I demanded, holding my hand out to receive my phone. While I waited, Brooke handed me my bag.

"I . . . I don't have your phone with me," Paolo stammered. "I didn't know I'd be seeing you so soon."

"Obviously," I said, turning quickly toward the door. Before I could stop, in walked the gorgeous Roman god/guardian angel in the Boateng suit.

"Wait! Please wait, I can explain," yelled Paolo, but Brooke held on to him tight.

"Hi . . . again," said the angel as I bumped straight into him in an even deeper state of anguish and confusion.

"Oh, hi."

"*You* two know each other?" Brooke said, twice as aghast, as I sped out the door, drowning in pain.

"Wait . . . please Imogene. . . . Wait . . ." I heard Paolo's footsteps closing in. Thankfully the elevator doors closed before he reached me.

"Your mother called. . . . She left a message. . . . She wants you to call her. Imogene, please, I can explain. How can I reach you?" Paolo desperately shouted as the elevator descended.

When the elevator finally opened onto the main floor, I bolted, desperate for fresh air. I pushed through the doors gasping for breath, feeling like a goldfish outside her fishbowl. Oh great. Just when I thought nothing worse could possibly happen, it was raining. And I didn't have an umbrella! There was thunder and lightning, and the rain was coming down in buckets. But that was nothing compared to the storm raging inside my head.

My train rolled out of Grand Central Station. I sat there drenched, torn, and tattered, with a crush that was over before it even had a chance to be official. I felt something in the pit of my stomach that I couldn't quite put my finger on. OHMIGOD, I'm getting one of Mom's ulcers!

chapter five

The Hautelaw Imogene

date: JULY 8TH

mood: MAGNETIC

Highly cultivated girls such as I always know when we're near a Prada Boutique. We can actually feel it pulling us like a super powerful magnet. However, the power of my commitment to my job outweighed even Prada. And the fact that I was flat broke helped a trifle.

✳   ✳   ✳

As my Dior No. 104 manicured finger pressed the on button, I said, "HelloMoto" cheerfully. (I mean, normally I'd be saying that to my cell phone but not to break with tradition, I repeated it to my Sidekick instead.) A daily affirmation flashed across the screen:

104

"I AM ON THE PRECIPICE OF SUCCESS."

I then shoved the substitute cell phone into my Chanel pink-and-black hip-hugging pochette. I picked up the Jeffrey shopping bag containing one dead pair of Lanvins as I did every day for the last week, and slammed the door behind me.

It had been a while since I'd actually written anything in my journal, not that I didn't have anything to say. I did, but life at work has been an absolute, nonstop, eighteen-hour-a-day loony bin on wheels and I hadn't had time to even think. I mean, it had been a week now since Evie and I moved our stuff into her parents' *pied à terre*, or as we called it, Villa Fantastique. (I mean how anyone can call 4,800 square feet of duplex in the heart of Tribeca a *pied à terre* is beyond me.) And, best of all, we had a separate entrance on the top floor, which Evie referred to as the North Wing. As our ever fortunate fate would have it, Evie's parents were usually not home. Evie's mom had been commuting to Brooklyn every day to be with an ailing Aunt Etta, and Evie's dad was either at one of his several restaurants or at his office a few blocks away, where, as "Page Six" has it, he was planning to branch out into London later in the year. Anyway, *my* parents believed Evie's parents were here at all times, and I intended to keep it that way.

Well, so far, living in New York has been amazing! I haven't even given Paolo a single thought these past fourteen days, twenty-two hours, and thirty-seven minutes since I saw him kissing Brooke. I've occupied my time with a whole lot of other things. My new resolve was to henceforth put all my energy into my new relationship (which is actually my old relationship): "the street."

I was determined to show Spring and Mick, and Brooke for that matter, what I could do if they'd just give me a chance. So, Cyber-shot in hand, I hit the streets like a style-seeking missile.

I revved up my Vespa, buckling in Toy and *his* toy, Booboo, and darted down Franklin Street. It was morning in Tribeca, one of the last New York-y neighborhoods in New York. Even the cobblestones are still intact on some side streets.

It was a perfect New York summer day. The glare of early morning sun sparkled brighter than a flawless cushion-cut diamond across the mirrored towers that scraped the cloudless enamel blue sky. I steered my way through the thick, bustling crowd of pedestrians meandering like some great river down the sidewalks and across the streets. I went through Soho, shooting the groovy gallery chic-sters, groovy pets, groovy cabbies and messengers, power brokers, bikers, and skateboarders. Then I zipped over to the East Village, where flocks of avant-garde funksters could always be found. I darted through myriad city buses, cars, and taxis to a persistent chorus of car horns, car alarms (mostly set off by *moi*), and sirens from emergency vehicles. I sped through the West Village, Chelsea, and Union Square, the last for rural farmer's market chic. Then I canvassed the Upper West Side for family chic and buzzed through Central Park to the uptown museums for urban chic, shooting everything that caught my eye.

At the intersection of 57th Street and Fifth Avenue, I reached a state of pure nirvana. (They don't call it the Upper *East* Side for nothing.) Everything anyone could ever lust for was on these four corners: Bergdorf Goodman, Bulgari, Prada, and Tiffany—360 degrees of sheer happiness. With Barneys being a short hop skip and a jump away, it was the gateway to bliss.

After all was seen and shot, I could envision the layout of my photos. And I knew I had my story. Spring would love it.

That part of the mission accomplished, I shoved my camera in my pochette and proceeded west on 57th Street. Last stop, Starbucks. I was commanded by Brooke to stop there on my way back because there was a big, and I mean big, creative meeting, which—Ohmigod, I'm late—was about to begin.

A pair of dazzling gold Gucci snakeskin heels walked quickly down a plushly carpeted hallway, revealing the trim, sexy back view of . . . *moi*! Thank you Evie. Little did anyone realize, I was an advocate of borrow and spend economics.

I found Spring's office in great commotion, as it apparently always was this time of year. The Autumn/Winter Forecast report was about to go to press. I slid in quietly next to Malcolm, who perked up when he saw me and very quietly whispered, "Where have you been you naugh-tee girl . . . late as usual." I ignored him (though how anyone can ignore a man wearing a T-shirt with "Prom Queen" emblazoned across the front is beyond me), and dispensed my cache of lattes, espressos, chai teas, cappuccinos, mochaccinos, macchiatos, grande triple-decaf iced vanillamochachocafrappacinos all around.

This week I was beginning to get into the office groove. I was mainly a gofer, but that didn't bother me at all. Sometimes I helped Spring communicate with her clients, or typed her crazy letters. At other times, I ran errands and did little things for Brooke, like RSVP'ing to her avalanche of invitations to this black-tie event or that gala. Malcolm says she's sent out anonymous press clippings on herself to every PR company in New York, to get herself onto every VIP list in the city. But mostly I Xeroxed, filed, organized, FedExed, messengered, and covered the phones at the reception desk for lunch breaks.

Malcolm continued teasing me at whisper level as I handed him his latte. Thankfully, no one else noticed I was late.

Ooops, I spoke too soon, I realized, catching Mick's displeased glance. I think he senses some semblance of potential in me. If you haven't guessed yet, Mick is the Roman god/angel who pulled me out from under the Fendi bag avalanche on the day of my Hautelaw interview, and ever since then I've felt some type of connection with him—kinship, sort of. Like a big brother, little sister thing, you know? Anyway, from that point on I was in with Mick, and he was in with me.

I shrugged my shoulders and mouthed "sorry," hoping he wasn't angry.

"I know that look. . . . It's *luv* . . . ," Malcolm cooed.

"Malcolm!" I whispered faux harshly. "I mean, I am only sixteen. I'm trying to concentrate on my *career*!!"

"Oooh, and a new *schmatte*. You aren't just looking delicious for me, are you *shayna punim*? Lunch date? Come on," he urged, niggling me. "Tell Mally, who is he?"

"Stop!" I snapped, feigning outrage. Malcolm continued taunting, ignoring my pleas. I adored him; he was forever teasing me about something. He was fun and flamboyant in a butch sort of way. His summer uniform consisted of camouflage cargo pants, vintage black Reebok high top sneakers, and either a black ribbed muscle tee or the one he was wearing today. He had a bit of a tummy, he dyed his mustache and sideburns dark, and he had glorious blond highlights that any girl would envy.

"Tell me who he is, or I shall have to paddle your cute little bot-tom. And talk to me about those *mahaya* shoes, dahling! New?" I didn't know why, nor did I ever think to ask, how it was that he was fluent in, of all things, Yiddish. Just another Malcolm mystery, I suppose.

"Later," I said with a wink and a smile. Just as the meeting was about to start I got up from my usual seat next to Malcolm and moved to a seat across the room, where a phone sat on a seventies chrome and glass table. Spring's new assistant slash receptionist, Duke, was out sick and I was answering the phones for the day.

"Quiieett, pleease!" Spring intoned. Two long snakes of velvety cigarette smoke spiraled upward, intertwining like the straps on a pair of Roger Viviers, a momentary ballet of haute haze, that only the reigning queen of fashion forecasting could produce. She slowly exhaled and another vast plume rose to form its own weather system near the ceiling above her. Her gaze slowly swept the hushed group huddled tensely around her desk. On top of it, an enormous ashtray piled high with petrified cigarette butts rested precariously close to the book; to Spring's right, towering stacks of magazines crowned with a soccer-ball-size übereighties crystal lighter. (For those of you into reruns, think Alexis Colby from *Dynasty*.)

"Mmmm, mmmm." Spring oozed as she flipped through the pages of the Autumn/Winter Forecast Report, otherwise known as The Book. "Mmmmmmmmmmmmmm." She stopped, fixated on one of the spreads, and then took another long, thoughtful drag from her cigarette holder. An ash the length of her index finger fell on the sacred images.

"Fabulous . . . FAAABULOUS!!!" She looked into the crowd standing closely around her. Malcolm and Ian nervously leaned forward, frantically blowing ash off the book. Spring took no notice. In the foreground, the larger of Spring's two charmed pugs dragged its rear end by its two front paws across the antique Aubusson carpet, while the other buried its face in its crotch. Their sliding, snorting, and licking went unnoticed except by me.

The group huddled tensely, waiting for Spring Sommer to speak. Her lips curled into a wry smile; her steely yet somewhat blurry eyes suddenly focused on a point in the far corner of the room. Everyone turned around and looked.

"There's nothing over there. I'm just thinking," she drawled. "Mick. Brooke. Malcolm. And uh . . ." Spring held up her jewel-encrusted cigarette holder and studied it.

"Ian," Ian offered politely.

She raised the holder an inch and gazed at him from beneath it.

"Yes, of course. Ian. You put together the swatches for the skiing in Somalia piece."

Ian brightened, his eyes full of anticipation, longing for praise.

"Yes. I did a lot of research and —"

"Let me ask you something . . ."

"Ian."

"Ian," she said, fumbling through piles of fabric, swatches, swipes, and magazines that mimicked the Manhattan skyline on her desk. Mick and Brooke exchanged a quick glance as Spring dug several sheets of fabric swatches and pictures from beneath the mess and scrutinized them with intense gravity, gravity much greater than the situation called for. It was a skill she'd developed into a high art — good for clients, great for business, totally meaningless. "What colors do you think of when you ski in the desert?" she asked.

"Well . . . ," Ian began.

"I always think of that reddish, hazel color . . . ," Spring continued. "You know the one, dahling. It has a little purple in it . . . maybe some azure. A cross between a dead sea and a living desert."

"Amethyst?" Mick ventured.

"Oh, that's close, but a little more Moroccan."

"Was it a purpl-y red or a reddish purpl-y?" asked Brooke.

"Ummmm, purpli-er red. But there's definitely something African about it."

"Tanzanian Cinnabar?" Malcolm suggested.

"Nooo. Too brown-y."

"Matanje midnight?" said Brooke.

"Too blue-y."

"Umtata passion," Brooke tried again,

"Botswana Bolognese," said Ian.

"Serengeti Surprise," Brooke again.

"Togo Tango," said Malcolm.

"Simpler, like brick but brighter, sparklier—pinki-er . . . like 'pinkle,' but deeper," she insisted.

"Red," intoned Mick.

With that Spring paused. Silence engulfed the room. Spring always, *always* listened to Mick. Maybe because he was never wrong.

"Yes, that's it! Genius, sheer genius Mick, dahling." With that she buzzed me from her desk phone. "Imogene, sweetie, please ring my decorator. I want this office painted red—I must have red. Red is the color for today, red, red, red, red, red! Got that sweetie?"

"Red. Got it," I assured her from the phone on the other side of the same room. Spring slammed the book shut and spread her hands across the desk, as if trying to touch the opposite tips of Manhattan. Now, back to the focal point of the meeting.

"Mick. Where's Mick?!" she bellowed through the thick fog.

"Still here."

Spring flashed her brilliant set of ultrawhite veneers at him.

"Well of course you are, dahling! You've outdone yourself this time! I mean this . . . this . . ."

"Book," Mick said patiently.

"Book . . . is just brilliant! It's fantastic! By the way sweetie, you're looking quite scrumptious these days," she added, taking him in fully.

"Thank you. Actually," Mick said reluctantly, knowing full well that Brooke didn't have an original idea in her head, but I could tell he was unable to endure another word from Spring, "those street snaps were Brooke's idea. She put the whole story together."

Beaming at Brooke with admiration and respect, Spring exclaimed, "Well, there's no surpassing my Hautelaw girls." Malcolm and Ian struck a pose, raised their eyebrows and pursed their lips. Brooke beamed, as Spring leaned back and stuffed another cigarette into her holder.

"Spring?"

Spring leaned forward and lifted a piece of bronze taffeta fabric off the phone speaker.

"Yes, dear."

"I'm right here Spring," I said sitting near the courtesy phone in the corner. "Oscar's on two and your ex is on three."

"Which one?"

"Four."

"Oh, Freddie!" Spring cast her iridescent grin at Mick again. "He's the one with the big feet, remember?" Mick flushed to his toes.

"I'm not sure I do," Mick said.

"Well he certainly remembers you." Turning her head toward the taffeta, Spring said, "Tell Freddie I'll call him later, dear, and tell Oscar I'll be right with him. Thank you all! You're brilliant, as usual!" Spring declared, dismissing everyone from the meeting as she smashed her cigarette in the ashtray and turned her sights on Brooke.

"Stay a minute, would you dear?" Just then, Spring's cell phone rang.

"Imogene, be a dear . . . ," Spring said nervously while picking up her Blackberry to the ringtone of "Ray of Light," and handing it to me. "I don't know how to use e-mail. Tell me who it is, dear."

"It's from the Kabbalah Center," I said. "It's your Weekly Consciousness Tune-Up."

"Oh, goody. Thank you dear," she said as I handed her the downloaded message. "That reminds me dear, my Kosher Coach should be calling to book an appointment. Just schedule it for anytime next week and put it in my diary. Thank you dear." She read the message briefly in silence, then handed me back the device to click off. "And Imogene, I know you're busy, but would you mind staying a bit to help me organize my desk?"

"No problem, Spring," I replied.

"Good. Oh, Imogene, that reminds me, did you have a chance to pick up that book I ordered from Rizzoli?"

OMG, I completely forgot to pick up Spring's new diet book, *Eat Right 4 Your Dog Type*!

"Oh, right. Spring . . . they . . ."

"They were closed for inventory," Mick said, saving me.

"Right, so I'll just be going on my lunch hour to get it for you Spring, if that's okay."

"Thank you dear, I need to have it for the flight. You

know, you are every bit as trustworthy as Nini said. We're so proud of you. Aren't we, staff?" No response.

"Should I use petty cash?" I asked her.

"Oh, no-no-no-no-no," Spring cautioned while rummaging through her bag. "Take my credit card dear," she said, passing me her Sri Siva MasterCard, which bore the image of Spring's smiling guru (gold teeth included). It would seem that her spiritual quest has brought her face to face with the latest and greatest spiritual trend, Swami Sri Siva.

"I use it for everything!" Spring cooed. "How do you think I got this free trip to the Himalayas? By June first I had enough Self-Realization Miles to take me to the Himalayas and back!"

I'm all for spirituality, but these days, in order to be a spiritual person, you've really gotta pony up the plastic. $25 sounds like nothing for a Bikram Yoga class, but you don't have to be an Enron accountant to figure out what that costs a year. And *les accoutrements* can really set you back. There's the Christy Turlington Yoga wardrobe, $2,000; the Marc Jacobs sticky mat, $150; and the Kabbalah candles at $20 each. But my best investment so far is my $26 red string. An absolute necessity working anywhere near Brooke.

As everyone else filed out of the room, Brooke sat down deftly, her full attention on Spring.

"I just wanted to tell you how *faaabulous* your trend story was. I read it last night and it really impressed me. That's the kind of insight that keeps us ahead of—" Spring cleared her throat, lit another cigarette, and blew out a large smoke ring that faintly formed what I could swear was the outline of a skull—"Winter Tan," she seethed.

Not to dwell on the Winter Tan thing at this juncture, but understand that this person was the owner of Haute & About, Hautelaw's sole competitor, otherwise known as Sasquatch on Seventh, the Blair Witch, that couture cretin, and other unmentionables, all of which were dependant on Spring's particular level of nastiness at the time. Theirs was a fierce and ongoing rivalry that, according to Spring, went back into several past lives in various historical epochs, including, but not exclusive to, Waterloo, the French Revolution, the Peloponnesian War, and the burning of Alexandria. In short, they've been at each other's throats ever since Adam and Eve strolled out of Eden wearing your basic fig leaves.

"I don't know how you do it, Brooke dear. You're . . ." Never at a loss for words, Spring blurted out, "Fabulous!"

"Thank you, Spring." Brooke beamed. "Working with you is an inspiration. You make it easy."

She was good. On the outside Brooke is perfect, perfect, perfect. Inside she had the instincts of a stone-cold killer.

"Let's do have lunch soon, shall we? Just my favorite future assistant editor in chief and me. We'll spend some quality girl time together."

"I'd love that."

"Excellent. Since Duke's out today, you'll have to schedule it with Imogene."

Spring finally picked up the phone.

"Oscar dear, so sorry to keep you. . . ."

Y ou won't forget to schedule that, will you Imogene?" Brooke asked as we walked toward her office.

"I can do it right now if you like," I said. "I'll just grab Spring's diary and be right back."

"Good, I'll check my schedule in the meantime."

N ot wanting to be presumptuous by taking a seat until invited, I hung out in the doorway of Brooke's office. The first thing I noticed about her workspace (aka Casa Blanca) was that everything in it was white. Not just the HL embossed walls, but the rug, her desk, the two desk lamps that flanked her work, her swivel chair, and the two Barcelona chairs opposite her desk. The only exceptions were of Mick's publicity photo and the gorgeous flowers that seemed to arrive on a daily basis (though who would/could be her boyfriend was completely beyond me). She was also quite the germophobe. If you so much as touched anything, she'd freak—another reason for waiting at her doorway for her to invite me in. She was in the middle of dialing someone on her cell phone. Brooke looked flustered when she saw me and threw the phone in the drawer. It began to ring.

"Your drawer is ringing," I said.

Brooke just stood there looking at me like a deer caught in the headlights of an oncoming vehicle.

"Didn't anyone ever teach you to knock?"

"Sorry, the door was open." After some more ringing, I just couldn't control myself. "Aren't you going to answer it?"

Though muffled, I heard what sounded like a familiar

voice coming from the phone in her drawer and then Brooke began rustling papers and shifting things around on her desk. She tossed a pen in the direction of the doorway and said, "Oops, I dropped that. Can you pick it up?" Her weird behavior was cut short when her desk drawer stopped talking. "Make that appointment for Thursday," Brooke asserted in her usual self-confident tone.

"One okay?"

"Perfect."

"Brooke?"

"Yes?" Brooke said, swiveling her chair back in my direction, and looking mildly annoyed.

"Did Spring see my 'Eco Warrior' story yet?"

"Oh, yes. The pictures. I *did* show them to Spring and, well, I'm afraid they just didn't do it for her."

She leaned back in her chair, and I felt as if someone was squishing my guts. Brooke sighed, her eyes filled with compassion. "I'm sorry, Imogene, but she's the boss." Then she brightened and tried to smile warmly. "I thought they were sensational."

"Really?" I brightened back, hopeful.

"Really. In fact, I think you should do more."

"I'd love that! I mean, of course I will."

"There's another meeting next Friday before we finalize The Book; it's on the schedule. Can you get me some coverage by Thursday?"

"Sure! I can have it sooner if you need it."

"No. Thursday's fine. I'll make sure Spring takes a good, long look at them over lunch."

"Great. Thanks so much, Brooke."

"Anything for you, sweetie," she purred.

Brooke's office phone rang. She pressed speaker on the key pad, and a voice boomed loudly.

"Brookie, darling. I just wanted to follow up with you about that opening for Fern—is it still happening? And what about what's-her-name?" Brooke picked up the handset fast, doing away with speaker phone.

"Oh, noooooooo, that position has been filled," Brooke said, smiling at me while nervously twisting the phone cord. "I'm so sorry, Candy. Why don't I call you right back. . . . Okay, ta!"

At this point, you may need to know something about New York. In this town hoards of super-chic, trendy rich girls roam in packs through the shimmering world of society parties, gala events, private clubs, and a variety of newsworthy functions where paparazzi can be found in abundance. They are possessed of a single, laser-focused purpose: POWER.

Brooke, as you may recall, was a member of the Wolfe Pack. So named not because its members belonged to the family of Canis lupus, though there is some speculation on that point, but rather because it's the name of their leader: Candy Wolfe. It is rumored that Candy did have a tiny silver bullet tattooed in an unverifiable location on her body. In any event, the other members of the Wolfe Pack included two sisters, Fern and Romaine Snipes, known to partygoers (generally between yawns) as the Salad Sisters. What these women lacked in personality they more than made up for with monumental pretense and sheer monetary bulk. Girls such as I, without the requisite pretense and bulk, were referred to, infrequently, as the PITS (Profesionally Irrelevant Teens) and were thought to be too young and naive to merit attention whatsoever.

Back at my desk I clicked into my e-mail account and began responding to the flurry of e-mails as expeditiously as I could while cradling my landline phone. I wondered, what was Brooke up to now?

> To: Imogene
>
> Fr: Ian
>
> Re: Urgent!!
>
> Malcolm wants you to hop like a bunny into our office as soon as She Who Must Not Be Named goes out to lunch. . . . We're hearing Carson Kressley will be working the tents at Bryant Park, and that in person he's MAJORLY luscious—please can you skosh us some tickets from somewhere—anywhere!
>
> Thanks,
>
> Ian

To: Imogene
Fr: Evie
Re: Home Improvement
I'm getting off early tonight. As we speak Mom and
Dad are leaving for the airport to open a new Heshi
Tokyo and we have the apartment all to ourselves for
the month!!! I'll call u later. I'm screaming!
Hugs!!!!
Evie

And there was a message from Caprice. Ever since that
night at Soho House, we've been friends. In fact we did meet
up at her friend's jewelry showroom. Unfortunately, my
budget being more Costco than Cartier, I wasn't buying,
but we had lunch and a great time. She loved my snaps and
"Daily Obsession" column and was very encouraging. And
I found out all about her. She came from a very tight-knit
family and grew up in the heart of Santurce, one of the oldest
districts in San Juan, a million miles away from the place
I grew up. She was the runner-up in the Miss Puerto Rico
beauty pageant last year and got a modeling contract out of it.

To: Imogene
From: Caprice
Re: You've Got Sale!
Hola Chica,
At last we girls have our own Superbowl! Do the words
"Super Saturday" mean anything to you? As in
THE annual mother of all sample sales SAMPLE SALE?

FYI it is the hardest invitation to score—and I have
4 tickets!!!! Don't tell anyone yet. I know you're dying,
you can thank me later!
Besos
p.s. I'm going to yoga class—might b late. It's so good
to b home.

Oh great, the mother of all sample sales, the one that I'm going to pull out my hair for and gouge my eyes out over, because I won't be going to it. That sample sale?

My office phone rang. Every time a phone rings it reminds me of Paolo, and the gaping hole in my life where my cell phone used to be. I mean, a teenager without a cell phone is like Madonna without a bullet bra. At our school, the cell phone is the *official* accessory of every student. Now that I think of it, what if Paolo'd been calling all over the planet on my cell phone? I mean, he could have been sharing it with all his friends. He could have been calling Italy to talk to his poor old parents who work in that dreary factory . . . and I don't have roaming! OMG! My phone bill's going to be $10,000 and I couldn't do anything about it because my parents would kill me if they knew it was missing. I was going to jail, that was all there was to it. I was already in enough financial trouble. How could I have been so stupid?! Maybe he wasn't answering it because it was on vibrate. I'd text him; I'd tell Evie to text him. Why wasn't he trying to find me? If I found someone's phone, I'd try every number in their address book. Or maybe the battery was dead, which was a very huge possibility. OMG, what if he was reading my last text messages to

Evie? How *très* embarrassing! I'd been texting Evie about his gorgeousness all night! Ohmigod how first-hand embarrassing! I mean I told her how cute and what a fabulous kisser he was . . . and oh the shame of it all. I'm sooooooooo embarrassed. And OMG, all my pictures and coverage were *on it*. I just had to get my phone back, no matter what!

My desk phone rang—it was Evie.

"How's your day?"

"Besides obsessing about my cell phone you mean?"

"Uh."

"I got my first paycheck today."

"Yay!"

"At first I was in a state of hyper-mental-exhilaration, but then I went plain old mental. I mean, I give my check to the teller and he hands me a receipt. It turns out when I was hired I had to give bank info—direct deposit/direct withdrawal to AmEx. I don't even see it. It goes in, I get a teensy amount of pocket change back (thanks Mom!), and the rest goes to Miss Stevens. Anyway, enough about me, how was your day?"

"Oh, just great," she said sarcastically. "Today I had KP duty. I must have seeded a zillion cucumbers and washed a trillion pots." Evie's dad was teaching her the restaurant business from the ground up. "I also shucked 3,000 oysters and my hands are pruney. Tomorrow's going to be a nightmare because I'm scheduled to work the sushi bar and you know I hate, repeat hate, sushi, and who knows what I'll do then!"

I just remembered Caprice asked me to keep quiet about Super Saturday Sale (which is actually on a Friday), so naturally I had to share it with my best friend.

"Girlena??? Are you for real?"

"But it's a bittersweet story," I said cradling the phone between my shoulder and neck in order to get my wand into the tube of Chanel Glossimer 13, maneuvering it to collect the last molecule of lip gloss that had in reality been used up weeks ago. "Yup. I won't be using that fourth ticket. I'm flat broke."

"Don't worry about that, I have a genius idea. Can you help me out after work tomorrow night? We're short one waitress."

"I don't know how to be a waitress."

"Oh, it's beyond easy. I'll show you everything. The tips are phenomenal."

I chucked the lip gloss in the trash.

"Did they use your trend story?"

"I haven't been able to find time to talk to Spring yet," I lied. "But she just sent me a very positive e-mail."

"Okay, listen, don't sweat it. You're brilliant. By the way, I have a surprise for you: We are going to the Tom Ford movie premiere tonight—every star in Hollywood that he ever, EVER dressed is in it!!!"

"Oh no we're not. We're—without fail—much as I hate it, going to my Spenders Anonymous meeting. I've only got three more, and if I miss this one, they'll kick me out for good and the deal with AmEx will evaporate! So, meet me at six?"

"Okay, okay, no problem, I'll meet you at six, right outside the store. We'll just see the movie when it opens. Oh and pullllllllleeeeeeeeease, don't forget the shoes this time! I promised Bee that I would return them for you."

"Gotcha. Later."

As soon as we hung up I remembered, ohmigod, I had to stop off at Rizzoli and get that book for Spring.

I mean, the Vespa is practically Italy's national symbol, I mused, parking conveniently in the Vespa branded stand just outside Rizzoli.

I pushed through the revolving doors of the landmark building. The coolest Brazilian melody wafted through the air, and everywhere beautiful people of every nationality were grazing through what is in all probability the world's largest collection of coffee table books. I spotted the perfect English garden book for Mom and a gorgeous DeKooning book that Dad would be thrilled to have. I made a mental note to return at a future date. Like when I had money. After a quick perusal of the to-die-for fashion books, it was time to pick up Spring's order.

"What CD is this?" I asked the cute clerk, referring to the new music playing.

"Vasco. Do you like it?" he said in an Italian accent. It must have been the combination of his accent, the music, and the Italian flag waving over my head, because visions of Paolo hit my brain all over again. Not the one-night Paolo I experienced, but the Paolo that could have been, the Paolo-and-Imogene Paolo. I had a hunch that a bad case of the gloomies was not far off.

"Sounds so familiar," I replied as he handed me the on-reserve book.

On my way downstairs to the cashier, someone caught my eye and it registered. It was Paolo! And he was carrying a gorgeous bouquet of flowers. My heart either took off or stopped completely, I wasn't sure which. I bolted. Upon spotting Paolo I inadvertently spilled my Acqua Minerale Frizzante, which caused an instant slip'n'slide down the ancient manuscripts aisle. Paolo left the store. Just as an old man with a cane slowly struggled to get in through the revolving door, I struggled to revolve out. I gave up and tried the outer door instead, but it was locked.

"Security!" someone behind me shouted. "Someone grab that girl!" I turned around to find two bald, overweight men in security uniforms heading toward me. I didn't realize that I had Spring's book in my hand.

"Wait," I said as a guard the size of a refrigerator took hold of my arm. "It's not what you think," I said, flustered.

"That's what they all say. Look girl, are you going to pay for that or not?"

"I was just about to, but I recognized an old friend and wanted to catch him before he left."

"Mmhmm," he said apathetically. Thankfully, that was all there was to it. I was in enough trouble and didn't need one more strike against me. I craned my neck around to see which direction Paolo went, while pushing the Sri Siva MasterCard in the security guard's face.

was in such a hurry to get out of there that by the time I'd reached the revolving door again, I dropped my package and had to revolve again. But by that time, it was too late. Paolo had disappeared. Then, as luck would have it, a city bus passed just as I turned the Vespa key, and I saw his face.

"Watch out!" I shouted as passersby yielded. It was heading east on 57th Street. I'll be late now for sure, but I was determined to see him.

"Hey!"

He didn't hear me.

"I said HEY!!!"

He turned around, and I almost had a stroke. I'd forgotten how gorgeous he was. At first he looked startled, disoriented even, and just when I thought I saw a glimmer of recognition settle on his face, the bus took off, and he was gone.

chapter six

The P.i.t.s.

date: JULY 8TH

mood: BLACK & WHITE

Someone has switched directors on the film that was my life because of late, things seem a bit more Woman on the Verge of a Nervous Breakdown *than* La Dolce Vita.

I arrived at the corner of 64th and Madison early. Knowing I'd have to wait at least fifteen minutes for Evie, who was nowhere in sight, I headed straight for a phone booth—a commodity which was becoming increasingly scarce in NYC. After unsuccessfully begging the Korean grocer around the corner to break his "no buy, no change" policy just this once, I scurried back and managed to solicit fifty cents off one in a string of limo drivers who were lined up in force outside Barneys. I think he felt sorry for me when I told him I didn't have a cell phone. But I do try to look on the bright side. I mean, after a couple of weeks on my Sidekick I was ready to qualify as a world champion thumb wrestler. With just a few keystrokes, you can add your name to the waiting list for your new it-bag, confirm your weekly beauty appointments, flirt, feed your Neopet, and check your horoscope, all while waiting on line for your morning coffee.

Slipping my two quarters into the coin slot of the aforementioned rare commodity, I dialed my missing-in-action cell phone and prayed. While my prayers weren't answered, I felt momentarily paralyzed when a voice on the other end did.

"*Pronto?*" a young woman's confident clear voice asked. Who is *this*? I asked myself in stunned silence. "*Pronto, sì? Con chi parlo?*" She repeated in a heavy Italian accent, sounding extremely sexy and most probably looking exactly like a gorgeous, younger version of Monica Bellucci.

"Hello, is Paolo there?" I stumbled.

"*Che?*"

"Hello, this is Imogene," I said. "I'm trying to reach Paolo. Is he there?"

"*Chi sta parlando.*"

"Look, I don't know who you are," I heard my rapidly-becoming-terse voice exclaim, "but you're speaking on *my*—Imogene's—cell phone, which happened to be, when last I knew, in the possession of someone named Paolo. Do you know who that is?"

"*Come? Con chi vuole parlare? chi è?* ELL-O, har yoo there? Ooo eez eet uh?" Blend one language gap with bad cell phone reception and sprinkle a healthy dose of rage, and you get the following:

"WHO ARE YOU AND WHY ARE YOU ANSWER-ING MY CELL PHONE?!!"

"*Hey, parli piu' forte! Parli in Italiano! Non la capisco!*" Which translated probably means, "Are you insane? What's your problem you maniac, I don't understand you, you imbecile!" *Im-be-see-lay!*

"What are you doing with my phone? Where's Paolo? Did Paolo give you my cell phone?!"

"Paolo, *si*, yes. You want to speeek weeth Paolo, eh? Ah, why you no say so?" Then without waiting for my reply, "Paolo!" the sexy voice hollered in the background, then back to me. "*Rimanga in linea per favore*—hold thee line. PAOLO! PAOLO!!!! *AL TELEFONOOOO*!!!"

This paroxysm of shouting was followed by another, even longer pause, in which I began nervously flexing my thumbs.

"Ell-oh—*Mamma dice che Paolo non c'e' ora. Capisce?*—*Mi capisce?* Ello? El-lo?"

"What mama? What's going on there?"

"Do you understand? Paolo eezn't ere right now. Do yoo want leave eem a message?" Which sounded more like "Would you care for a sausage?"

"Yes, absolutely! It's very important! Please tell him to call me at 212—"A sudden blip interrupted our bilingual tête-à-tête and the sound of a prerecorded voice, compliments of Verizon, said, "Please deposit fifty cents."

Although I knew I had no change, I tore frantically through my bag, finding nothing more than the half eaten apple that I'd skoshed from Ian's desk and the leftover crumbs of a stale buttered bagel, which Brooke threw back at me this morning.

How was I to know when she asked me to order her break-fast that in the fashion world, butter is a capital offense?

"Please deposit fifty cents," the pre-recorded voice repeated.

"But I don't have fifty cents," I answered anxiously, knowing full well I was speaking to no one.

"Please hang up and try your call again." I was discon-nected. Slam. I was that close! Now what? I thought, check-ing my watch. Great, now I'm the one who's late.

I was supposed to meet Evie at six, but by the time I was finished with my quasi-international phone call, I was a half hour late.

While dutifully pushing past the waves of girls pit-stopped for a quickie pre-date touch-up at the Dior cosmetics counter on Barneys main floor, I caught a quick glimpse of my own reflection, shimmering in a radiant mid-summer faux glow — *Affirmation: I look cute, ergo I am.* I raced down the aisles chock full of Estee Lauder, Lancôme, and Shiseido in search of Evie, stopping only long enough for a quick spritz of Lanvin Femme, my current infatuation (well, at least I can *smell* French). Evie and I had forgotten to say where in Barneys we would meet, but I had a hunch where she would be — upstairs at Chanel. Whenever we get separated in any place that has a Chanel boutique, I can always count on finding her there, usu-ally blissfully wandering amongst the suits, counting stitches and mumbling about the garment's construction, while simul-taneously deconstructing it in her own mind. She'd say: "See how tiny these stitches are?" Or, "look at this hem, it's hand rolled and hand sewn, and *blah blah blah* . . ." or, "look how clever this is," pointing out the metal chain sewn inside the hem, "it allows the skirt to hang just so." And as usual, when Evie talks fine print, garment construction or otherwise, I totally zone out.

"Girlena!" she squealed when she saw me. Evie, it turns out, wasn't upstairs counting stitches, but at the next counter over—right in between the free-gift-with-purchase bags and the celeb-u-scents. She was standing with a pretty young girl about our age with curly blond hair, who appeared, by the way she was alternately blinking and squinting, to have something in her eye.

"There you are girlena! Look," she said, referring to blinky, "we're twinning!" They were both wearing the same Marc Jacobs bag. That, however, is where the similarity ended. While this new girl was attired in a cool vintage-circa-spring-2006 way, Evie was decked out in Marc Jacobs head to toe. "I'm helping Cinnamon with a makeover," she said.

"What do you think of this shade, Evie?" asked the girl, looking *très* lost. Note to self: When sampling makeup one must consider the "ick factor" before jumping in, because chances are there's more culture lurking in those samples than in the entire city of Paris! Evie and I both stared at each other. "Oh, introduction time. Imogene, this is Cinnamon. Cinnamon, this is my best friend, Imogene."

"How nice to meet you." She smiled, looking over my shoulder. While extending her hand to greet me, she stepped forward and bumped into the makeup chair, which was right in front of her. How could she not have seen that?

"I really can't see a thing without my glasses," she said, unzipping her hobo bag and placing an oversize pair of eyeglasses on the bridge of her tiny upturned nose. "I just hate the way I look in them." Removing her glasses once again gave me a chance check her out without her noticing. She looked exactly like a hippie Barbie Doll. Boho Barbie. Then I noticed her feet. (Normally the first thing I check is shoes.) *Quelle horreur!* Uggs! (Cringe!)

This girl was a serious good taste offender. Evie was right—this girl is in desperate need of a fashion intervention. (Or at the very least, a prescription upgrade.)

Evie handed me a flyer while Cinnamon felt her way carefully around the counter. It read:

Psychic astrology and tarot card readings
by Cinnamon. Advise on all matters of life,
love, and success. Spiritual cleansing
for the mind, body and spirit.
Call 917-555-6657. Act now!

"What, you called this person??"

"*This* person is *that* person," she said, pointing to Cinnamon.

"Are you losing it?"

"I did it for *you*," Evie whispered. "And it turns out she's really nice. I like her and I think you will too."

"Not you, too! That's all I hear all day long. Spring's psychic this, her astrologer that. I mean it's absolutely rampant!" I whispered back. "Something bizarre has definitely gotten into the New York City water supply this summer and someone had better report it soon, because everyone's going completely bonkers!"

"Shh, she'll hear you," Evie hissed.

"Well she sure can't see me," I hissed back.

"Listen girlena, just give it a try, and be open. Anyway, what took you so long?" she asked, changing the subject. "And I hope you brought the shoes with you because Bee's having a total fit. You are about to officially be the first girl from Greenwich to face excommunication from JEFFREY!"

"First of all, I don't have a cell phone, re-mem-ber?!" I was beyond annoyed. "Secondly, just tell Bee I'm having the shoes um, cleaned . . . uh, or something. . . ." It's completely low lying to your best friend.

"Well, have you tried calling your cell phone?"

"Of course I've tried my cell phone! Every time I call, someone different picks up. And they all sound glam and gorgeous, and girlfriendy."

"You know, if I didn't know you better, I'd say you're completely in love."

"Love? Ha! You're crazy!" In truth it was just a baby crush. There, poof, it's gone. "I mean, love? Me? Hardly. In fact, on the rat-o-meter, I give him a ten!"

"Then why are you lining your eyes with, of all things, *kohl*?"

"Ick!" I said with a shiver, tossing it back in its tray.

"Look Imogene, I know you better than anyone. Admit it, you're head over heels."

"It's just a crush, for your information. No more. Can we move on?"

Cinnamon returned. (Thank God.) Maybe Evie's right. I wasn't being very gracious. I'll compose myself and try to make conversation.

"So Evie tells me you're a full-fledged psychic."

"Well, actually I'm doing a bunch of stuff this summer. So far I've temped at a PR company, a real estate company, and an advertising company. I've been a concierge, waited tables, and, oh, I read cards twice a week at Serendipity. That's when I'm the most psychic. You should come sometime, or something," she said a bit awkwardly.

"Cinnamon's trying to save up money for singing lessons. That's what she really wants to do. Isn't that *sooo* exciting, girlena?"

Concierge, astrologer, tarot card reader, singer, temp. And I thought I was confused.

A pert cosmetics saleswoman arrived. "Have you seen these?" she interjected. She held out an exciting teeny tiny satin box with the gasp-inducing letters *P-R-A-D-A* affixed across the top and leaned over the counter, engulfing everyone in a giant puff of Chanel No. 19. She elbowed Evie out of the way, eyelash glue in hand.

"They're not just ordinary lashes. They're made of mink!" she said. "Real mink." She gushed. "It's the ultimate luxury for fall. They add the cutest flutter to your wink. Oh and by the way," she said to Cinnamon, "they're semi-permanent. They last up to six months. They're more like hair extensions than eyelashes. Can I interest you in a pair?"

"Absolutely!" Cinnamon replied.

"They're triple-divine!" Evie exclaimed.

"I didn't know Prada made mink eyelashes," I said.

"Why just five minutes before you sat down, I sold ten pairs of them to J.Lo," she said while applying the finishing touches to Cinnamon's upper lids.

Just next to us, a girl chattering away on her cell phone lifted her chin at our saleswoman, tapped on the counter, and shouted, "Is anyone here?"

I mean, press 1 for obnoxious!

"Hell-oooh?! Really, do you mind?" she asked our saleswoman. "I'm in a terrific hurry! All I want is this one little thing," she said, holding a jar of Crème de la Mer, which, at $192 per ounce, is roughly the equivalent of 80 hours of a fashion forecasting intern's salary.

"Will someone press her mute button," the cosmetics lady said under her breath. "I'll be right with you, dear." And then to Cinnamon, "Will that be cash or Barneys charge?"

"Charge," Cinnamon answered, handing over her the credit card.

Just then something the chattering cell phone abuser said got my full attention.

"Brooke, dahling, those photos are beyond fab. How'd you do it?" I turned around to get a better look at this BFF of Brooke's. I didn't recognize *her*, but right there standing next to her were Brooke's two trained bookends, the salad sisters from Soho House, Fern and Romaine. I spun back to the counter before they could spot me, and having no choice but to swallow my fear, I dipped into the "icky" makeup samples. I was just about to apply a second coat of Stiletto liquid eyeliner when a voice sounded behind me, interrupting my new found blissful state of make-upness.

"Welllllllllllook who's here. I would have thought Duane Reade was more your speed," said Fern, as I proceeded to poke myself in the eye with the wand.

"Why, it's that little girl from Kansas again, Ro. The one we met at Soho House. The one poor Brooke has to hand-hold all day long while she learns the ropes."

Helloooooo, will somebody deport them, please?!

I fumbled for the box of tissues Romaine was slowly pushing out of reach. Evie pushed them back. She was not missing a word of this exchange and I could tell she was getting mad. Fern pursed her lips together and narrowed her eyes.

"You know, Dorothy," she oozed, ignoring Evie while slithering closer to me, "Spring *was* going to hire someone *much* more experienced than you. Isn't that right, Ro?"

"Very right, Fern."

"But, as it happens, Spring Sommer's loss is Winter Tan's gain."

"Indeed."

"Now we both work with Winter, and Haute and About has the benefit of *both* our fashion senses."

This was news. Big news, which I pondered while blotting my eye. It explained why Brooke was so nasty to me.

Well, aside from her personality. I suddenly didn't feel so meek about being new and not knowing stuff. In fact, it felt pretty good to know one of these namesakes of the vegetable kingdom had been rejected in favor of *moi*.

Well, I had enough problems with Brooke and I didn't want to make things worse by being rude to her friends, however *impolite* they may be. Evie, apparently, had not come to the same conclusion.

Quicker than you can say "moisturize," Evie reached into the sample jar of Crème de la Mer on the nearby counter, scooped out a humongous dollop, and squished it right in Romaine's face.

"OHMIGOD! What have you done, you little witch?!" Romaine said, now dripping with something other than sarcasm. "Look at me!"

"I am looking at you," the saleswoman said, returning with Cinnamon's eyelashes, "and I'm sorry, dear, but you are using way too much of that product."

"Fern! Fern! Don't just stand there, get me a tissue! I can't see!"

"Let's go girls," the cell phoner said to Fern and Romaine. "This place has really gone to the dogs!"

"Good riddance," said the saleswoman, and then turning to Cinnamon with a sympathetic expression, she said, "I'm sorry to have to tell you this, but your card has been confiscated."

"Oh not again. And I promised myself I'd only use cash from now on."

"Don't worry dear, it happens all the time. Just call the business office when you get home, and they'll work it out with you. But I'm afraid you'll have to give the eyelashes back."

"But you said they're permanent, for up to six months."

"Oh wow girlene," Evie whispered excitedly. "Cinnamon's binge means she's officially one of us. Well, one of you. Now you can do a good deed and sponsor Cinnamon at Spenders Anonymous."

"Don't worry, Cinnamon dear," Evie consoled. "We're actually on our way to Imogene's support group—they'll help you. Besides, Imogene might go crazy and make a spectacle of herself, so we better be there to watch."

"Evie!" I said indignantly. She laughed and made a goofy cross-eyed smiling face back as if to say, *lighten up*.

I t was fitting in a completely twisted way that my bi-weekly Consumer Debt Counseling and Rehabilitation meeting, otherwise known as Spenders Anonymous, was held in the ninth-floor penthouse conference room of Barneys.

I have to confess I'd rather be sitting through Uzbekistan Fashion Week than baring my shopper's soul to a group of strangers. I mean, were it not for this credit conundrum, I'd be strolling through Paris right now with Toy, Aunt Tamara, and Evie. Instead Evie, Cinnamon, and I took the last few chairs, carefully avoiding the sea of shopping bags and mostly Manolo-clad feet of those already seated at Spenders Anonymous.

"All right then, ladies," announced Margaux, the Bulgari-bejeweled chairperson.

"Ahem," said the man in the front row twirling his Gucci shades.

"And man," she amended. "Let's settle down and get started, shall we?" she said from behind a small table at the front of the room.

"Before we begin, I'd like to thank Myla Greenberg, who so generously provided our upscale refreshments. I would also like to thank our host, Barneys, for graciously allowing us to feel right at home, as for many of us, it *is* our home away from home."

"I'll be right back," Evie whispered, entranced by the scent of sugar wafting from the treat-laden table. Cinnamon followed, bumping into people and knocking over a chair along the way.

Evie returned with the super-deluxe sampler assortment. All set for an hour-long snackathon.

"I thought you were on a diet!" I growled.

"This is my diet."

Oh, great, she's back on the Easy-Bake Oven diet again.

"Their vanilla cupcakes are killer!" she said. "Try one."

Was she really in this much denial? To tell the truth, her deranged diets were starting to get on my nerves. After some thought, I had come to the conclusion that Evie was transferring her pent-up need to design into a need to eat. And she doesn't just eat from her own plate. She absolutely has to always pick off mine too — which drives me bonkers.

Just to make her happy, I bit into the cupcake and well, it was delicate and scrumptiously moist and in less than a nanosecond I was transported to my blissful, carefree kindergarten days before I had become the hyper, over-ambitious lunatic I am today.

"Thanks pal," I said, half smiling. The thing about Evie is no matter how annoying she can be at times, she *is* completely wonderful, the world's greatest trouper and portable support group. I'm so glad she's my best friend.

"Don't mention it," she mouthed, smiling a cherubic, chocolate cheesecake smile.

Quiet finally fell over the room, the door swung open dramatically, and Caprice made her entrance. Every head in the room spun around and the group gasped in collective awe. You could see why men went gaga over her. When she walked into a room, her body said *hello* before she even opened her mouth.

She spotted me right away. Her hair was damp and her clothes limp.

"We'll begin by reviewing our twelve-step program," Margaux directed. "Repeat after me ladies—and man. One: We admit our addictive fashion cravings render us powerless to resist shopping, especially during times of sales."

The group recited her words in unison.

"Two: We believe that a power greater than charge cards can restore our dignity. Three: When in doubt, employ the buddy system. . . ."

"What happened to you?" I whispered to Caprice as she collapsed into the seat I'd been saving for her. "You look like you just climbed out of a sauna."

She exhaled. "It was so hot and crowded in that yoga class, I'm ready to commit *OHM*-icide!"

"Why are you working out so hard? You don't need it," I said, glancing in the direction of her gorgeous figure.

"Do you know how many days there are to Fashion Week? Sixty-two!"

"Ohhhhh, *Capriiiiiice*," I exclaimed in joy. I hadn't noticed her new puppy until he just then poked his head out of her supermodel-y messenger pouch.

"Who's this wittle, wittle bayyybeeee?" I said, touching his teeny ears and frail little head. "He's adoooooorrrable!"

"Yes you are, Diablo," she said sweetly, picking him up for a kiss. "He's my little papillon puppy." (Heads up non-New Yorkers: The number one model accessory is at least one miniature dog from the following breeds: Chihuahua, papillon, teacup Yorkie, teacup dachshund, Pomeranian, min-pin, or toy poodle.) "I got him from a shelter. Isn't he the sweetest?"

"How was your trip?" I whispered, referring to her recent extreme modeling gig.

"Swimming with sharks in Belize for a bathing suit photo shoot may sound totally exotic. But when you're the one in

142

the cage and hungry sharks are circling you like you're the bait, well . . ."

From what I gathered, it ended much the same way most of her gigs do. She was fired. Not because of any bad attitude. The problem was, as previously mentioned—her big butt.

"Ladies, please," Margaux said to us. "Thank you. Now that we've reviewed the twelve steps, I'd like to officially welcome everyone. My name is Margaux and I'm a shopoholic."

"Hello, Margaux," the room responded in unison.

"Who'd like to start us out this evening?"

This was the part I dreaded. I always felt guilty about not raising my hand. I mean, it's a well-known fact that I'm a natural born hand-raiser.

"Come, come ladies, there are no secrets in this room, no need to be bashful. Do we have any newcomers tonight? Who's going to break the ice this evening?"

Cinnamon put her knitting back in her bag and raised her hand and I asked myself the question: Is knitting the new black? How cute! Maybe I'd ask her to teach me.

"Have you met Cinnamon?" I whispered to Caprice.

"Oh, eew, she's a knitter. Very *Ladies Home Journal*, if you ask me," Caprice said, squashing my hope.

Margaux beamed at the new arrival.

"My name is Cinnamon," she said, standing up.

"Hi Cinnamon!" raved the group.

"Welcome, Cinnamon. Can you tell us about yourself?"

"I'm an astrologer, psychic, realtor, PR specialist, singer, vintage slash resale junkie, Marcaholic, and faux-lash fiend."

"Oooo I see," said Margaux, looking at her like fresh meat.

"So, Cinnamon, can you give us some insight into your spending state of mind?"

"Definitely," she said. "I can attribute my shopping of late directly to the fact that Jupiter is transiting my second house of material things and squaring my Leo midheaven."

"If she's such a good astrologer," Caprice whispered in my ear, "why didn't she predict the monthly credit card bill transiting her mailbox?"

"Thank you, Cinnamon." Margaux smiled.

Caprice nudged me, but Evie got up instead.

"I'm Evie, and I'm a sugar junkie."

"Oh, I'm afraid that you're in the wrong meeting, dear. The Sweet Tooth Anonymous meeting isn't until Tuesday."

Caprice cleared her throat righteously and declared, "My name is Caprice. I am neither a Marcaholic nor a sugarholic. I don't have compulsive shopping disorder. I am merely here to support my friend." She smiled in my direction proudly, to which the group replied in unison, "Hi, Caprice! Way to go, Caprice! Awesome!"

"I hardly even shop. I have a personal shopper who takes care of most everything I need. So what if she's number two on my speed dial?" she added, giving greater thought to the matter. "And we do chat at least three times a day, weekends included," she mused on. "In fact, I saw her just an hour ago," she said. "And . . . she . . . bought me . . . this. . . ." Caprice looked down at her gorgeous new Bea Valdes bag, seemingly ashamed for the first time. Then she rallied, "It's unavailable in this country. . . ."

"Ooooooooh," the crowd murmered.

Even I was salivating over Caprice's new bag—all crystal beads and satin ribbons. I mean there's style, but beyond style is the ultimate 9-letter word: "exclusive"!!!

"My personal shopper got it directly from Paris," Caprice added. "Who could resist?! After all, I'm only human! Besides, I'm spending much less than last month," she rationalized. "It's Sale Season."

"But Caprice," Margaux interrupted, "did you really need that bag, or are you simply consumed, no pun intended, by the vulgar, substanceless yet intoxicating buy-buy, consume-consume culture we live in, where we are driven to have the newest, latest, and greatest? All in an overriding urge to impress people who don't in fact give a hoot about you."

"You're right, I don't need this . . . icon of consumerism." Caprice affirmed. "I'm an individual, and I don't have to impress anyone. . . . I'm returning it. That's it."

The crowd is visibly moved and applause fills the room.

"Good idea, Caprice, why not phone your PS right now while we're all here to support you. We'll wait."

Caprice paged her personal shopper. Soon her cell phone rang. Silence filled the room as Caprice answered.

"Hi Ivy. About the new bag, I have to return it." Pause. "What do you mean it's non-refundable? . . . Because it's so exclusive? . . . It's not even for sale yet? It's the only one made so far?" Caprice clicked off and without so much as a beat someone called out:

"I'll buy it, Caprice!"

Another voice rang out. "I'll give you eight hundred."

"I'll pay a thousand for it right now."

"Twelve hundred, in cash."

"Twelve fifty."

"Two thousand."

"Three thousand!!!"

"Going once, going twice . . . sold! To the gentleman in the front row," Caprice said in the midst of rabid applause.

"That was very compelling," Margaux said. "Thank you for sharing."

"Thank *you*," Caprice sighed, looking as if she'd gone through another round of Bikram. "I feel purged!"

"Is there anyone else who would like to say a few words?" Margaux asked. "How about you, Imogene?" she asked, craning her neck to see past the scrawny size-two Kelly Ripa impersonator in front of me.

"Hi Margaux," I said. "For the record, I haven't spent a dime in at least a month. Come to think of it, I just may be cured."

"Come now, Imogene, it doesn't serve you to fudge the truth. You're among friends here," Margaux encouraged.

"Well, I don't know what everyone is making such a huge fuss about. Spending is an American citizen's patriotic duty! In fact, they should give me a medal for all the shopping I've done in my few short years on this planet. I mean, were it not for we consumers, what would the state of our economy be? I know, it looks bad," I said, "but really, I haven't bought a thing in two weeks. I couldn't buy anything even if I wanted to—I'm maxed out on my credit card. I'm even debt dieting— I've been living off everyone's leftovers."

"Well Imogene, I know you're trying very hard, but this is a twelve-step program. You've been coming here for a few weeks now, and you haven't even moved out of step one. Now, we're all here to support you, aren't we, group? "

"Yes, Margaux," they answered in unison.

"So, for your own sake, Imogene, why don't you get it off your chest."

There was a long pause — I took a deep breath and whispered, "My name is Imogene and I'm a shoe addict."

At 10 pm, the exterior of Barneys is as quiet as a Wal-Mart on Park Avenue. (As if.) We had just left the Spender's Anonymous meeting. I stared longingly at the Greek goddess themed window display. The atmosphere was that of a forest, all mossy and woodsy, and the goddess Diana held a bow, and a quiver full of arrows was strapped across her back. "Haven't you had enough of this place? Let's go," called Caprice.

"Unfortunately, I only get visitation privileges — once every two weeks. Anything more and I'd have to endure a court-appointed chaperone," I said, coveting the dazzling Versace ensemble.

"Don't mind her," Evie said. "Thursdays are when they change the windows. Imogene always goes a bit psycho then."

"It's not just that, it's everything . . . or rather, nothing — no cell phone, no cash, no plastic, and no reason to live! And something has been really fishy at Hautelaw. I mean, every time I walk into Brooke's office, she slams her top drawer and hangs up on whomever she's talking to. I think she's been stealing my ideas. I just have a hunch."

"I knew it! You're psychic, like me!" Cinnamon radiated.

"I already caught her clipping my name from my report and I think she substituted her own. She got all flustered when I asked about it and made like I was crazy. Today she gave me a big stack of papers to staple and file, and when I got back with everyone's lunch—"

"Don't worry about her," Caprice interrupted. "She's just your run of the mill, power-hungry, back-stabbing wannabe, who, like everyone else in her pack, is bucking for a big promotion—at someone else's expense!"

"Maybe it's not too late to go back to Greenwich and take that library internship."

"Bite your tongue," Evie admonished,

"But Evie, I'm just an assistant junior intern nobody!"

"This is your dream! Remember, you're the 'HAUTE' in Hautelaw! It's just a matter of time; you've got to hang in there. You'll see, the klieg light will swing your way. Just give it some time."

"She's right," said Caprice. "Are you going to let that punk and her friends shape your whole future? Don't you see, by piling up the paperwork and giving you all those personal errands and that mindless busy work to do, she's trying to break you down?"

"Besides, you're not the only one with problems. Look at me," Evie said. "I'm stuck in a kitchen all day long learning the nuts and bolts of the restaurant business against my will, when all I really want to do is design clothing."

"What about me?" Caprice added. "Do you know what it

feels like knowing that as soon as you turn around, everyone's laughing behind your back because you've got a butt the size of Kansas?"

"But you're completely totally drop dead hot," I said. "So what if your butt's a tad large? It's sexy—totally sexy."

"And what about you, Cinnamon?" Evie asked.

"Well, I know it sounds way corny, but my dream is to be a singer. The problem is I get stage fright every time I step in front of an audience. If only I were braver. I'm trying to overcome it. I've been singing karaoke for a couple of months now. Of course mostly in my apartment when I'm alone."

Evie said, "If I could only convince my dad that all I want to do in life is design clothes."

Caprice said, "If only big butts were happening, I'd have more work."

"Look at us," Cinnamon said. "*We're* goddesses—more than those mannequins in the window—no matter what our tribulations."

"Yeah," Caprice said, nodding to the display of Diana in the Barneys window.

"Goddesses have inner powers," Cinnamon said, taking out her tarot deck. "I think it's high time for each of us to embrace our own inner goddess."

We walked to the curb where my Vespa was parked. "Let's all pick one card and see how we each can overcome our problems right now." She placed her bag on the curb and shuffled the cards, continuing, "We are the goddesses of our destinies, and as such, we banish all evil people and circumstances from our lives." She arranged several cards on the narrow seat, turning one over under the sun card. She studied the cards. "I'm getting a vibe about Caprice. I'm feeling a shift coming on—big butts are going to be making a comeback! And," she said, turning over two more cards, "somehow, you're involved with it, Imogene, as are you, Evie."

"But how?"

Caprice interrupted, saying, "Look, guys, I could talk about this forever, but this has been a long day and I have an early morning go-see, so why don't we all go home, have a good night's sleep, and think about everything in the morning."

Everyone agreed. Cinnamon asked, "Is anyone going uptown?"

"Yeah, I am," said Caprice. "Where are you going, I'll drop you."

"Eighty-second and Park."

"Nice address," Caprice said, looking her over as if for the first time.

"Yeah, I'm house sitting for the entire summer. And you should see the place, it's like a palace. Actually, it's an interesting situation because it's going to be the location for a reality television show. Anyway, who cares? All I know is I have it rent free, until production begins."

This was too weird, I thought. It couldn't be. "Which building is it?" I asked,

"It's on the northeast corner, penthouse B."

"That's Nini Langhorne's penthouse!"

"Who's Nini Langhorne?"

"She's my . . . my . . . oh, it's a long story."

"Wow! Talk about a cosmic coincidence!"

After we said our good-byes, Evie and I sped off into the night's inky cauldron of stars that swirled seamlessly amid a sea of city lights on the West Side Highway, and I contemplated in silence my newly found friendships that I hoped would last a lifetime. And I wondered what I had to do with Caprice's butt.

chapter seven

Wintergate

date: JULY 14TH
mood: AS BLACK AS
MY STONE COLD DOPIO

It all began with Wintergate, which is to say, your basic paranoid corporate espionage debacle taken to the outer reaches of space, which became, I'm sorry to say, my undoing.

As you know, I possess a deep affinity for closets — my preferred sanctuary for inner peace — so when I was put in charge of Hautelaw's sample room, which, like my office, was merely a converted closet, I was totally transcended. For one whole hour a week, I organize (between gasps, coos, and drools) the absolute latest and greatest clothes, accessories, jewelry, shoes, hats, bags, fragrances, and beauty products, which Mick brings back from shopping jaunts all over the world. Unfortunately today wasn't the

usual ecstatic, kid-in-a-candy-store kind of closet day because some samples have recently gone missing and Spring had asked me to do a complete inventory. Meanwhile, Hautelaw was still losing clients to Winter Tan. To make matters worse, certain proprietary information had mysteriously found its way from our private files onto the pages of Haute & About's most recent report.

In response, Spring hired this super-hunky private-investigator-type guy named Lance to "sweep" Hautelaw for listening devices. Aside from locating Choux-Choux's Miu Miu Chew-Chew (an adorable locomotive-shaped chewy toy) and Spring's third ex-husband's wedding band, up to now he had found bupkes. He did, however, distribute a handy guidebook, complete with pictures, on how to identify listening devices—should we stumble across any in the future.

Needless to say, paranoia had gone into overdrive as Hautelaw's quarterly report was due to come out in two weeks. Major freak-outs were commonplace these last few days, the worst of which were Spring's, whose growing suspicion was surpassed only by her growing exasperation.

Anyway, all this office craziness was compounded by the fact that I had a tad of ennui, no doubt brought on by cell phone withdrawal, Spenders Anonymous meetings, Mercury retrograde, and the long-term damaging effects of negative cash flow. There I was in the sample closet when I realized I had forgotten to re-sort the pile of clothing Brooke had so graciously dumped on my desk earlier in the day. I exhaled unhappily and grabbed the doorknob, which, of course, was locked (Mercury retrograde, hello!), and began repeating to myself, "Stay calm and never, under any circumstances, panic."

Intercom! I thought suddenly.

Within seconds I was on the intercom to Malcolm — who wasn't there. Nor were the other ten people I called after him. Having been unsuccessful with the intercom, I tried knocking loudly on the door and shouting things like "Hello?" and "Can someone let me out of here?" Anyway, after a few minutes of that, I settled down to some serious kicking and screaming, eventually collapsing, hoarse and exhausted, on a pile of faux fur. I had pretty much given up and was about to drop off when the door flew open and Mick, arm full of samples, stepped in.

"Oh, there you are," he grinned. "Everyone's been looking for you." I clutched my throat and rasped as the door began to swing shut.

"Wait! The door!" Too late. It slammed behind him leaving us trapped together.

"The door locks from the outside," I wheezed. "And nobody's answering the intercom." I fell back.

"Well, someone will come along sooner or later," he said cheerfully.

"I've been in here for half an hour," I croaked, my voice slowly creeping back from the dead.

"Don't you have a cell phone?"

"It's in Italy," I frowned. "I mean, not really. I lost it. Well, I left it with this guy Paolo, who . . . never mind. It's really confusing." How embarrassing, I mean when am I going to be able to converse normally? There was a pause as we stared at each other uneasily. This was definitely the most alone time we've ever spent together.

"So," Mick said, "how's everything going?"

"Great," I chirped. "I love this business."

"Me too," he said as more awkward silence followed. "Spring mentioned you had some prior experience. You never told me that."

"She did? I mean, yes, I do. I mean"—oh God—"I write a column for my school paper. It's called 'Daily Obsession.' Actually, I spent all day Saturday zoooming around town and got some great photos, because—"

"I'd love to see your work."

"Really?" I croaked, further injuring my voice box. Mick smiled patiently.

"Sure. I'm always looking for new ideas." He stood up and glanced at his watch. "I'll be leaving on a three o'clock flight, but how 'bout if you show me when I get back."

"Oh Mick! That would be super, thank you!" I gushed, as the door flew open.

"Malcolm! You got my message. And you came!" Malcolm looked at me, then Mick, then me again, and said, "Of course I came. What, I'm going to leave you in a closet all day? Silly girl!" he snapped. "*Oy vey*, it's hotter than the Tenth Street baths in here!" He looked down at the pile of mush on the floor, which was me. "My you're a sight!"

"Thank God you had a key," I said.

"Oh, this isn't just any key. This is *theeee* key," he smiled, dangling a brass key ring from his finger. "This unlocks every door in the office. How do you think I know what's going on around here?" I dusted myself off while Mick and Malcolm chatted on about keys. Then he said, "Let's go. There's an emergency meeting in Spring's office. Chop, chop!"

"What's the meeting for?" Mick asked as we piled out of the closet and hurried down the hall.

"*Oy*, pick something. First she's *meshuga* with this *kakameyme* spy thing. Now she's on a tear about Jock Lord."

"What about him?"

"This just in. We didn't get an invite to his fashion show."

MICK! Darling! Oh, thank GAWD you're here!" She cried, running toward him. "Did you hear about Jock Lord?!"

"Malcolm told me," he said seriously.

"The show of the year, and we're not invited!"

"Are you sure?" he asked. "Maybe the invitation's lost in the post."

"Dahling, you can't possibly believe that! Can he, Imogene dear?"

Before I had a chance to answer, Brooke magically appeared between us.

"Of course not, Spring," she said, as if the very thought were offensive. "We would have received ours the same time as everyone else."

"I called a friend of mine over at House of Lord," Deborah said. "We're not on the list."

"I would absolutely *die* to get coverage of that show!" Spring cried.

"They're not allowing any photography, either."

"Imogene, open that window! I'm going to jump! I no longer want to live!"

"How can we not be on the list?" Mick said quietly to himself.

"I'll tell you how that can be!" Spring spun around, seething. "It's that couture clown, Winter Tan. She's behind this. I just know it!"

"That horrible woman!" Brooke exclaimed.

"Deborah, dahling, is you-know-who on the list?"

"Well, yes, but—"

"You see!" Spring stormed over to her desk, sat down, and fired up a cigarette. "Would someone hand me that pillow?" Of course, Brooke rushed to prop the needlepoint remnant of office past, the one that read "Kabbalists do it better," behind Spring's back. Mick rolled his eyes. I thought I was going to be sick.

At that point Lance the spy guy entered the room and beamed at Spring who, making a speedy recovery, beamed back.

"You've all met Lance, I assume," Spring sang out. "He's been helping me locate bugs in my office." It was Deborah's turn to roll her eyes.

"Oh Lance, what's this?" Spring pointed casually to something on her colorful Zandra Rhodes chiffon caftan.

"Don't anyone move or speak. It may be a listening device," Lance warned, feeling the front of Spring's caftan.

"All clear," Lance announced when he'd completed his search of Spring's clothing. "Just a random hair clip."

"Oh!" Malcolm cried. "I think I have some listening devices on me, too."

"Is there a point to this meeting?" Mick asked.

"A point? Of course there's a point!" Spring plunged her hand into a drawer and yanked out a tiny metal object about the size of a dime. "Look what the Kaiser found today!"

Everyone stood around her desk and peered at the miniscule object.

"This, my *dahlings*, is a bug!" she declared.

"Zhang Ping model A4," Lance read from the handy guide of listening devices. "Made in China." Mick and I exchanged wide-eyed looks then stared at Spring as she took a long, satisfied drag from her cigarette.

"Your dog found it?" Malcolm blurted out.

"Don't look so surprised," she purred. "You remember Madame Blatskovitch, the medium who was here last week?"

Oh, yeah, I almost forgot. Spring hired a medium: one Madame Blatskovitch, who came in for an hour to teach us how to communicate without the use of speech. Telepathy, you know? The object, of course, was to prevent any alleged listening devices from picking up Hautelaw business. The rest of the afternoon was spent practicing our "silent speech" with each other while working. Needless to say, not much got done that day.

Spring widened her eyes and began to stare at the group for a very long time. Talk about uncomfortable.

"Spring, are you all right?" I asked.

"I was communicating telepathically."

"Oh. Sorry, I haven't been practicing."

"Me, either," the group added in unison.

"Never mind." Spring waved her hand dismissively. "Anyway, while she was here I had her train Choux-Choux and the Kaiser to sense the vibrations of illegal electronic devices."

"Really?" I know. It was a stupid question, but I couldn't help asking.

"And here's what they found." She held out the disc in the palm of her hand and grinned wildly. "A listening device planted by a spy. Yes, we have a spy in our little family." She looked around the group suspiciously. "And I intend to find out exactly who that spy is."

"Maybe Lance is right. We shouldn't be talking in front of this thing," Deborah said.

"If you had practiced Madame Blatskovitch's techniques, you wouldn't need to."

In the midst of this cloak-and-dagger routine, Ian huffed into the room.

"Sorry I'm late everyone. Had to pick up the wool swatches for the new trend—"

Spring pressed her finger against her lips and held out a hand with the metal disc on it. Ian attempted to speak but Spring shook her head violently, pointing at the disc repeatedly, then cupping her ear as if listening, then bulging her eyes and staring at him in a telepathic way. Ian placed his fingers on his temples and mouthed *Sorry, I haven't been practicing.* Ian then held up three fingers, as in charades. Everyone nodded. He then began prancing around the room, opening his mouth and bobbing his head rapidly like he was doing a power hurl or something. Long story short, he was being a sheep—as in "baaatery."

"Battery?" Deborah said quietly.

"It's a battery. See?" Ian flipped it over. "Two-point-oh V. That stands for volts."

Spring stared at it thoughtfully. "Well, that explains why my camera's not working."

"Glad we got that sorted out," Mick fumed quietly on the way out. And the rest of us followed suit. "I'll be back late Friday."

"Oh, and don't forget, people!" Spring hollered after us. "I'll be in the Himalayas all next week."

Everyone mumbled their good-byes. I myself was halfway out when Spring called me back.

"Oh, Imogene dear, don't leave yet."

I made a wide turn and headed back to her desk. She sat down, lit a cigarette, and said, "Imogene, I just want you to know what a *wonnnnderfulll* job you're doing here."

This was out of the blue and I blushed from head to toe. "Thank you."

"I'm *sooo* glad I listened to Nini, but then, I *always* do, and Mick has nothing but nice things to say . . . as does everyone else, for that matter."

With the exception of Brooke, I imagined.

"So, what do you think?" she asked, her eyes wide with expectation. Okay, what did I miss? With Spring you never knew. I stood and stared at her, desperately applying what little I could remember of Madame Blatskovitch's brief but intense telepathy lesson. She furrowed her brow and asked, "Are you all right, dear?" Then she leaned forward and felt my forehead.

"I'm fine," I lied.

"Hello?!" she boomed. "The column, I want you to do a small piece on retail windows around the city."

"What?" I gasped.

"Brooke didn't tell you? Well," she chuckled. "She's *sooo* busy these days."

I would have gagged at this if it weren't for the fact that I was on cloud nine. Spring smiled at me indulgently and lit another cigarette. "Maybe you should sit down. You really don't look well." She led me by the elbow to a deep chair, into which I collapsed. "Then it's settled. I've discussed it with Mick and he agrees that *L'Hiver Bleu*, our next book, needs something extra. Something fresh, something new and exciting. Ian or Malcolm or whoever over in that department will give you the digital requirements, and you'll check in with Brooke and Mick for the creative. Well, I don't want to keep you any longer. Duke will be driving me to the airport shortly and Brooke knows how to reach me should any of you deliciously talented young creatures need me!"

"Are you ready, eager young fashion forecasting intern, for your first major assignment?" asked Spring brightly.

I decided to wait until I left the room before I started screaming in ecstasy.

I was on my way to meet Evie at Serendipity for lunch and just couldn't wait to tell her my good news. I snaked in and out of midday traffic feeling on top of the world. With my first major assignment and lunch with the girls—everything was positively perfect! My thoughts suddenly boomeranged back to Paolo. Maybe I've been wrong about him . . . you know? Like, maybe he *has* tried to return my phone. Maybe he even tried to find me. Then somewhere deep inside the recesses of my mind, an errant brain cell sparked the question: Am I falling in love?

I walked into the back room and found Evie and Cinnamon sitting at the rear table, scrutinizing the oversized menu. Evie was jotting something in a notebook.

"What are you guys up to?"

"Girlena!" They both jumped up, and after hugs and hellos, we sat down and chatted until the waitress came over.

"Hi. Are you ready to order?" The words "Need you ask" were on the tip of my tongue when Evie chimed in with something so completely out of character, I nearly fell off my Stella McCartney wedges.

"Are your vegetables organic, seasonal, indigenous, and GMO free?"

The waitress stared at her.

"What?" she finally managed.

"GMO free. You know, not genetically modified?"

"How should I know?"

"Then I'll just have an egg. Lightly poached."

"What happened to your usual Frozen Hot Chocolate and Bleu Burger?" I asked.

"That way of life is so over. I'm onto the next phase, girl-friend."

"And for you, miss?"

"I'm starved," Cinnamon said. "Um, I'll have a cheese-burger and an Apricot Smush . . . and a small cappuccino to start, please."

"Oh no you're not," Evie huffed. "Do you know how many thousand of gallons of jet fuel are used to get those apricots here? And the burger—have you any idea how much methane gas cows produce?! I mean, hello?! Global warming?!"

"When did you become an eco-warrior?" I asked.

"And your cappuccino? Is Serendipity buying fair-trade coffee?" Evie glared at the waitress. "Are you?"

"Hey, I don't even know what that is!" she barked.

"I guess I'm not really very hungry," Cinnamon sighed.

"Me either," I murmured. "I'll just have what she's having."

"Ditto," said Cinnamon.

"Three eggs," the waitress scrawled furiously on her pad and was gone.

I looked up at Evie, who was studying me. "You want to tell us what's going on?" she asked.

"I'm fine," I lied.

Enter Caprice nonchalantly sipping an Odwalla diet Vanilla Al'mondo. All heads turned, and as usual, all conversation ceased. She was wearing sparkly sandals, black fishnet stockings, and a scant, sequined satin spangled, saffron-colored, leotard—in other words, a circus costume.

"Why are you wearing a trapeze costume?" Evie asked.

"Oh this?" she laughed, casually. "*Mira*, I'm on my way to a *Cirque du Soleil* audition. Why, do I look all right?"

"You look great!" said Cinnamon.

"Have you eaten yet?" Evie asked.

"Yeah. I'm down to seven Tic-Tacs a day. Fashion Week is looming and I still have this," she slapped her visible hip. "What's up, chica," she looked at me. "You seem a little down."

"It's nothing, really," I lied again.

"I see. Boy trouble."

"It's that guy, Paolo!" Evie cried.

"Who's Paolo?" Cinnamon leaned forward, hungrily.

"Oh! This is such a good story! I mean, he totally kissed her then stole her phone, and then he turned up at her job, well, I mean, before it was her job, and he was like making out with Brooke."

"Evie!" I objected.

"This is making you upset?!" Caprice looked shocked. "*Mira*, this is how they are! They tell you they love you then they steal your phone!"

Cinnamon touched my hand and smiled behind her nerd-chic glasses. "This might be a really good time for me to do a reading." She pulled out a tarot deck.

"Oh, uh . . . ," I said hesitantly.

"Go ahead, girlena. They're only cards."

"Don't worry, nothing bad is going to happen," Cinnamon said. "All you have to do is shuffle the deck and think about your life, or any questions you want answered. When you're ready, put the deck down in front of you and pull out a card. Any card."

I nervously felt through the deck, trying to choose the right card. A card that would tell me about my destiny, about the big, spectacular life I was going to have. A card that would reveal what I secretly wanted to know about Paolo . . . and me. A card that would answer all my questions the way *I* wanted them to be answered.

I yanked one out and opened my eyes. Of all the cards in that big, fat, stupid, deck *I* had to pull the *death card*.

Nobody spoke. We just stared at the picture of Skeletor riding a dead horse. Why couldn't I have picked the pretty princess, or the beautiful world, or the sun card, with those lovely twinkling rainbows and stars all around it?

Evie broke the silence, "Does this mean someone's going to die?"

"No! Definitely not!" Cinnamon protested. "It's not about physical death." She looked at me carefully. "It indicates a transformation in the works. It can mean death of an old way of life . . . to make way for a new way of life. You know?"

"Kinda like, one door closes so that another one can open?" Caprice asked.

"Exactly. It usually has to do with some important and necessary changes in one's way of life or way of thinking. Like letting go of an old way of life, preparing for the new."

I finally breathed. "Well that doesn't sound *too* scary. What am I supposed to do?"

"Nothing. Just be ready, because I'd say big changes are on their way."

On the way back to work I realized I had completely forgotten to tell Evie about my good news.

chapter eight

Breaking News: You're Toast!

date: JULY 14TH

mood: YOUR FORECAST:
Sunny with a high of 90 degrees, and a chance of complete and utter devastation.

You know what they say, life's what happens when you're making other plans.

The sound of music—humming to be precise—was emanating from behind a gigantic flower arrangement on Brooke's white desk—an arrangement remarkably similar to the one Paolo had been carrying at Rizzoli. One might even say exactly like it. I peered around the floribunda and saw a curl form on Brooke's lips as she flipped through the pages of some thick, spiral-bound tome.

"You wanted to see me?" I asked the snow queen.

"Imogene." She smiled pleasantly.

Okay, whenever Brooke is pleasant, it's officially creepy. I stepped into her office, carefully scanning the room for possible defensive strategies should she go over the deep end. Due to the sparseness of the room, my only choice of weapon was a stapler. I could imagine the headlines: "Girl staples co-worker to desk in freak attack." I decided to seek safe haven in a chair but was stopped mid-sit by Brooke.

"Don't bother. This won't take long," she said, studying her nails. "Spring has asked *me* to speak to you in her absence."

"What about?" I asked, balancing between confusion, dread, and chair.

"Well," Brooke said innocently, "I'm afraid there's been a little bit of a misunderstanding."

"Misunderstanding?"

"That's what I said, Imogene. Misunderstanding." This time she rolled the word in her mouth, tasting it.

"What kind of misunder—"

"The unfortunate kind." She slapped the book shut and shoved it toward me. "Here. Hot off the presses."

I picked it up and stared. The vibrant purple cover was inscribed with the title *Haute & About: Summer Trend Guide*.

Normally, I would have been eager to check out Haute & About's work. I'd never actually seen any of their publications before, but everything about this seemed wrong.

"And?" I said, trying to sound casual.

"I think you'll find pages twenty-seven through thirty-two *especially* interesting," she purred. Slivers of ice slowly crept up my spine as I flipped through the pages . . . twenty-five . . . twenty-six . . . at twenty-seven I stopped dead. I mean dead. I felt like I was falling into a deep, endlessly dark well. Only worse. There, amid Haute & About's swatches, patterns, and color combinations were *my* photos, the ones from *my* cell phone, the cell phone that *Paolo* had.

"I don't have to tell you how very upset Spring was when she saw this. Especially given her, how shall I put it . . . dislike for our competitor."

"This is some kind of mistake," I stammered. "I don't know how these got in here."

"Don't you?" Brooke looked at me with her big, ice blue eyes. "Does the name Spenders Anonymous ring any bells in that empty head of yours?"

"What?!" Okay, now it was time for shock, closely followed by severe anger. "How do you know about that?!"

"Oh, well," Brooke exhaled blithely—she was enjoying herself. *Really* enjoying herself. "It just so happens that some of my . . . less fortunate friends are members of the same chapter of SA as you. And guess what?"

I didn't have to. Those cretins, Fern and Romaine, must have followed me to the meeting. Suddenly the idea of stapling Brooke to death didn't seem far-fetched at all.

"Please understand, I don't blame you for selling your pictures to Spring's competitor, Imogene," she continued. "I mean a girl's got to do what a girl's got to do to make ends meet. What with your parents being financially challenged and all. Oh, don't look so shocked. One should be proud of one's heritage, however disadvantaged."

I couldn't help it. I wanted to scream out some expletive, but all that came out was, "You, you, #%@*$!" Ohmigod! (*CONTROL-ALT-DELETE!*) It just popped out.

"There's no need to get nasty. Besides, you brought this on yourself."

"I haven't done anything!" I cried. "I don't even have those pictures. They were on my cell phone, which was stolen!"

Brooke looked at me innocently. "I don't doubt you in the least. In fact, I tried telling Spring this was probably some kind of mix-up. Unfortunately, with samples missing from the closet and clients leaving, and now this . . ." She shrugged her shoulders and sighed.

I couldn't move. All I could do was stand there and stare at her across the wintry landscape of her office, fighting back tears so as not to give her the satisfaction, while my entire body quaked. Finally she said, "I think that's all . . . Oh, wait, I almost forgot—Spring did leave you a message before she left." With this, Brooke's lip curled again. "She said to tell you, you're fired."

I don't know how I let Evie talk me into this, but after my nervous breakdown, she said she wouldn't let me out of her sight. And since she had to be at the restaurant, so did I. I mean, some people would be horizontal right now, as in, in bed, as in unable to move. Some people would remain that way for days, or weeks or even years, but *I* didn't stand a chance because of Evie.

After Brooke fired me, Evie was the first person I called. I mean, she was the only person I could call.

Although according to her, it's a good thing I'm like mired in debt, desperate, completely broke, and as of today, absolutely directionless in life, or I might not be sitting here right now, which is to say waiting tables at Heshi. Which again, according to Evie, is a good thing because a) it keeps me from thinking about everything that's gone wrong with my life, b) it forces me to be around people, and c) it prevents me from having conversations with Miss Stevens — which I couldn't do anyway because I have no cell phone. Trouble is, a, b, and c remind me of d) the kind of man who steals your heart, then your cell phone, then sells the pictures (on your cell phone) to the competition, which gets you fired from your dream job and everything you had hoped for disappears before your very eyes.

So there I was on a very humid Tuesday night in the middle of summer, sitting at a little table and writing in my diary while all around me churned a category 5 tornado of organized chaos known as the kitchen. Takeshi, after Evie told him about my miserable life, took pity on me, and made me a mouth-watering array of whisper-thin slices of sashimied red snapper set off by a to die Peruvian hot sauce. Any other time I would have been in heaven, but I couldn't bring myself to eat.

Evie sat down with her own version of God knows what.

"Evie, I don't know how I let you talk me into waitressing. I don't know what to do!" I whined, feeling the discomfort of navigating in unchartered territory. "What if I trip or drop something? I mean then what? Nothing on the menu cost less than eighty dollars."

"Okay, calm down. Let's just go over it one more time." Evie rolled her eyes, tried to remain patient, and proceeded to explain Waitressing 101 for the zillionth time. But I still wasn't getting it. Aside from the total decimation of my emotions, I was beyond anxiety-ridden, fearing yet another something would go wrong.

"Just try to relax," she said. "The tables by the door are reserved for the bridge and tunnel crowd." (Which, for you out-of-towners, are out-of-towners.) "They usually ask for the front room tables anyway, to see which celebrities are coming and going. If those tables are taken," she said, pointing like an air traffic controller directing planes on and off the tarmac, "David, the manager, will seat them next to the patio door. Regulars generally prefer to be seated further in. For the ultra-cool ones: The bar is the place to sit. And the major players are consigned to the enclosed patio, otherwise known as the boardroom because so many deals go down in there."

"Okay, got it. I think."

"But like I said, you don't have to worry about seating because David takes care of all that. You just have to do as I told you. In fact, girlena, you could do this job blindfolded, it's that easy." Well, it's refreshing to know someone still has some faith in me. "Besides, you're going to make enough money tonight that you will pay off that stupid AmEx card plus have lots left over for Super Saturday!"

"You think?"

"Of course. It's just like McDonald's, remember?"

Unfortunately I do remember.

"Just follow me, and relax, it couldn't be easier. All you have to do is walk over to your table, smile, take their order, go to the kitchen, give it to Takeshi, and bring the food back to the table that ordered it. Simple, right?"

The place was really beginning to fill up now, which was making me nervous all over again. The main dining room was absolutely buzzing! At any other place in New York I would say having a packed house on a Tuesday in July was weird, but at Heshi it was business as usual. I mean anyone and everyone who was not out in the Hamptons was here. Table-hopping was rampant. I mean it's like everyone knows everyone else, just like summer camp.

"Break over," the blur that was David hollered into the kitchen where Evie and I sat. In restaurant parlance that meant DO NOT THINK, MOVE NOW.

Needless to say, I jumped to my feet and scrambled to my station.

"Three euro chicks on thirteen. Get moving honey." That would be my table—one of them, anyway. I grabbed some menus and sped out in the direction of table thirteen, dodging waiters, waitresses, and the rare child. On the way, I spied Missy Farthington (I guess she finally found an in at Heshi) sitting with a small coterie near the door. The last thing I wanted at that moment was to be reminded of the McDonald's fiasco. So, shielding myself with menus and crouching low, I circled behind the bonsai forest, crept around the rock garden, and snuck over to my table like a hunted animal.

I approached it with a powerful silent affirmation that made me feel much more confident.

The table was set for four but only three of the guests had arrived and all of them looked like Sophia Loren: major cleavage, Italian, gorgeous. A blonde, a brunette, and a redhead dripping with enough diamonds to light up a small city.

"Good evening. May I get you a drink?" I asked, raising myself from a crouched position and smiling as if everything were perfectly normal.

"Are you all right?" the blonde asked with genuine concern and a genuine Italian accent.

"Me? I'm fine." I laughed inappropriately and glanced over my shoulder.

"You seem a bit . . . nervous." She smiled gently. They all smiled gently. They really cared. I could feel the tears coming. Oh God . . . get a grip Imogene!

"Come. Sit down and tell us about it."

"It eez a man. No?" The redhead feigned anger then grinned from ear to ear.

"It is always a man," added the brunette.

"No, really. I'm okay . . . really." I pulled it together and smiled for real. "Thanks."

The blonde put her hand on my arm.

"When you are ready you will tell us, no?"

"No. I mean sure," I took a deep breath. "Okay. Let's start over." I passed out the menus. "Would you care for something to drink?"

"We are waiting for one more . . ."

"Who is always late," said the brunette.

"A man, of course," added the redhead, and they all laughed. I laughed too.

"Some Dom Pérignon, I think," said the blonde. This was going to be a piece of cake, I smiled. When I returned with the champagne, the fourth chair was still empty and the women were all chattering away in Italian.

"Would you like an appetizer while you're waiting?"

More conferring, then, after a quick glance at the menu, the blonde asked, "What would you suggest?"

"Well." I smiled to myself because I adored Takeshi's food and knew every dish by heart. "I would go for the broiled black cod with miso; rock shrimp tempura with ponzu sauce, delish. Or the new-style sashimi on a bed of pickled cucumber, seared toro, or sizzling Kobe beef. There's also the Kumamoto oysters with Maui onion salsa. Yummy. And an aromatic broth of Matsutake mushrooms and rice noodles."

After much deliberation, "I think we will try them all," the blonde beamed.

Works for me, I thought, and went to fetch more champagne.

Okay. To make a long story short, after I made the rounds of my other tables (being totally careful to ever-so-casually hide my face behind the menus at all times so Missy Farthington wouldn't ID me), I gossiped briefly with Evie and explained my scrunching-down-behavior to David. Then I whisked table thirteen's order to them. Due to the number of dishes, I'd had to pile them on top of one another which, happily, covered my face. The disadvantage was that it was a bit tricky crossing the floor in traffic with my arms full. Anyway, I successfully reached thirteen, unloaded the last of the plates, and was about to set down a large bowl of rice noodles when I noticed that the ladies' guest had arrived.

You know that expression "I was so mad, I saw red"? Well it's true. I really did see the color red. Actually it was tinged with fuchsia, but you know what I mean. I stared at him in disbelief for a few seconds while a gigantic wave of anger welled up inside of me and found its ultimate expression in a single, defining word.

"YOU!" I exploded. "You . . . rat!"

Paolo slowly stood, his mouth agape. His expression changed from surprise to glee to shock to horror. The entire two thousand square feet of guests and staff went silent and looked at him: He looked absolutely gorgeous. For a split nanosecond a guilty fantasy played itself out in my head. Imagine: I keel over right now; he rushes over and administers mouth-to-mouth. Reality? My knight in shining armor had turned out to be a rat!

"Do you have any idea what you've done?! DO YOU?! How *COULD* you sell me out like that?!" Paolo's mouth began to move in an unsuccessful attempt to speak. I looked down at the three women who had seemed soooo nice, soooo sympathetic. "And I suppose these are your girlfriends who you have answer *MY PHONE* for you. Which *BY THE WAY* I demand you return. Or are you planning on selling any more of my pictures?!"

"What pictures?" Paolo stammered. "Imogene . . . I . . ."

In the corner of my eye I saw David moving slowly toward the table.

"You sold my cell phone."

"I didn't."

"Well how in the world did the pictures on my cell phone get into Haute & About's book? The only way was if they had my phone. Don't even bother making something up," I seethed, noodle bowl in hand.

"But I don't have your cell phone. I gave it—"

"OH! I can't believe it!! You're actually going to lie to my face!"

David's voice spoke softly nearby. "Put the bowl down, Imogene."

"Chill out, girlene," Evie said.

"Please, Imogene," Paolo pleaded. "Just listen to me for a—"

"And to think I actually liked you!" I cried, furiously. David stepped forward and grabbed for the bowl, but he was too late.

"Oooo!" I groaned in exasperation, and dumped the rice noodles on Paolo's head. There was a collective gasp. Then, it was as if a tornado touched down right inside Heshi. I must have caused a chain reaction. Glasses, sake bottles, and plates flew through the air. Stunned waiters dropped their trays; ornamental objects fell off shelves; people turned around and dropped their drinks out of sympathy, surprise, or just plain fear. I imagined diners from Manhattan to Montauk frantically speed-dialing their news contacts about the incident as television helicopters buzzed overhead . . . and somewhere a flash went off.

Then there was silence again, as everyone in the entire restaurant was frozen solid. They all stared at us. And without so much as a shred of anger, Paolo, noodles and all announced, "Everyone, I'd like you to meet Imogene,"

Everyone burst out laughing; some people even clapped.

"Hi Eemogene!!" one of the ladies with Paolo said. "You must be the Eemogene I spoke to the other day, yes, no? But we got disconnected."

"Look, obviously this is a big misunderstanding. The only thing that matters is I'm seeing you standing here again," he said. Rice noodles draped his shoulders, mushroom broth plastered down his hair, flash bulbs went off. Flash bulbs still?

"Do you have any idea what my life has been like without my cell phone?"

"Do you have any idea what my life has been like without you?"

Melt.

I wanted more than anything to believe him, but it was too late. The pain stabbed at me one last time, and I ran.

I don't remember much after that, other than hitting the night air in a blind panic, sobbing miserably. Everything I had dreamed of and hoped for up to that point in my life suddenly looked dark and blurry through my wet tears.

"*Ciao, amore mio*"—which translated means something like . . . well I think it means, "Good-bye, my love."

chapter nine

Truth or Dare

date: JULY 15TH

mood: TO DO:

1. Floss
2. Walk Toy
3. Drink 8 glasses of water
4. Jump off the Brooklyn Bridge

Draped from head to toe in a breathtaking champagne colored evening gown and matching shoes, I gunned my Vespa and sped up Sixth Avenue toward 59th Street. I was in hurry, a big hurry, but funny thing, I couldn't remember why. Toy gazed up at me with a look of sublime satisfaction as the wind flapped his cute little ears. Then he turned his eyes to the street ahead and grinned.

I shot past FAO Schwarz, waving to crowds of people who packed the streets and cheered as I flew by. Someone held up a sign that read, "You have an important phone call to make."

"Stop in the name of the law!" shouted a vaguely familiar voice. I looked back and saw the cop who had chased after me when I got stuck on the weenie cart, only this time he was driving it. Directly behind him was the weenie cart man, running and shouting, "My veenies, my veenies!" Riding on his shoulders was Miss Stevens, who waved a pink credit card slip and pen, shouting, "You forgot to sign!" A hoard of others chased behind them, including a string of angry diners from Heshi. Bringing up the rear was the entire staff from Hautelaw. They were on what appeared to be a McDonald's parade float. They were wearing off-color, polyester outfits, except for Spring Sommer who was dressed as Ronald, and Brooke as the Hamburglar.

And they were gaining on me. I tried to make my scooter go faster, but it wouldn't respond. Someone behind me yelled "Imogene, Imogene, Imogene," over and over. I spun around and saw Toy pointing forward, his eyes widening in panic.

"Imogene! Imogene! Imogene!" he shouted louder and louder. I looked ahead and saw a giant maraschino cherry rolling right down the middle of Madison Avenue, heading straight for me. All I could do was watch . . .

"Imogene! IMOGENE! HEY, IMOGENE! WAKE UP!"

Real time unfurled and I opened a bloodshot eye. There was Evie, sitting on the edge of the bed, shaking me with one hand and waving the *New York Post* in the other. I was pretty sure this was reality, but the way things had been going lately, it was becoming increasingly hard to tell.

"Listen—you're not going to believe this, girlene! I mean it's totally awesome!" Evie was usually a fast talker, but this morning she was setting new speed records.

"Evie," I mumbled sleepily, squeezing my eyes shut. "Can't you see I need sleep?"

She whacked me with the paper. "You've got to see this—NOW! You're on 'Page Six'!"

She threw open the Donghia drapes and my eyes struggled feebly to adjust to daylight.

"You can't shut the world out," she said, sending the empty ice cream container and numerous cellophane candy wrappers skibbling across the room as she walked. "Now for the last time, are you going to get up or do I have to take stronger measures?"

"Why don't I sleep on that and get back to you in the morning," I said, covering my head with the cool cotton comforter.

"News flash: It is the morning! Did you hear what I said?" This time Evie threw the newspaper at me. "YOU'RE ON PAGE SIX!!!"

"Oh God." I heaved myself up and reassembled the paper. Suddenly visions of last night washed over me like an enormous, sickening wave. Sure enough, there for all the world to see was a shot of Paolo, post noodle shower, with the caption: "TREND WATCH—FASHION SCION SPORTS NOODLE DOO."

As I sat there staring at the picture, something kept nagging at me. Then it came into focus and my heart began to sink, and sink, and sink. "What fashion scion?" I murmured.

"Duh! That's what I've been trying to tell you," Evie said. "Your ex would-be boyfriend is the only son of Renzo Glamonti! As in the chicly famous House of Glamonti!" she said as if I were a complete moron, which come to think of it, maybe I am. "As in, they've been around for ten thousand generations?"

Speechlessly, I scanned the article.

IT'S RAINING NOODLES AT HESHI, OR SO IT WOULD seem for Paolo, son and heir to the House of Glamonti fashion empire—you know, the guys who clothed the Medici family. Last night a bad weather system formed over the impossible-to-get-a-table-at Tribeca sushi palace, Heshi, while guests were treated to a freak storm of rice noodles and thunderous tempers as a crazed waitress pummeled the Prince of Palermo with a pound of pasta for reasons yet unknown. According to sources, the errant waitress had a score to settle with the scion over a missing cell phone containing some photographs of a rather private nature.

"Ohmigod!" I dropped the paper on the floor, curled up, and pulled the pillow over my head just to have Evie pull it right off.

"Oh come on girlena, it's not all bad. If you hadn't run out like that last night, you would have found out—oooo, I'm absolutely getting goosebumps all over, because it's like a real-life Cinderella story—this guy, the prince, who really is a prince, is going out of his mind trying to return a cell phone to some girl he's head over heels in love with, as in you, my best friend! WOW!" She shivered.

As she spoke, a couple of frazzled, die-hard memory cells have just fired off in some murky recess of my brain. It all started to come into focus and was now in major reverb mode ricocheting around in my head and I asked myself: Self, did you really do that?

"After you left, it was amazing!" Evie forged ahead breathlessly. "I mean absolute bedlam! First of all, David almost had a heart attack. I've never seen him so worked up."

My heart was now in my stomach.

"And then my dad called in the middle of everything and started screaming at David and then David screamed at him and then he screamed at me and would have screamed at you except nobody could find you, but that's not the best part. Oh, this is *soooo* romantic. The best part is that Paolo ran after you! Can you believe it?! He actually ran out into the street covered in rice noodles and tried to find you . . . and everyone was yelling and running around and Missy Farthington was screaming for a camera crew. Did you know she's doing the local news in New York now? She's the one who took the picture, by the way."

None of this was making any sense. "Wait," I whispered. Evie stopped talking, though she looked like it was causing her a great deal of pain. "But he sold my pictures! He betrayed me. . . ."

"That's why I tried calling last night, to straighten you out. And to make sure you weren't going to do anything stupid like eat ten pints of ice cream." She looked around at the evidence. "Well, too late on that count."

I crawled back under the covers. "Evie . . . I feel sick."

"Of course you do, with that part sugar, part emotional hangover you're nursing. Wait here. Don't move," she said. "I'll be back in a flash with something to fix you right up." On her way toward the kitchen, she said, "By now the whole city must be talking about you!"

Oh great, I'm officially the poster girl for firsthand embarrassment. The laughing stock of the whole demographic of "Page Six" readers. I'm about to cross the poverty line, and to make matters worse, if that's possible, I've sprouted one huge pimple on my forehead.

Evie returned with a big silver tray.

Well despite everything, at least I still have Evie, who was clearly experiencing an early morning frizz attack and sporting what vaguely resembled an evening gown made entirely out of video tape.

"Is that annoying sound coming from whatever that is you're wearing?"

"Oh, this fabric? It's a blend of video cassette tape and cotton. I tossed all my old movies on video and replaced them with DVDs—I wove it myself. Do you like it? Look, it's dual purpose—if I run it through a VCR," she said, flattening a loop of the fabric into strips, "we could be watching a scene from *Annie Hall* right now. Completely genius, don't you think?"

I dove under the covers again.

"C'mon, girlene, snap out of it. Here, drink this, it will make you feel better," she said.

Goody, coffee, I thought, taking a sip.

"Ohh, ewwww, ick! What is this? It tastes like dirt!" I yelped, wiping the grit off my teeth. Just when I was getting used to peanut butter and maraschino cherry blender drinks, Evie pulls a fast one.

"That's because it *is* dirt," she said. "But, don't sweat it, it's been recycled. It's completely clean."

"Clean dirt?"

"It's called DirtiCleanse—today is day one of my total cleansing detox," she said, taking a sip. "What's the point of eating healthy if you're dirty inside?" Fine print time: I didn't have the foggiest idea of what she was talking about.

"How much does this dirt cost?"

"Don't ask."

After a moment, and another sip of DirtiCleanse I said, "Evie, listen, I'm really sorry about last night."

She sat on the edge of the bed.

"It's okay, don't worry about it. Besides, you think you're the first person to dump a bowl of rice noodles on some guy's head?" she said accommodatingly. She picked up the newspaper I'd dropped on the floor. Then suddenly she screamed out, "Ohmigod, girlena! Check this out . . . quick!"

"Here's your answer, here's your

chance to turn everything around and get your job back. And I'm going with you."

"Where?"

"To the Jock Lord show, of course!" I grabbed the paper she was pushing at me, and read.

COMEBACK COUNTDOWN
(PART II)

Jock Lord ♥ New York.

Nicole Kidman, famous muse to Jock Lord, has been confirmed for the hotter-than-hot Jock Lord Comeback Couture show. The Oscar winner, who is between film projects, as Page Six reported earlier, is expected to be seated in the front row next to the legendary editor formerly known as Andrew Lyford Tilley. The show is shrouded in secrecy and is scheduled to take place at a special showing in Bryant Park. Kidman and company have all been invited to Jock Lord's new Madison Avenue boutique for a cocktail party later that evening fêting his hotly anticipated comeback of the century.

"Ohmigod! That's the show that Hautelaw didn't get invited to. Spring will have a cow when she reads this!"

"And this is it—this is your answer!" I could tell by the look on her face that she was hatching a plan.

"Oh no. No way."

"Listen, okay, so Hautelaw didn't get invited, and without

an invitation, no coverage. All we have to do is get in to the show, and . . ."

"Evie, I can't,"

"Excuse me, girlene, but your life is waiting! Don't you see, this is your chance to get back in Spring's good graces. Hautelaw is your dream internship which is going to some day launch your entire career, the job you dreamed about since you were a little girl. This is how dreams begin. They're not given to us. We're only given opportunities to grab them. So, get up and get dressed. There's a whole world out there waiting for you. Besides, in two days tomorrow will be yesterday and what will you have to show for all your yesterdays?" Evie folded up the paper and lifted herself up off the floor. "Cheer up, girlena. Things are already turning around."

"That's what I'm afraid of."

chapter ten

The Big Faux Paw

date: LATER
mood: RESOLUTE

As usual, we had a plan. Not such a good plan, but a plan nonetheless. And whenever Evie and I have a plan, you can be sure that something is going to happen, though usually not what we planned in the plan.

"Come on, girlene," Evie said. "Let's go or we're going to be late!"

"I can't find Booboo and Toy will be too neurotic without him," I said, ducking back inside the Villa while Evie waited outside, Toy in hand. "Besides, creativity can't always be on time," I replied, using one of Evie's overused axioms.

"Imogene, please, it's going to be a zoo. We have to leave now!"

188

"Okay, okay," I slammed the door, without Booboo. "It's okay Toy boy, we'll find your Booboo later."

I set an all-new speed record, making it all the way from Villa Fantastique to 42nd Street in less than fifteen minutes, determined to give my future one last shot. From a distance I could just make out the white peaks of the tent above the crowd filling Bryant Park. It looked like a circus had landed in the middle of Manhattan. I gunned the scooter, navigating around a plethora of limos, town cars, Hummers, Bentleys, and custom SUVs, which converged around the perimeter of two city blocks, double- and triple-parked to disgorge the first rung of potentates, whose hierarchy began with alpha-female magazine editors, buyers, and moguls and extended up to a heaping helping of celebrities, and a galaxy of pop stars, rap stars, rock stars, actors, actresses, and it-girls. Some of the world's wealthiest A-list Super Socialites would be there, many with their ASS-ettes in tow. All of the above would have cut short their summer holidays in order to attend what promised to be the most mind-blowing event of the season, the Jock Lord comeback show.

By six o'clock it was hotter than Hell's Kitchen in Bryant Park, where the temperature hit a sweltering ninety-five degrees.

"Remember what Cinnamon said," I reminded Evie. "Whatever you do, don't press the red button. That turns on the music."

"Right," she said as together we stared at the large, impossible-to-miss button on Cinnamon's karaoke microphone.

"How do I look?" asked Evie who, like me, was disguised. I, in an oversize newsboy cap, and Evie as my trusty producer, complete with clipboard and Motorola headset. It was a trying-to-look-edgy-but-not-offend-any-viewers-type outfit that she put together at the last minute, with enough makeup to make her look passable for twenty-five-trying-to-look-twenty, and studious but fashionable vintage DKNY glasses and of course, a blond wig from her mom's Raquel Welch collection.

"Brilliant."

The plan was to mix in with the press that was bound to be crowding the entrance and wait for an opportunity to slip inside the tent.

"You think this will work?" I regretted saying it as soon as it came out. I mean in the old days (two months ago seems like an eternity), that thought would never have crossed my mind. I remembered all the stuff we'd done in the past that was, to be perfectly honest, not exactly sane by most people's standards. And here we were again.

"Okay," I heaved. "Have we got everything?"

"I think so," Evie's eyes were shining with excitement. I held out the karaoke microphone with its big red button.

"Microphone."

"Check," she said officiously.

"TV personality hairstyle."

"Check."

"Digital camera."

"Check."

"Memory sticks."

"Check."

"Lip gloss."

"Check."

"Adorable pooch."

"Check."

"I think that's it. . . ."

"Oh, wait!" Evie gasped, plunging into her bag. "We almost forgot the most important thing. Our press passes!"

"That would be helpful," I laughed. We had spent the afternoon making phony passes on my computer. Hopefully no one would look too closely, since we used Evie's old Barbie pretend passport for the basic layout. We took one last look at each other and dove into the teeming crowd now bottlenecking the entranceway to heaven.

"Evie!" I said, yanking her arm as a security guard walked by. "We're not going to make it—the security's tighter than a Joan Rivers facelift, for crissakes!"

"Of course we will!" she reassured me. "Oooo, girlene!" she said, squeezing my arm, already on to the next thing. "Do you see what I see? Look, over there, it's the freebie tent!"

"Evie, wait, I sense a disturbance in the force."

"What?"

"Look, it's those creepy girls." Emerging from the hospitality tent were two suddenly blond, very blow-dried salad sisters, multiple pairs of sunglasses and about 30 boxes of Jacques Torres chocolates in hand as they rifled through their VIP goody bags.

"The freebies have never been better, Fernie!"

"You are so right, Ro dahling!"

"Hide!" I said, grabbing Evie and spinning around.

After what seemed like an eternity, probably closer to five minutes, we reached the entrance and stood before a solid block of muscle, tall enough to have his own cloud system and a haircut you could land a jumbo jet on, otherwise known as Security Chief Nash, whose laser vision scanned my person for the conveniently-tucked-behind-my-bag Barbie press pass.

"Press yes, cameras no. . . ."

"Ohmigod, what do we do now?" I whispered to Evie. "How are we going to shoot this show?"

"No different than the original plan. Your Cyber-shot's tiny. Nobody will even know."

"Name," he said as we got to the front of the line.

"Farthington," I smiled. "Missy Farthington. And this is my producer." I yanked Evie forward to share in the scrutiny.

"Where's your camera?" came a grunt from the stratosphere.

Evie held up the microphone and beamed, "Radio."

"Good, because Mr. Lord insists that this is a photo-free, paparazzi-free event."

Evie and I exchanged suppressed but uneasy looks while Nash went back to his clipboard, brow furrowed.

"Farthington . . . Farthington," he mumbled. Then suddenly, from somewhere deep inside, a light went on. "'Page Six,' right? That was your story this morning about that wacko stalker chick who dumped spaghetti on that Italian guy?"

I silently recited my favorite mantra.

"Yeah, talk about being in the right place at the right time."

"I couldn't stop laughing. What a nut-job!"

"Yeah. That girl was *completely* out of control," Evie chimed in. I glared at her.

"So, can we go in now?" I blurted out.

Nash paused and eyed us carefully.

"Aren't you forgetting something?"

Evie and I stared at each other then at Nash, when a nervous flush of panic trickled under my skin. Finally he leaned forward and spoke confidentially.

"Mr. Lord. You know. He's making a statement to the press. Should be any second now." He winked. "You'll want to be in on that, of course." No sooner had he said that than a wave of excitement swept through the crowd as reporters and fashion groupies lurched forward like a school of fish that suddenly darts, en masse, in a single direction.

"There he is!" screamed an *E! Entertainment News* reporter.

Evie and I were pushed forward with the tide and wound up close to the front, packed like sardines between the CNN and E! crews. Jock Lord appeared at the back door and was met with a mix of paparazzi, fashion press, and a cornucopia of hysterical fans. He smiled easily, waiting as people fell still, flashes stopped, and voices grew hushed. The clamor and bustle of the entire city seemed to pause for a moment in anticipation of his first words after years of self-imposed exile.

Jock Lord said simply, "I'm back."

A roar of applause shook the air as the crowd went wild. Jock Lord, looking every ounce the returned monarch come to sit once more on his couture throne, raised his hands to calm his fevered subjects.

A forest of hands shot up as the reporters began shouting, each trying to talk over the other. Evie and I just stood there, pointing the microphone in his direction like everyone else and waiting for the Q and A session to end so we could sneak in.

"Mr. Lord, Mr. Lord! Where do you get your inspiration from?" someone asked.

"From my muse . . . and from my imagination, of course," he said with a great flourishing hand motion. "I create women's dreams, which stem from their innermost desires and fantasies. When a woman wears a Jock Lord gown, it's a cause for celebration."

"Word on the street is that your muse has taken a powder and defected to LaCroix. Is there any truth to that?"

"Julie," Jock Lord whispered to his assistant. "Has Nicole arrived yet?"

"No JL, not yet. We have calls in to her camp—no one knows where she is."

"Well, find her now—quick, fast, and in a hurry!" Then to the crowd defiantly, "Absurd! Who's next?"

In truth I had a few questions of my own. But just as my hand went flying in the air, from the street came the sound of drums, bells, cymbals, and chanting.

"We love you Lord! Praise the Lord!" A group of passing Hari Krishnas happened by chance to be dancing by—Indian instruments, shaved heads, bare feet, and all. They were wearing pink robes and chanting, "Hari Krishna. Praise the Lord; praise the Lord, Hari, Hari, Krishna Krishna! Praise the Lord."

"Why thank you," Jock responded, shouting over everyone's head. "Thank you all—all you interesting, trendsetting people out there," he shouted to the chanters. "Fab frocks by the way," he called after them, but by then they were out of earshot. "Julie," he murmured to his assistant again, "those frocks rock. . . . Did you see? Go sketch, sketch, sketch! Quickly!"

The crowd began moving forward. At last! Unfortunately, as we were about to cross the threshold a reporter mistook my foot for solid ground, causing me to yelp in pain, a cry that was taken up by Toy inside my bag, which in turn was understood to be a fit of reporter angst by Jock Lord, who immediately, and with great dramatic flair, stopped the proceedings and selected *moi* for a final sound bite.

"One last question," he announced regally, gracing me with an indulgent smile.

I was just about to ask my question when, anxiously pointing the microphone toward him and, true to the way my life was going I accidentally pushed the big red button and the faux mic began blasting "Like A Virgin." I fumbled to shut it off as I imagined myself, and Evie, slowly shrinking.

Before the crowd had a chance to react, a screaming match broke out at the front gate. The voice, loud, obnoxious, and insistent, began moving in our direction, cutting a swath through the dense crowd and leaving behind it a path of bruised egos and verbal destruction. Nash immediately went on alert, speaking rapidly into his shortwave radio and stepped in front of Jock Lord, preparing for the worst. Funny thing was, the voice seemed, somehow, all too familiar. I looked at Evie, who stared in the direction of the voice, paralyzed.

"Ohmigod," she murmured. "It can't be."

"What?" I was getting nervous.

"It is." Her eyes widened and she began pulling me in the opposite direction.

"Who?" Now fully alarmed.

"Later, girlene. Time to go," Evie said. We turned to leave, only to bump into a wall constructed of two XXL security people who had not been there a second ago. Meanwhile, the voice was now very close and very angry. It came back to me in a rush of panic and OHMIGOD! It was . . .

"Missy Farthington, you idiot!" she screamed at a security guard as the crowd parted. "Channel Four News! Don't you own a television?!"

Missy stopped in front of us and stared. For the first time since her arrival, she was at a loss for words. She did however manage to turn several shades of Sahara dusk while attempting to recognize Evie *et moi.* I pulled my newsboy cap down over my face in an unsuccessful attempt to crawl inside. Slowly Missy's eyes widened then bulged out of her head. She pointed her finger and shook it frantically. Her mouth dropped open and a garbled, choking sound came out. Needless to say, the crowd (including XXL security) backed away, forming a circle with me and Evie and Missy standing in the center. Jock Lord stepped forward.

"Who is this woman?!" Nash jumped in. "She claims to be Missy—"

"So it's you," she hissed, lifting the front of my cap and pushing her face into mine. Her eyes narrowed and slid toward Evie, who slinked behind me. "And you!" Eyes bulging again. Toy yipped with fear as her gaze spotted him nestled in my bag. A thin smile curled the edges of her equally thin lips as she stepped back and announced to the crowd, "I am Missy Farthington! And this person . . . is the Noodle Girl!"

'm not going to bore you with what came next. Let's just say that after a supremely embarrassing silence followed by yelling, screaming, pleading, and barking (and that was just Mr. Nash), Evie and I were sent on our not-so-merry way. By the time we reached my Vespa, the last of the summer sky had faded and the lights of the city began to glisten. I turned toward the park for one last look. Inside the tents glowed with brilliant white light. Clinking glasses and laughter rose upward, echoing off the surrounding buildings. A group of paparazzi lounged around the rear gate waiting for something to happen. I felt dead inside.

"I'm so sorry, Im," Evie whispered. Even Toy managed a whimper of sympathy. I picked him up and held him close.

"Let's just go," was all I could manage. I put Toy into his carryall, climbed onto the Vespa, and waited for Evie to put on her helmet. In front of us two men unloaded covered racks of clothing from a truck—no doubt outfits for the Jock Lord show. I couldn't wait to get out of there. To make matters

worse, a white stretch limo double-parked right next to me was boxing the scooter in. I was about to yell at the driver when one of guys with the racks (name tag: Vito) shouted, "Look, it's Mariah Carey." Minor pandemonium broke out around us as the clutch of frustrated paparazzi pounced on the limo like a pack of starved jackals. The curvy diva emerged, followed by friends then bodyguards then friends of bodyguards. "I gotta get her autograph," name tag Vito gasped.

"Me too," said the other guy. And with that they disappeared into the fray.

"Can you believe that?" Evie fumed. "They left the racks just sitting there. Anybody could come along and . . ."

Evie and I looked at each other with exactly the same thought.

"Let's go!" I said, and we clamored off the scooter and hurried behind the racks while everyone was frothing over Mariah.

Racks upon racks of garments stood shrouded in Jock Lord emblazoned plastic covers—no doubt Jock Lord's entire new collection. They stood ready to be delivered and fitted on the waiting models.

"Evie, you go under that one, and Toy and I will slip in here," I said.

"Awesome!" Evie squealed as she lifted a cover and climbed inside. Toy barked as if to say, *What's going on here?* as we slipped under an adjacent rack.

"No, Toy. Shh. We have to be quiet," I said. He tilted his head and stared at me this time uttering a barely audible arf. "Good boy," I whispered.

All we had to do was wait for Vito and company to come get us, which I knew would be any second now. Four, three, two, one. The sound of loud steps approached up the metal ramp and we started moving. The rack jerked and I nearly lost my balance, covering Toy's mouth just as he was about to let out another yip. He licked my hand. So far, so good.

We bumped and shook a while, eventually banging into a wall somewhere unknown as Vito and company's footsteps vanished with the slam of a door. Aside from muffled voices somewhere nearby, all was quiet. The cover lifted and Evie's face appeared.

"Ohmigod, did you look at the clothes on your rack?! You should have seen mine. Unbelievable workmanship. I mean like I could hardly keep from screaming."

"Shhh! I know." I tumbled out of my hiding place and looked around. We were parked with about twenty other racks in a short hallway.

"Quick, lift up that cover!" I whispered, pulling out the camera. For the next fifteen minutes I shot clothing like I'd never shot clothing before—like my life depended on it, which it did.

We just looked at each other,

"Eeee!" we silently screeched.

"Now for the show," I said.

"Awesome!" Evie grinned. We moved toward a double door at the far end of the hallway and slipped through.

"We did it! Evie," I said hopefully. "Do you realize that in just a few short minutes, we'll be witnessing the biggest fashion event of the year!"

"And you'll have your job back in no time."

Before anything had a chance to register, I was hit by the overwhelming scent of gardenias, which triggered one of those weird moments when you instantly go from like, so normal, to like, so somewhere else in like, a nanosecond. Suddenly I was back in my childhood in my mom's garden and I remembered how things used to be happier at home and how gardenias only bloom in summer and how Mom didn't have a green thumb anymore and I didn't have a job anymore and I suddenly felt like crying, which made me angry and I swore then and there that I would make everything all right again. I just had to.

The room snapped back into focus. We were finally inside the show. I stood there, momentarily dazed by the perpetual motion of people and things all around us. A mega jewel-encrusted JL logo chandelier plunged downward from the center peak of the tent, shimmering white diamond light throughout the tented room. But the runway was the most awesome part. It was paved with gold bricks spiraling outward from backstage and winding a path beneath the chandelier, just wide enough for super-skinny models to wind their way to center and back.

Needless to say, the room was filling fast. Hollywood

royalty, moguls, editors in chief, all sipping champagne, anxiously awaiting the clothes, the music, the models, and the magic that was a fashion show.

"Imogene, this is beyond!" Evie gasped. "I mean, look where we are."

"Someday," I smiled, "in the not too distant future, you'll be showing your own collection and I'll be sitting right out there."

"Best friends forever!" Evie hugged me.

"C'mon. We've got to find a place to sit," I said, and yanked her into the crowd. Of course, we immediately headed toward the best location in all of North America — the front row.

"Ohmigod!" I said to Evie, spotting two free seats. "Grab them! Quick."

No sooner did we sit down, than someone said, "Hello!"

"Is he talking to us?" I whispered to Evie.

"Hello, I say," boomed an extremely tall, middle-aged man draped in an astrakhan coat that must have required the sacrifice of at least 25 lambs for its construction — no doubt the reason for the young assistant frantically waving two Chinese rice paper fans in the tall man's general direction.

"*Hellooo.* Hell-oh! You there in rip-off Chanel sunglasses and newsboy cap," he exclaimed, pointing a long finger in our direction. Evie and I slunk down in our chairs, hoping he was talking to someone else. He stopped right in front of us and glared. I looked up. "Me?"

"Do you see anyone else around who'd have the audacity to come to a Jock Lord fashion show wearing those H & M rags?"

"Quite vulgar," the fanning assistant chimed in. "Then again it has a certain Oliver Twist chic-ness to it."

This prompted a brief discussion over the veracity of H&M. I mean if Miss Stella and Karl Lagerfeld could get down with H&M, I'm with it too. Although a girl such as I has to be careful, because it's a well-known fact that wearing too much H&M can actually lower your IQ into the single digits.

While they debated Evie pinched me. "That's EFKALT! A very, very important editor from *Vogue*, and someone whom I would very much like to show my collection to one of these days."

"Does he have a real name?"

"Only the Editor Formerly Known as Andrew Lyford-Tilly. But he goes by EFKALT."

"Oh, yoo-hoo," EFKALT twittered. "I'm going to close my eyes, and when I open them again you and your little friend will be gone. Ready?"

"These aren't your seats," I said acidly, feeling my temper rise. "There's no reserved seating." So there, Mr. Stupid EFKALT doody-head.

He gave a loud sigh and cast his eyes heavenward as if for some sort of otherworldly support. When that had no effect on us he struck a defiant pose and a photographer with enough gear to make even David Bailey envious appeared out of nowhere, snapping him from all angles.

"Hey," I said. "I thought no photographers were allowed in here."

"Correction, my inexperienced young vagabond. No

paparazzi! There is a difference, you know." He turned and beamed at the camera. "This is Serge—my *in-house* photographer, here to snap me and me alone."

It was Evie's turn to pull me. "Let's just go. We'll find other seats." She, of course, was right. Then his assistant, Tim, stepped forward and made a sour face at us.

"In the future, I suggest you avoid all contact with the EFKALT, verbal or otherwise." He turned to bask in the glow of EFKALT's approval but was met with eyes turned heavenward again. Tim turned and peered into my bag. Toy growled at him.

"And take your little rodent with you," he seethed, poking his finger into my bag. Toy, being a good judge of character, nipped.

"Ow!" he cried.

"Ohmigod" I gasped.

"Ohmigod!" EFKALT bellowed.

"Ohmigod!" the photographer screamed.

"Ohmigod," Evie sighed.

The photographer jumped into action, wildly shooting pictures of Toy, which scared the hell out of him, so he jumped out of my bag, peed on the floor, and ran under a chair.

"Not the dog, you idiot!" EFKALT hollered at the photographer, then posed in mock panic. "Over here!"

"That animal is a menace!" Tim yelled, hiding behind Evie. A nearby rent-a-cop began moving toward our happy little gathering.

"Guard! Guard!" Tim whined. "These two ragamuffins

are harboring a wild animal. I insist you arrest them!"

Evie and I ducked down on the floor, crawling around on our hands and knees, trying to grab Toy. To make things worse, the lights dimmed and house music began to thump. Loudly. Toy (poor thing) panicked and bolted toward the backstage curtain.

"Toy! No!" I hollered, feeling my way through the darkness with Evie at my heels, praying Toy hadn't gone backstage. We reached the curtain as the runway lights came up and a model, wearing the first House of Lord creation in two years, strutted onto the golden spiral to a breathless chorus of "oooooooos" and "ahhhhhhhhs."

"Evie," I whispered. "You stay here and keep an eye out for Toy. I'll go inside."

"But you'll miss the show. What about your coverage?"

I handed her the camera. "I'll meet you back here as soon as I find him. Shoot some pictures for me, 'kay?"

Behind the scenes was beyond insane—the ultimate in crazed excitement as models, makeup artists, dressers, hairdressers, design assistants, seamstresses, PR people, producers, caterers, and—oops!—security guards frantically buzzed around a long row of makeup tables that divided the room in half. A solid line of clothing racks butted against one another encircled the entire frenzied scene. And buzzing around in the middle of everything and everybody was the Queen Bee himself, Jock Lord, who quietly but firmly went from model to model checking clothes and hair, making last-minute changes and

adjustments that no one else but he, could.

As cool as all this was I had to find my dog, and the best way I could see was to jump in and hope nobody would notice, which was probably do-able, since people were talking nonstop and focused on what they were doing. Except, of course, for security. Clearly the best tack was to slink around pretending to be a model. So I looked bored, stole a cigarette, acted like I was looking for a match, and stared at myself in a mirror.

While performing this charade I desperately scanned under tables, between clothing racks, and anywhere else Toy might be hiding. In the midst of this search and rescue, the dreaded Mr. Nash appeared on the other side of the room and began chatting with one of the dressers, his beady little eyes restlessly scanning the area. At one point I stumbled over someone's curling iron and, convinced Nash was watching, which he was, freaked out. I grabbed a book from a nearby table (*Siddhartha* by Hermann Hesse—don't ask), spun around, and pretended to be absorbed. I could tell Nash was like trying to remember where he'd seen me before. I needed to blend more. I grabbed the first model that wandered by in the hopes of appearing to know someone.

"Does this book make me look fat?" I asked.

"Yes," she said blandly, looking me up and down then lilting away. A hand touched my shoulder and I froze; I thought I was busted for sure.

"Imogene?" said a familiar voice.

I turned to see Caprice standing there, in the classic hand-on-hip pose.

"When did you start smoking?" she said, pointing to my unlit cigarette.

"Caprice! Thank God. What are you doing here?"

"What am *I* doing here?" she said, blinking her gorgeous brown eyes. "One of the models ran off to Tahiti with her boyfriend and they called me." She was still in street clothes—jeans and a cami—hair pinned up, stylist-ready, no makeup, with only a faint spray of teeny pink diamonds around her neck. If I were a guy, I'd definitely be smitten. "What are *you* doing here?" she practically hollered. "And more importantly, what is your dog doing here?"

"TOY?! You've seen him?! Where?!"

"He ran off with my dog, Diablo. I was trying to find them when I ran into you. Now, again, Imogene. What are you doing here?"

"Evie and I—"

"Evie?!" she hollered again, looking around.

"She's out front. We snuck in to get coverage for the show but EFKALT's assistant frightened Toy—"

"EFKALT?!"

"Caprice, let me finish."

"Fine."

"So he ran backstage—"

"EFKALT?!"

"No, Toy! And I can't find him. And he's teething. And I'm afraid he might chew on something, you know? Something valuable."

Caprice looked alarmed.

"Caprice!" someone shouted.

"I'm on soon. Stay here . . . understand?"

"I can't just stand here. I mean security—"

"Just read your book . . . and look bored. I'll be back in five minutes." And with that she was gone.

The show was now in full tilt to the thump, thump, thump of DJ Majestic MC. Models shuttled out on the runway and back, changed, and went out again in an endless conveyor belt of chic. In the midst of all this, I heard, or imagined I heard over the din, a yip. Toy's yip. I spun around and ogled a large, white screen in the corner of the room. From behind it came Toy's yip again—this time I wasn't hearing things. Fearing that Toy and Diablo might have found something to chew on, I weaved my way toward them. I was nearly there when a truck suddenly stepped in my way. A truck named Nash.

"Excuse me," he grinned, flashing his gold tooth. "You look familiar. Have we met before?"

"Me? No, we've never met," I mumbled nervously, staring at my feet.

"Are you sure? Recently, I'm thinking—"

"I would have remembered. Can I get by please?"

"Yeah, we've definitely—"

"Oh, there you are, Princess!" An arm latched on to me.

I looked over at a tiny man with shortish, red spikey hair and a matching red goatee—in other words, a complete stranger. One who also recognized me. "I've got her!" he hollered over his shoulder.

"Who, me?" I asked.

"Who, you?!" He laughed wildly. "Of course you, Princess." He frowned at Nash. "Excuse me, Gigantor, the last time I checked security was not allowed in the dressing room," he said, and dragged me toward the makeup tables. "Has anyone ever told you that a dab of Nars purple shadow in the crease here would bring out more blue in your eyes?"

"Not really."

"I'm shocked!" He feigned surprise and pressed me into a folding chair. Yes, I had joined the rank-and-file models who sat patiently while being dabbed, poked, painted, brushed, curled, pulled, parted, and blown out under the heat of temporary industrial clamp lights.

"Look, um . . ."

"Phillip."

"Phillip. I'm really flattered, but I'm not Princess or even *a* princess. And I really can't have my hair and makeup done right now 'cause I have to get my dog."

"Oh, so humble! She takes care of her own dog! I heard you were nice but—"

"I have to go now," I said firmly, getting up. I glanced over and saw Nash still standing in the same spot, frowning at me. Clearly I was short on choices at that moment—

best to go with the flow. I slumped back in my chair, took a deep breath, and resolved to be Princess Whatever. At least for now.

"That's right, Princess, just relax," Phillip cooed. "I'll be done in a sec." And he was. If I put my makeup on that quickly every day I could add five years to my social life.

From then on everything moved at the speed of light. I mean all I remember is being passed from one station to another like a Quarter Pounder at lunch rush, crimped and primped and photographed repeatedly. At one point I had no less than six Polaroids of myself in various stages of transformation. I re-entered reality when a dresser started pulling my clothes off.

"Hey!" I shouted.

"Hey, yourself," she said matter-of-factly. "Get those rags off, honey, and put this on!" That was absolutely the last straw. I could not go through with this charade any longer. I mean time was running out, and I had to find Toy before he ruined something. I had to get back to the show. I had to get my coverage.

"Excuse me. I'll be right back." I pushed past her and plunged into the crowd.

"Imogene!" I looked over and saw Caprice in mid-outfit. "I've been looking everywhere for you."

"Look, I have to go."

I was in mid-step when suddenly the room fell silent. Dead silent. The crowd parted like the Red Sea as a totally upset Jock Lord appeared and stopped right next to me.

"Where is she?!" Jock Lord thundered. "Where is my muse?!" He turned toward one of his entourage, presumably his publicist, and stomped his foot.

"Where is Nicole?!" he demanded.

So much for Nicole Kidman, I thought. The poor publicist proceeded to physically shrink in size while simultaneously mumbling and gesturing in a frantic and somewhat frightening manner.

"You absurd buffoon!" Jock Lord interrupted. "She's supposed to wear the wedding dress . . . TODAY . . . NOW . . . NOW TODAY!" He turned a lovely shade of Nars purple. "WHERE is the DRESS! Bring me the dress! I must see it! I must see it now! . . . And the bridesmaids! I want those as well!"

"Here they are!!" someone yelled from behind the big white screen. You know, the screen where I had heard Toy's yip coming from.

"Now then," JL said quietly as the rack arrived. "I need a new muse; someone fresh, someone fabulous, someone completely new!" He spun around and pointed at me.

"YOU!"

Mantra time.

"Me?" I asked.

"Yes, you!"

"I?"

"Enough already!" He held out a hand. "Come to Jock!" With Nicole Kidman a no-show, Jock Lord decided that I was to be the bride, the last girl remaining, standing alone at the end of the show, the finale, the denouement. I, Imogene. It was impossible.

I slinked over and stood face to face with Jock Lord. He calmly gazed at me with those famous electric blue eyes. He furrowed his brow then half smiled. "You've got . . . freckles. I hate freckles!"

Then it hit me. I grabbed Caprice and pushed her in front of me.

"She doesn't have freckles!"

Jock took a step back and examined Caprice from head to toe, alternately rubbing his chin, blinking rapidly, and making a sort of clicking sound with his tongue.

"Yes. She'll be a gorgeous bride," he said. "Get her in the dress." And with a snap of his fingers, assistant designers, dressers, and makeup artists instantly surrounded Caprice. I was *soooo* happy for her. I mean at last she was getting her big break.

When they unwrapped the dress and slipped it on her there was a collective intake of breath followed by a shriek from one of the assistant designers, who proceeded to faint into Jock Lord's arms. I, along with JL himself, took that to be a shriek of divine ecstasy. I mean, the gown, all form fitting white lace, with a voluminous organza overskirt, was truly breathtaking. Unfortunately, the assistant designer's blackout was actually due to the fact that a good deal of the dress was shredded—backside and all, thanks to a couple of small, teething dogs with a penchant for clothing. The sordid details of screaming, mayhem, riot, and dog chasing are best left to the imagination. Suffice to say that cool heads prevailed and Jock, the consummate professional and every inch deserving of his reputation, tossed a floor-sweeping cape over the dress which completely covered the back and looked absolutely intentional and fabulously stunning. Yours truly was unwillingly drafted as a bridesmaid, freckles and all. Needless to say, those dresses were just as shredded, so we also wound up wearing capes to cover the damage as well. And where were the dogs?

We bridesmaids hit the stage, strutting our way toward the center, looking like spun sugar. It was terrifying in a sort of exhilarating way.

Caprice finally came out looking magnificent, if somewhat unsteady. I thought her shoes were bothering her, but when the hem of her cape lifted briefly, I spotted eight little doggie feet running in step beneath. Caprice finished her walk, stopping at the center of the spiral. I could tell she was freaked. I risked a sidelong glance at her and saw, to my complete horror, Toy's little head peek out from beneath her gown. This was quickly followed by Diablo, which was followed by both dogs running out on to the stage yipping, growling, and chasing each other around the dress.

"Diablo! No!" Caprice hissed, trying desperately to maintain calm.

"Toy! Stop that right now!" I chimed in to no avail. At that point all bets were off. I broke character and went after the dogs, running, as best as anyone can run in couture, around the dress. I managed to wrangle them after several orbits around Caprice, but when I grabbed Diablo, his jaws were clamped to the edge of Caprice's cape. He pulled it off to reveal the shreds where the back of the gown should have been, which as an added bonus, highlighted Caprice's figure. It was an absolute booty fest.

A mass gasp nearly vacuum sealed us all to an early death by suffocation, and left the tent in deafening silence. Seconds ticked by until somewhere in the darkness, a pair of hands began to clap.

"Bravo!" shouted EFKALT, rising to his feet, followed by his assistant. One by one, the audience stood up to applaud the mad genius that was making his way out to the runway. The applause grew louder and louder into a deafening crescendo. Shouts of "Genius!" and "Brilliant!" filled the room. The doors burst open, admitting an army of crazed media and paparazzi. A million flashbulbs popped. Tossed flowers covered the stage at Jock Lord's feet. He was holding a sketch book. Caprice and I were wedged on either side of him. Jock Lord stopped momentarily to quickly erase the sketch of Nicole Kidman, and in a jiffy replaced it with Caprice. He turned to the television cameras, holding Caprice tightly, then flashing a million dollar smile, he turned the sketchbook around in the direction of everyone and said, "Meet my new muse!" to which more flowers, gasps, and general ecstasy rose up from the frenzied audience. Then he looked over at me holding the dogs and frowned.

chapter eleven

Escape from New York

date: JULY 16TH
mood: GRAY

As in somewhere between black and white, neither here nor
there. In other words, limbo.

I let the purifying water wash over me. For one brief
moment, space and time disappeared; nothing else existed
in the universe but me. No cell phones, no Paolo, no
Brooke, no Spring, no Miss Stevens, no Mom, no Dad, no
country, no home, and no fashion. I was naked and alone —
pared down to my innermost, essential self. It had only been
a few moments earlier when a ray of dawn light broke
through the window, where I'd been seated, huddled with my
PowerBook and bathed in sweat at the kitchen table, for the

last eight hours, laying out my Jock Lord coverage, running on the few last fumes of what I hoped would be the last all-nighter of my life. To say that I was beyond spent would be an understatement, as these last few days, sleep, tranquility, and self-esteem have been rare commodities.

I ran a Ted Gibson orchid-infused hair sheet through my damp mane, wrapped a fresh towel around my body, and then it hit me. If I hurry, I can just make the 8:10 train to Greenwich. So I quietly ran down the hall to Evie's bedroom. She'd been up half the night with me, poor thing, poring over all the photos from the Jock Lord show. Evie did a great job and I couldn't wait to send them to Mick, even though I wasn't sure what his reaction would be. Deep down I knew that our photos were sensational and my coverage of the show was the best I'd ever done. I just prayed that Mick would feel the same way. I took a big chance and included some of the street scenes I'd shot over the summer along with some shots of Evie's brilliant collection as well. Who knows, maybe he'll like them.

I scribbled my future whereabouts on a Post-it, stuck it to the Gummy Vites bottle on Evie's nightstand, then headed back to the kitchen, determined to finish my reportage.

I started writing my cover letter to Mick. When I really thought about it, the show had eventually worked out fabulously for Jock Lord and, best of all, for Caprice, big butt and all. Backstage after the show, Jock Lord made it official when he offered her a contract to be the new face of the entire Jock Lord brand, including cosmetics, fragrance and the Jock Lord Couture and Ready-to-Wear Collections. I mean in a few short hours, Caprice would be the hottest supermodel on the planet. And as much as I wanted to go to the after party, I decided to get back to Villa Fantastique and finish what I set out to do.

I was a hair away from e-mailing my report to Mick, waffling back and forth between adjectives, when the phone rang.

"Imogene!"

"Hi, Mom," I said wobbly.

"Where have you been? I've left messages all over town for you. I don't know why we pay for that cell phone of yours if you never answer it." I couldn't think of what to say, but, probably due to my vulnerable state, I suddenly felt the strongest urge to confide in her. I wanted to tell her I was getting on a train and coming home, that I was leaving New York for good. I wanted to tell her everything.

"I called your office yesterday and some nice boy named Malcolm told me that you weren't in. Are you feeling all right? Has something happened?"

"I'm fine, Mom," I said with the last drop of fakiness in me. "Listen, Mom . . . I . . ."

"Honey, before you say another word," she said breathlessly, "I have to tell you the most amazing news. Are you sitting down?"

"Yes. I'm sitting down."

"Your father is finally having his own gallery show! Isn't it just thrilling news, sweetie?!"

I was dumbstruck.

"Imogene, are you there?"

chapter twelve

You Go-ddess, Girl

date: JULY 16TH

mood: REFLECTIVE

"If you can see your path laid out in front of you step by step, you know it's not your path. Your own path you make with every step you take. That's why it's your path." —*Joseph Campbell*

I couldn't hold Toy a nanosecond longer. As soon as I opened the taxi door, he went completely bonkers—his little legs hit the gravel and he and Booboo were off. All the familiar sights, sounds, and smells were so reassuring to him. Me too.

I grabbed my Kate Spade straw weekend bag, tipped the driver what little change I had, and headed toward the front door. The cottage glowed in the summer sun and a warm feeling

rolled over me. If I had to put it in a word, I would call it "appreciation."

I assumed I'd find her in the kitchen in front of the TV as always, but I was wrong. Before I reached the front door, it swung open and Mom appeared and my mouth nearly dropped open, not because Toy skittered past me, almost knocking me off my feet on his way upstairs, but because she looked so un-Mom-ish. She hugged me hard, like she hadn't seen me in years. Until now, I hadn't realized that I missed her as much as I missed Dad. I hugged back tight and didn't let go. Suddenly all my tension drifted away and for the first time in a long time, I felt like I was home.

"How'd you get here so fast? Dad was just getting ready to pick you up at the station." Truth was I couldn't wait a second longer. After Mom called this morning, I dashed my report off to Mick, crossed my fingers, and jumped into a cab. And before you could say "reverse commute," I was in Greenwich.

"Wow, Mom, you look amazing." For once I wasn't lying. The yawning style gap that had always been a wedge between us had, in an instant, grown a tad narrower.

"I had my hair done. Do you like it?" she asked, atoning for the sins of a lifetime. I mean I've only made it like my entire life's work trying to convince her to lighten her mousy brown hair with a few well-placed highlights—as anticipated, they really brought out her beautiful eyes, which, for the record, were twinkling like mad.

"I *love* it Mom!"

She took my bag and led me into the kitchen.

"Isn't it wonderful about your father?" she said, setting my bag down on the center island. Before Mom called, I must admit I had a temporary lapse of maturity. Assuming I'd be the center of attention, I thought that I'd just go home and cry on everyone's shoulders. How childish. And how thrilling about Dad's news.

"How did it happen?" I asked, anxious to hear every detail.

"Just like that really," she snapped her fingers. "One day, out of the blue, Nini called, just to"—she reflected wistfully, then her eyes lit up—"chat! We hadn't talked like that in years, and well, one thing led to another." She sighed happily. "She casually mentioned that her set decorator needed some original art for the show and asked if your father would mind a studio visit from her production team. Well, the set decorator had an art dealer friend, who turned out to be a really big art dealer friend, and the rest, as they say, is history."

"Wow!"

"We had no idea it would be this spectacular though. He's already sold all of your father's black-and-white drawings and pre-sold several canvases."

"Oh Mom, that's so exciting! Dad must be thrilled! Is he in the studio now?"

"These days he practically lives there. He's still got some

painting to do, but he'll be ready by the time the art movers arrive. He can't wait to see you. He's so proud of you, dear."

Mom always tells me how proud Dad is of me, but my heart practically stopped when she added, "And so am I." I mean, who was this person? "Now, I want to hear all about Hautelaw. Oh, and by the way," she said, "I've never heard of Fashion Day. What exactly is that?" She knew. "Is the garment center really closed or is there some other reason you're not at work today?" Thankfully at that moment, Dad sauntered in. Great timing!

"There's my butterfly!" Dad shouted. I know. It's a smidge embarrassing, but it's been his pet name for me since I was a baby. He reached out to deliver one of his famously big bear hugs.

"Hey, Dad—congratulations! I'm so happy for you!"

He wrapped his arms around me. "Thanks." He grinned. "So . . . let's have a look at you," he said, stepping back. "You look like a million bucks! As usual." No matter how old I get, I always blush when my dad compliments me—always will.

"Your mom and I are so proud of you. I just know you're setting the world on fire!" I held on tight as he hugged me again. I was beginning to feel better already. No wonder Mom fell head over heels—he's kind, and gentle, and the sweetest dad in the world. The last thing I wanted to do was make them unhappy (again) with my miserable life. Especially now that he's finally getting the break he deserves.

Affirmation: From this point on, I will appreciate having such caring parents; and most important, I will try harder than ever to make them proud of me.

"We've missed you so much," he said in the tender voice he always reserved just for me.

"Me too," I said with a trickle of guilt.

Dad wrapped his other arm around Mom's shoulder, pulling us into a Dad sandwich, and stealing a kiss from her.

"So . . . when do we eat?" Dad asked Mom, who had begun peeling carrots.

"About fifteen minutes."

"In that case, it's back to the salt mines! We'll have a real chat over lunch, Im." He kissed Mom's cheek and winked at me and was gone. There was a long, silent pause in the kitchen. Without Dad around as the buffer zone, it was just Mom and me and my nagging subconscious. I tried to put recent events out of my head, but they just wouldn't go. I struggled, trying to work up the courage to tell her I was fired. Her radar was unfailing.

"Imogene," she asked, "is something bothering you?"

"Uh . . . no . . . ," I said, nervously crunching the carrot Mom handed me, "I'm just excited about Dad's show. I mean I can't wait to see his work hung in a real gallery."

The urge to unload my baggage wouldn't stop nagging me. I just had to tell her the truth and then it happened. Before I could think about it, I just sort of gurgled something like, "I was fired."

Mom's reaction was blank. I wasn't sure if she heard me so I said it again, this time with more conviction.

"Mom, I was fired." It was weird. She had no expression whatsoever. I mean, she was completely calm—unnervingly calm! Too calm!

Then finally she said, "Go on."

So I did, and once I started, I couldn't stop. I told her everything. It just gushed out like some long, pent-up volcanic eruption. I told her how I'd lost my cell phone. I told her about Brooke and the Wolfe Pack and my new friends, Caprice and Cinnamon, about Jock and Mick and Missy Farthington. It just poured out in one long-drawn-out continuous lava stream. Finally she spoke.

"Imogene," she said opening the kitchen door, "why don't we sit in the garden, where it's cooler." About to acknowledge her suggestion, a brilliant flash of color caught my eye from the open door. The rambling old roses which formerly had been a jumble of dried out thorns against a row of old wooden post fencing were in full, luscious bloom, as were the wisterias, jasmine, peonies, poppies, phlox, lupines, lavenders, and foxgloves. The two cherry trees that had been planted a century ago and so far sprouted only an occasional blossom were now bearing heavy bundles of fruit. And the perennially overgrown lawn that at this time of year would have been fried to a crisp was groomed and . . . green!

"Mom, your garden . . . ," I said, whirling around to face her at the kitchen door. "I can't believe it. It's stunning!"

"Yes, I know," she said, holding two iced teas, leading the way to the patio set beneath the huge Japanese maple that had been my favorite tree since I was little. "Isn't it something?"

"But how?"

She set the glasses down. Dappled sunlight danced across her hair, forming daubs of rich gold and red. She was still beautiful.

"I've done a lot of soul searching since you've been away. And this"—she gently waved her hand at the intense greenery,—"is the result. Imogene, when you did that with the credit card, your father and I were so disappointed in you."

"I know, Mom."

"When a person receives something without going through a process of earning it, it hurts them. Not today or tomorrow maybe, but eventually. That's why your father and I insisted you work this summer instead of spending it with your aunt." Her brow furrowed. For the first time, I think she felt guilty. "Look, I know it's fun shopping and having beautiful things, but that's just icing on the cake. Money and things do not define a person. In time, it makes you lose sight of what you really are." She looked sideways at me; a tentative smile barely flashed across her lips, then disappeared. "Besides, you have something money can't buy. You're like a candle . . . you just glow. Not because of what you wear or how many pair of shoes you have in your closet. You're a talented, wonderful, caring, and gifted human being—and you're driven. And I admire you very much for that."

Mom leaned forward to touch a tiny bud on a nearby gardenia bush, its green leaves sprinkled with tiny drops of water. "The mistakes and dramas you're going through now are just a learning process. You're growing. You'll come out of this a better person than you were going in."

I felt good and bad all at once and I didn't know what to say, so I just sat there and blushed.

"Oh. And one more thing," she said.

"What's that?"

"I love you very, very much."

"In spite of everything?" I asked, fighting back tears.

"I love you *because of everything* you are."

"But Mom," I heaved, "I just feel so lost right now. Like . . . lost like I've never felt before. I mean, before I was always so sure of myself. I never questioned it. But now . . . I'm not sure who I'm supposed to be. I don't know where to look."

Mom nodded her head, thinking. Then she raised her eyes to mine and spoke softly, from someplace deep inside. "You don't have to look anywhere, Im. All you have to do is listen. Because what you're looking for you already have . . . in here." She patted her heart and smiled.

When did my mother become Yoda?

Then she suddenly brightened up and asked, "So . . . when are you going back?"

"What?" I was stunned. After all these years we're finally getting close and she pushes me away?

"Back where?"

"To Hautelaw."

"Hautelaw? Mom, they fired me, remember? I can't go back. There's nothing to go back to."

"You have to fight for what you want, Im."

"I did fight, Mom. I fought all summer."

She looked at me carefully. "You've always known what you wanted. And you've always been right about it. Go back to New York, Im. It'll be all right, you'll see."

We sat in silence for a moment.

"There is one other thing," I paused, trying to come up with a sentence to best describe my feelings. "There's someone I like very much, someone I can't stop thinking about."

"Is his name Paolo?" The surprise overwhelmed me. How did she know about Paolo?

"You don't have to look so surprised Imogene, I read 'Page Six' too—Noodle Girl."

I must have looked completely dumbstruck because she started laughing, and then I started laughing, then we both cracked up for a long time.

When the laughing finally died down, I asked her something I'd wanted to know my whole life.

"Do you have regrets about . . . you know."

"If you're talking about marrying your father, the answer is no. I haven't regretted that choice for one second. I knew it was right for me. And I didn't care what anyone else thought."

"How will I know?"

"You'll know. Your heart will tell you."

And I had known. At least I thought I had. I mean my heart had been crazy about Paolo from the very beginning.

"Look, Mom, I know what you're saying, but Paolo—"

"Don't be so sure about him, Imogene. Sometimes people are not what they appear. Besides, hearts never lie."

Maybe if I had listened to my heart in the first place, none of this would have happened. But none of it mattered because I knew I'd never see him again, and for the first time in my life I was coming to terms with reality. I wondered how long hearts stay broken.

✳ ✳ ✳

When my train pulled into platform 24 at Grand Central Station, I was beyond shocked—Mick was standing right there, waiting for me.

"What are you doing here?" I asked in disbelief.

"There's no time to talk . . . we're late," he said urgently, grabbing my bag, and my elbow, shepherding me in the direction of the main concourse, while I held tight onto Toy.

"Late for what?" I said, dragging my feet while Toy made a low growl.

"For our deadline. I'll explain everything to you shortly; right now we have to hurry." Why is everyone I know completely mad? "Suffice it to say that I know who the spy is and that Paolo is innocent."

"Did you say Paolo? Is innocent? How do you know about Paolo and what do you mean he's 'innocent'? And where are we going?" I asked again, beyond bewildered.

"Just trust me," he said. "I know who's been selling us out—and it isn't you."

"*I* could have told you that."

"You did. Not in so many words, but with the coverage you sent me. Which, by the way, was spectacular."

"Really?" My heart sang.

"Yes, really. But we have to go."

We hurried across the great room, past the clock, but it didn't feel like walking anymore. It felt like floating. Like I was lighter than air and could float all the way up to the ceiling and touch the painted stars. I was innocent. And Mick knew it, which meant that Spring knew it, which meant that . . . calm down, Imogene.

"Imogene! Waaaaaaaaaaaaaaaait!" Evie's voice echoed across the station. Okay, weird and getting weirder. She was running toward us like crazy in a crinkly vanilla paper bib dress that looked like a used FedEx envelope. With her tangled, newly colored pink and red hair wantonly clipped with baby barrettes, her vanilla and pink striped anklets, and pink pumps finishing off the ensemble she looked half-lollipop, half-human. By the time she caught up with us, we were heading out the door.

"Stop for a second," she panted.

"What are you doing here?"

"Didn't you get my message?"

"No, I—"

"Listen girlene," she said panting. "I know everything . . . and you have to listen, because . . . your boss . . ."

"Spring?"

"No, what's her name . . ."

"Brooke?"

"Yes. She and that Wolfe Pack girl . . . what's her name?"

"Candy?"

"Yes! Well, I have the evidence right here, and . . . what on Earth were you doing in Greenwich anyway, you dope! You're never going to believe this. I know the truth about Paolo because he's for real. He came over looking for you. Together we got it all figured out . . . and . . . I know how you're going to get your job back. I have evidence on Brooke. Luckily your mom told me what train you were on."

"Isn't anyone going to introduce me?" Mick said.

"Oh, I'm sorry," I said, flummoxed. "Evie, this is Mick. Mick . . . Evie."

"As in, Mick from Hautelaw?"

I looked at Mick, who was staring in more than an amused way at Evie. I mean it was bad enough she looked so weird . . .

"Are you the famous Evie Goldstein Nakamoto?"

"I'm Evie," she smiled devilishly, tickled by the sound of that, "but I'm far from famous."

"Well," Mick said, "not if I have anything to do with it."

Evie and I exchanged puzzled glances, though if Mick was thinking what I was thinking, I was about to jump out of my skin. "Your collection is wonderful!" he said.

"Where did you see it?" Evie asked, confused.

"Oh, Evie sweetie, I umm, hope you don't mind, but I sent Mick the snaps of your collection." I had submitted it for the "Up-and-Coming Designers" section.

"Right, in fact I'd love to feature you in the next issue," he said, checking his Cartier Roadster watch.

"OHMIGOD, really? Wow, are you serious?!" She looked at me, then Mick, and then me again. "That's incredible! Thank you!" Evie gushed.

"Thank Imogene. She's the one with the great eye," he said with a wink. "But if that book's ever going to see the light of day, we have to hurry, ladies. Malcolm is pasting it all together as we speak."

Evie and I squeezed hands and exchanged a quick silent squeal of joy. Evie smiled at me sweetly, her eyes tearing, a faint line of mascara ran down her cheek.

"Here." I handed her a tissue.

Mick said, "We've only got a couple of hours. If we hurry, Sidney can pull a proof tonight. So let's go ladies," he said, picking up my bag. "Time is running out!!"

"Wait!" Evie suddenly screamed. "I completely forgot why I met you at the train!" She dove into her bag and pulled out Cinnamon's karaoke mic. "Paolo didn't *do* anything! Listen!" She flipped a switch, pressed a button, and the mic began to play back a stream of garbled noise until suddenly the icy voice of Brooke began to speak.

"That little [static here] doesn't have a clue. She thinks Renzo's son sold you the pictures. [Laughter] Of course, I knew *Spring* would fall for the whole thing. She's even more clueless than that [more static here] from the suburbs. Besides, it serves her right for not hiring Fern and Romaine in the first place." Evie flipped off the mike and beamed.

"Cool, huh?"

"Where did you get that?" Mick stared at her in amazement.

"We used it to get into the Jock Lord show. It must have been on record the whole time I was in the audience. I hit the play button by accident and this popped out. Who knew?" she shrugged.

"You must have been sitting right next to Brooke without even knowing!"

Mick smiled coyly. "I think I have the perfect image to go with that."

The art department was like tornado season in Kansas. Papers, swatches, dummy layouts, and font styles covered every surface. Malcolm sat at the far end staring into a flat screen monitor a tad smaller than a football field.

"Okay, this is what I want the two of you for," Mick explained as we picked our way through the piles of flotsam and jetsam that covered the floor and stood behind Malcolm.

"How are we doing?" Mick asked quietly.

"See for yourself," Malcolm said, lightly clicking the mouse. In a nanosecond a layout filled the screen. MY LAYOUT!

Blazoned across the page was the title "An Insider's Guide to the Jock Lord Comeback Collection." I was beyond stunned. I think my pulse even stopped for a few seconds.

I was so proud, but I wasn't sure what the reaction would be. I held my breath as Mick exclaimed, "Fantastic!"

"I'm kvelling!" gushed Malcolm, with Ian nodding.

Evie said, "Fantastic!"

Mick said, "Let's see the rest."

Malcolm flipped through the spreads, each one better than the last, while Evie and I watched in awe.

"I don't understand," I said breathlessly. "I thought the book was at the printer already."

"I pulled it after I got your coverage," Mick said. "Nobody else has this material except us. We've been working on it for the last thirty-six hours and we're not going to

press without it. That is, of course, with your permission."
He raised his brows at Evie and me.

Evie and I stared at each other for a second then grabbed
hands and jumped up and down screaming "Eeeeeeeeeeee-
eeeeeeeeeeeeeeeeeee!!!"

"That would be a yes," laughed Ian.

"Show Evie 'What's Haute,'" Mick said, and with a flick
of the mouse another layout opened, entitled "What's Haute,"
which featured Evie's entire Goddess Collection. It was
beyond gorgeous.

"Evie," Mick said, "I'd like you to sit with Ian for a little
while and give him some thoughts about your collection. You
know, what you were thinking, your inspiration, for the edi-
torial, if that's okay."

"Are you kidding?!" Evie gushed. "Try and stop me!"

While Evie was off giving Ian insight into everything from
fashion to diet to the best way to assemble a salmon skin hand
roll, Mick, Malcolm, and I settled down to work on the last of
the pages. At one point Mick looked at Malcolm and nodded.

"There's something else you need to see, *maideleh*,"
Malcolm said, handing me a proof sheet filled with pictures.
I leaned forward.

"Look familiar?" Mick asked.

They were all my photos. Mostly street coverage—some
that Haute & About used in their report, others from Soho
House the night I lost my phone.

"Where did you get these?" I gasped.

Mick reached in his pocket, pulled out my cell phone,

and handed it to me. For the second time that evening I was stunned.

"Where . . . ?" I stammered. Malcolm held up his infamous key ring and grinned from ear to ear.

"I accidentally found it in the back of Brooke's bottom drawer."

"Brooke had it?" I could feel the hairs on the back of my neck starting to tingle. "Brooke, as in the Brooke that works in this office?"

"We found these, too." Malcolm handed me a stack of telephone messages and notes—every one addressed to me, and every one from Paolo.

I could feel my face flush and my hands tremble. I was beyond livid; I was broiling. I think I literally staggered.

"Brooke's been intercepting my messages? He really did send me flowers, and my phone?"

"Apparently."

"*Nisht uguteh*," Malcolm noted.

"Before you go ballistic about Brooke, and you have every right to," Mick said soothingly, "I want to impart some ancient wisdom to you. Something that sages have known since the dawn of time."

"And what would that be?" I hissed.

"As you sow, so shall you reap."

By 2:00 a.m. the last trickle of adrenaline was just about spent. Ian was asleep under the conference table, Malcolm was fiddling with a last-minute font change, and I was sitting next to Mick, head propped up, listening as he gave final instructions to Sidney, the printer.

When he got off the phone, he pulled open his desk drawer and handed me an envelope.

"What's this?" I yawned.

"Compensation."

"For what?"

"For your brilliant coverage."

I opened the envelope, and just stood there staring at the figure in the middle of the check, because it did not register.

"But . . . it's a fortune," I gasped.

"It's what we pay all our contributing editors," he said matter-of-factly. "No more, no less."

I'd never seen that much money in my life . . . not in person, anyway. I mean, it was the equivalent of my entire summer's salary times ten.

"This is some of the best work I've ever seen," Mick added. "And your 'Street Trends' were spot on. But the Jock Lord coverage . . . well, thanks to you, not only will we scoop everyone else, it will enable us to get our clients back. I knew you were amazing the first time I saw you. And so did Spring."

"But she fired me."

"Yes, sorry about that. You might be surprised to know this, but she suspected Brooke all along, we just needed proof." He turned to the Jock Lord coverage and said, "Does this girl look familiar?"

"Yes, that's—"

"That's Candy Wolfe—Winter Tan's right arm, and look who's sitting next to her," he said, pointing to a teeny spec in the audience.

"It's Brooke!" I shouted. "And she's sitting right next to Evie! But I thought we didn't get an invite."

"We didn't. With the evidence on your mic, Evie, and this picture, well I guess you could say we've got our proof."

"What do we do now?"

"The only thing we can do now is wait."

"Mick," Malcolm said, poking his head in the doorway, "I need you to see this one last thing." Mick blew me a wink and he and Malcolm were gone. So I curled up on Spring's sofa with Toy and Evie (both of whom were snoring loudly), and I found myself pondering bedtime prayers that hadn't been spoken since I was a little girl.

The last thing I remember before losing consciousness was, did Mick say "contributing editor"?

chapter thirteen

The Darwin Code

date: JULY 20TH

mood: EVOLVE OR DIE!

I mean it was too awful. The gossip, the thievery, the plotting, the backstabbing, the Machiavellian scheming. And the doors hadn't even opened yet!

Hundreds of hipsters, fashion students, trendy moms, couture-dressed-(sub-zeros) (and I'm not talking refrigerators), stiletto-wearing women, and a smattering of well-groomed young men, waited anxiously in a line that stretched around West 17th Street, and down Seventh Avenue, and ended somewhere near the South Pole. Every one of them was desperate to get inside the Barneys Friends-and-Family-Super-Saturday-Sample-Sale-on-Friday.

It had been a long night's journey into day. Like good little fashion junkies, Evie, Cinnamon, and I had made a

235

concrete plan of attack for the sale, including getting there the night before with lots of stuff—teepee, sleeping bags, Coleman stove—to make sure we'd be rested and comfortable. We didn't end up getting there until midnight, which did not exactly constitute getting one's beauty rest. Then there was Evie's teepee, which was especially nice during the pre-dawn hours when we hunkered down in our little cradle of comfort. We reviewed the basic guidelines to sample sale etiquette, which are:

1. There are no rules.

2. Only the strong survive. Nowhere on Earth is the mantra me, myself, and I more applicable.

3. Adrenaline is your ally.

4. The best time to go is just after that wicked fight with your assumed boyfriend. You know, when he says he wants to date other people.

5. This is no time for a fashion detox. That's what New Year's resolutions are for.

6, 7, and 8. Rainbow dyed cashmere is a complete CLW (can't live without). Dip-dyed crocodile is a complete DO (daily obsession). And last season's tea-dyed peasant skirts are a complete no-no.

9. No claiming. Only non-pros do that.

Well, all of this thinking about sample sales made me feel a little queasy. I mean, for one thing, we were somewhat far from being first on line, like fifteenth or twentieth or something, and I was seriously worried that everything on my CLW list would be gone by the time we got in. On top of that, Caprice had the tickets and like should have been here an hour ago. I had already called her cell several times, but she didn't answer. Major stress aside, there was something else going on and I couldn't figure out what it was. I mean under normal circumstances I would be approaching a state of pure bliss by now, thinking about the abnormally large bank deposit I made yesterday, and the final payment I made to Miss Stevens—yay! And as a personal reward to *moi*, the deeply gratifying shopping spree I was about to *sooo* dive into. But for some reason the thought of it wasn't the least bit satisfying. Which was totally incomprehensible to me so I instantly banished any doubts from my mind.

I checked my watch again. It was rapidly approaching eleven a.m. Where was Caprice? The line lurched forward a couple of baby steps, causing anticipation levels to skyrocket. This crowd was beyond psyched.

We stowed our teepee in a conveniently provided storage locker near the entrance (once again, Barneys thinks of everything!) and were whiling away the last remaining minutes reviewing the rules for sample-sale-ing, when an out of breath Caprice found us just as the line began moving again.

"Listen, here are the tickets," she panted.

"Aren't you staying?" I cried. I really wanted her to be with us today.

"Can't. So much has happened since the show. I have a million go-sees today. We're shooting Jock's ad campaign before Fashion Week begins."

"Ohmigod!" Evie practically screamed in my ear.

"Oh, and you'll never guess what else." The three of us waited breathlessly. I looked around and noticed everyone within a fifty-yard radius was also listening breathlessly. "I'm walking the Dolce show in Milan!!!" she shrieked. The surrounding crowd broke into wild applause. Caprice bowed with mock seriousness.

"That's wonderful!" we all shrieked back.

"*Mira*, I have to run." She shoved the tickets in my hand. "Good luck and call me later!" As she turned to leave, she spotted Margaux, our shopaholics guru, in the crowd and waved.

"Remember," Margaux hollered. "Don't go crazy!"

Suddenly the main door opened. A deafening hush fell over the crowd and the ranks closed tightly. Very tightly. The pungent aroma of *eau de bargain* oozed out of the celebrity dermatologist-administered pores of a million nearby fashion zealots, filling the air with the promise of cheap chic. Then, without warning, *ready, aim, shop!!*—the line shot forward, hurtling us inside like human cannonballs.

Once inside we headed toward the tables. Which designer one gravitates toward is quite revealing about one's innermost state of mind. For instance, if you find yourself heading straight for Dior, you're chic, but probably a tad mentally unstable. If it's a Zac (Posen) attack, you may suffer from attention deficit disorder. If you can't help yourself with Chanel, you suffer from princess envy. And if you choose Prada, you're most likely dying to be popular.

We, of course, headed straight for Prada, which, unfortunately, turned out to be mostly bags. I mean hush-hush time, but of late, "it" bags have started to have a strange effect on me, as in, they make me gag. I mean why shell out like $2,000 for something that is going to be so five minutes ago in like two minutes?

"There's nothing here," Evie said, pulling me toward the next table. I was just about to stuff a gorgeous Gucci dress in my basket when the rudest person grabbed it right out of my hands, which is completely out of bounds!

"I claimed that!" the wild-eyed maniac barked.

"You can't claim anything at a sample sale!" I yelled, grabbing it back. "Duh! Haven't you ever heard of rule nine?!" I shouted after her.

"Back off my dress, creep!" screamed yet another woman.

"That's mine!" snapped a third, grabbing it as a school of fashion piranhas grappled for my dress. Cutting my losses, I dove into the adjacent Pringle of Scotland table (Pringle makes me tingle!) drowning my sorrows in gobs of cashmere. Score! I found the most irresistible argyle twin set and matching panties.

Before I could show Evie my fabulous find, I heard "DIOR-GIOUS!" from Evie. She held up the chic-est, one of a kind tie-dyed, crocodile Dior bag and beamed.

"JACKPOT!!!" I hollered. The bag was one of a limited edition number in the $18,000 range. "Maybe if we all chip in we can time-share it," I added sarcastically.

"Girlene, look!" she yelled in complete disbelief. "Can this be right?"

The price tag read $400. Unfortunately, in her blissful excitement, Evie let her guard down and before she had a chance to react, an over-buff 20-something snatched it.

"Hey give that back!" Evie shouted, lunging forward and yanking it from the miscreant's hand.

"Girlena!" she hollered. "Help!!!"

The two of them were now locked in a battle to the death. I put my feelings about "it" bags aside and joined the brawl. I mean this was about honor and fair play, God and country, the inalienable right to shop.

"Let go, you little twirp!" hissed the savage. She elbowed Evie in the left rib, knocking her into another savage, who was in the middle of a Chanel grab-fest at the next table.

"Hey!" yelled savage two. "You made me miss that sequin camisole!" She braced herself to shove Evie but stopped abruptly as her eyes lit on the Dior-gious bag. In a flash her expression went from anger to menace—then she pounced. Evie reeled back in horror.

"Evie!!" I waved my arms and she lobbed it over the head of savage two.

"Get her!" she screamed.

I caught it and ran like a halfback heading for the end zone. Savage one swung around and cut me off near the Narciso Rodriguez table. I was trapped. Cinnamon came barreling down the aisle, full speed.

"Hang on, Im!" she shouted, throwing a full body block at savages one and two.

"OOOF!" They went down together, knocking over shoppers like bowling pins as they skidded across the floor. Hard-won merchandise scattered everywhere as women fell on top of one another. Nearby shoppers seized the opportunity for extra goodies, pouncing on the stray items, creating an even larger pile. As I stood there clutching Dior-gious and staring in disbelief, security disentangled bodies from the ensuing melee. I glanced over at the table next to me. "OMGICAN'TBELIEVEIT!!" I screamed. "Evie!"

"What?!" she hollered from somewhere beneath the pile.

"Evie! Look!" I held up a brand-new, unscathed pair of bright red Lanvin shoes. *The* Lanvin shoes. The same ones I borrowed from Bee. The same shoes I've carried with me like a carcass since day one of my Hautelaw life. Maybe they've been reincarnated, I thought. All this time I had been so afraid to confront Bee knowing I couldn't replace them.

After the riot police had left, I pushed my cart up to the register. It was now filled with Pringle cashmere; a classic Chanel bag; the replacement Lanvin shoes for Bee; books; and a heavenly pink J. Mendel mink shortie jacket and mini pleated chiffon skirt—shades of Tinsley Vogelzang's capelet (but chic-er).

When I got there, that queasy feeling started again. My heart began pounding and my palms began to sweat. At first I thought it was adrenaline leftovers from a morning of extreme shopping. But the more I thought about it the more I realized this fashion-burdened zealot wasn't me. At least not anymore. Maybe Dad's butterfly was finally beginning to emerge from her chrysalis. Maybe I was changing. When all of this finally clicked—when the message from my heart made it all the way up to my head—

I knew I was leaving behind one life and entering a new one.

I abandoned my wagon, taking only the Lanvins and a couple of nice books I had picked out for Mom and Dad from the Rizzoli table.

"I'll just take these," I said to the cashier. She raised her eyebrows in disbelief.

I mean, after a lifetime of fantasizing about this very moment, well, I changed my mind. Just like that. Right there in the middle of the most wonderful, insane madness I had ever imagined.

I hate to think what menopause will be like.

Well, I thought Evie would have a thermonuclear meltdown when she saw what I had done — or rather, hadn't done. It shook her to the core. I, on the other hand, was experiencing a new thrill. I mean, I absolutely can't believe the rush of excitement I felt just by saying no. It was completely weird. I felt free as a bird.

Now that all that was settled, it was time once and for all to replace the dead pair of Lanvins with the brand-new pair, size 6 and 1/2 and return them to their rightful owner.

I put the new pair in my bag — the old pair had been in there so long I didn't even think to remove them. I was almost out the door when the phone rang. It was Mick asking if I could stop by Hautelaw for a few minutes.

"There's something I need your opinion on."

"No hints?" I asked playfully.

"Better you should see it in person," he said.

I jumped on my scooter and headed uptown in the last of the summer heat—Jeffrey first, then Hautelaw. Bright, hard late summer light was just beginning to soften, giving way to the warm, dreamy radiance of the first hints of autumn. But, like everything else in New York, summers don't give up without a fight, and I was glad to finally breathe the air-conditioned ecosystem of Jeffrey.

"Bee said to tell you she'll be five minutes." The pretty concierge smiled warmly, hanging up the phone. "Can you wait?"

"No problem."

"Feel free to shop around and I'll direct her to you when she gets downstairs."

"Thank you," I smiled back.

I just couldn't help taking a peek at the new inventory. A month ago I would have died for these glittery ruby red Mary Janes, or these Sonia Rykiel red sequined pumps, and would have found a way by hook or by crook to have them. But now, not even the assemblage of the world's chicest styles could have tempted me to break my budget. And yes, you heard correctly, I am in the process of creating a budget. I, Imogene.

"Hello, Im," Bee's voice was flat.

I spun around to face her. She looked completely adorable, smiling her cute little bumblebee smile. Her classic pearls, flattering pink knit twin set, voluminous print skirt, and chic Chanel double C pink-and-black flats gave her trademark china doll haircut an au courant vibe.

"Hi Bee," I said, lamely. There was a long, uncomfortable pause between us while we just stood there staring at each other. "Bee, I'm so sorry. I don't know what else to say. I mean, it's not like I forgot, well, not exactly anyway. I just lost my phone, well, actually it was sort of stolen, and, well, I knew I had to return the shoes but something happened to them on the way to my interview and, well, I was afraid you'd be really angry when you saw them. So by the time I finally found a new pair it was, like this morning, and I knew you were calling me and, well, here they are."

I reached in my bag and accidentally pulled out the tattered pair of shoes.

"Oops," I flushed. I quickly shoved them back, but Bee's hand shot out and stopped me.

"Wait! Let me see those!" she shouted. Customers stopped and stared. What the hell, I thought. I may as well explain the whole thing in grisly detail.

"Bee, I'm so sorry it took me so long to return these, but more than that I'm really sorry for what happened to them. But not to worry, because luckily I found the exact same pair . . . so here." So I offered her the new shoes but instead she remained transfixed by the tattered ones, and a big smile returned to her face, even bigger than the first one.

"Oh Imogene, thank you!"

"Oh, no, no, don't thank me," I said briskly. "It's the least I could do. I'm the one who should be thanking you."

"No, I mean thank you because these shoes are exactly what I'm looking for! In fact I have a meeting in twenty minutes with our design team. I don't know if you've heard or not, but Jock Lord's new show was all about tatters. They're the latest thing. He's calling it 'rich little poor girl.' How fabulous is that! He's *soooo* brilliant! I would have died to be at that show. Anyway, these shoes are exactly what I'm looking for!" she said giddily, holding up the shoes for us both to inspect. I stood motionless, waiting for the next surprise. (I was going to say that I was waiting for the other shoe to drop, but how corny is that?) "In fact, I'd really like to bring you in on the meeting. Can you stay a little while?"

"Wow. Umm, I'd love to but, I have to be somewhere soon."

"I'm disappointed. Well, of course I'll tell everyone who the genius is behind the shoes and let you know how it turns out. I'm sure they'll want to meet you, though. You have so many great ideas . . . so maybe you can come back another time?"

"Sure . . . why not?"

"Okay. I'll call you. See you soon. And Imogene, thank you again!" she said, hugging me in last burst of gratitude. "I can't wait to show them off!"

Walking into Hautelaw was a totally different experience that day. For one thing, I felt like a different person—cleansed, morphed, turned inside out, a little older, and much wiser. I mean, knowing what I now know, I didn't feel the tiniest shred of firsthand embarrassment or insecurity like I had when I first walked through these doors. It was as if I had finally stepped into my own shoes.

I headed over to the temp receptionist—Derek or Jason or Oliver or whoever Spring's flavor of the month was.

"May I help you?" he asked.

"*Shayna punim!*" Malcolm's voice trilled as he hurried toward me with a big hug while slyly winking over my shoulder at Oliver, who stared at him in horror. He took a step back and sized me up. "My, aren't you looking quite the gorgeous young thing!"

"Just for you," I laughed. I had on a sexy little Conspiracy Eight top I'd borrowed from the new and improved politically correct Evie and a funky chic pair of embroidered Brazilian jeans that totally emphasized my figure (which I don't remember having until recently), along with a stunning pair of ultra strappy Dolce & Gabbana sandals, donated by Caprice, who had them sent over direct from the factory.

"We're going to meet in Mick's office," he said as officiously as ever, and headed down the hall with me in tow.

"Who's we?"

We rounded the corner and headed into Mick's office. At the far of the round table sat Mick, his feet propped up on his desk and a big grin on his face.

"Glad you could make it," he said. "Nice ensemble."

"Thanks," I blushed.

Deborah leaned against a huge built-in cabinet, her arms folded, a knowing smile playing on her lips.

"We've missed you, Imogene," she said.

"I've missed you too, Deborah."

Mick nodded to Malcolm, who closed the door.

"I thought you might want to see this," he said, pulling a thick tome out of a drawer and setting it on the desk in front of me. It was the fat new Autumn/Winter book.

"Hot off the presses," Malcolm said excitedly.

OHMIGOD! The cover was one of my Blue Village shots—pictures I shot in the East Village while looking for the perfect shade of blue. The whole book was so fat and juicy and totally TDF I didn't know what to look at first.

"So this is really it . . . the real thing?" I asked, hungrily flipping through the pages. "Malcolm, your layouts are gorgeous! I mean, it's all gorgeous. And it's for real." I started laughing.

"It's for real," Deborah started laughing too.

Mick leaned forward and flipped to the front of the book.

"This is what I wanted your opinion on." He pointed to the masthead and scrolled down to my name, which I was flabbergasted to see, but then he pointed to the line directly next to it, which read, "Senior Intern and Contributing Editor." As Malcolm would say, I nearly *plotzed*!

"I can't believe it," I said softly, shaking my head. "I can't believe what I'm reading. Mick . . ." I turned to Malcolm and Deborah. "Guys . . . I don't know what to say." I was laughing again but this time I could I feel tears welling up.

"I'm the one who doesn't know what to say," Mick stood up. "Except, thank you."

Of course, right in the middle of our touching moment, who should barge in unannounced but Brooke.

"Hey, what's going on? Oliver told me . . ." Her voice trailed off as she spotted me and her eyes hardened into ice. "What is *she* doing here?" she asked, working hard to conceal a snarl.

"I invited her," Mick said casually. She stared at him them

spotted The Book. "Is this The Book?" She snatched it up. "Why didn't anyone tell me it was here?" Her voice gained volume (or was it panic?) as she rifled through the pages. "Wait a minute, this isn't the layout we agreed on. Whose pictures are these?" Definitely panic. When she hit the Jock Lord coverage her mouth dropped open.

"Did you see your picture?" Malcolm pointed to a small insert of Brooke and Candy Wolfe sitting in the audience. "Right there."

Brooke looked up at him. "Where did you get this?"

"Oh, Imogene's friend shot it at the show."

"Her friend? What friend?"

It was Deborah's turn to jump in. "Her friend with the karaoke microphone that also acts as a recorder."

"Karaoke recorder? What are you talking about?!"

"The one that recorded you telling Candy Wolfe what a nice job she had done with Imogene's pictures. You know, the ones from her cell phone." Okay. I was stunned, as in could not move because what I was hearing was impossible to believe.

"I don't have her cell phone," Brooke snarled.

Mick nodded to me and I pulled out my phone.

Imogenious!

"See, I don't have it. She does!" Brooke argued.

"But where did it come from?" Mick asked. The color drained from her face. Malcolm pulled his hand out of his pocket, a key dangling from his finger. Brooke started, "You've been in my drawers?!"

Malcolm pursed his lips. "I have no interest in your

drawers, honey. Your desk however—" At that point my cell phone rang. Mick leaned toward me and whispered, "Let me get that for you."

Mick casually flipped it open.

"Hello?" he said lightly. "Oh, hello Spring. Yes, she's here." He looked at Brooke and smiled pleasantly. "Speaker?" He looked at me and raised his eyebrows.

"Uh, right side, push twice then green," I said, amazed that I could remember much less speak. He pushed the buttons and Spring's voice boomed out of the tiny phone.

"Can you hear me?" she asked. Somewhere in the background people were chanting.

"Yes, we can hear you," Mick said.

"Good. Listen, I'm in the middle of my daily chakra therapy so I only have a few seconds. All I have to say is Imogene, you're hired! Brooke, you're fired! Gotta go."

Mick flipped the phone shut, grinned at Brooke, and said, "Spring gets all the fun jobs."

Suffice to say that after Brooke was gone, which took ten rather intense minutes of drawer slamming, door banging, and muffled cursing, things calmed down a tad. Well, as calm as they get in the fashion-forecasting business.

On my way out Mick stopped me. Holding out an engraved envelope with my name written in the most luxurious script, he said, "I almost forgot. This came for you this morning."

"What is it?"

"Your last assignment of the summer," Mick said. I slowly pulled out the elegant, deckle-edged stationery. It was a VIP invitation to the Glamonti fashion show.

"What? This is Paolo's father. I can't go to this."

"Why not?"

"Are you kidding? I accused his son of selling my photographs to Haute & About. Oh, yeah, and there's that little matter of dumping a bowl of rice noodles on his head."

"I saw the article. I haven't laughed that hard in ages."

"Oh God. You see, everyone knows. Besides, as soon as they find out who I am, they'll throw me out."

"They sent you the invitation, didn't they? I'm sure they know who you are."

"Well, I can't go anyway." I said, feebly trying to hand the invitation back to him. "It's the same night as my dad's opening, which I wouldn't miss for the world."

"Your father's opening is at six-thirty—I'm going, remember? The Glamonti show doesn't start until eight. You have plenty of time." He pushed the invitation at me and walked away. I made a face at him.

"I saw that," he said.

chapter fourteen

Imogene Rising

date: AUGUST 1ST

mood: TUTTO POSSIBILE!

Having your feet on the first rungs of the ladder of success is absolutely breathtaking, as long as you're wearing your chic-est Louboutins!

Gifts in hand, I swept through the gallery doors into another universe, where the frisson of excitement overflowed like icy champagne froth, gushing down the floral-etched side of a magnum of Perrier Jouët. Wall-to-wall people of every ilk packed the cavernous gallery tighter than a Japanese subway car. The already too loud DJ offering bounced off the hardwood floors and pressed tin ceilings.

Dad's gallery opening was looking like a clear and unequivocal success and my heart was spilling over with happiness, because after all the years he spent as a struggling artist, no one deserved it more. I spotted one of his paintings and I remembered how I'd sit in his studio doing my homework when I was little. His paintings were always haunting and beautiful, but in this gallery, his work was transformed somehow—larger, more important. And here, on this night, they became what they had really been all along: magnificent.

Through an opening in the crowd, I caught a glimpse of a waiter and went straight for him.

I held my breath (due mostly to the nauseating jumble of assorted perfumes, food, alcohol, and body odor which combined to set off an olfactory mushroom cloud), and thrust myself into the mob weaving my way between a dramatically feathered, Philip-Treacy-hatted, modelly girl and a belly dancer. When I finally reached him, he sighed and asked the obligatory question, "Something sparkling?"

"Thank you," I said, helping myself to one of several fluted glasses elegantly arranged on his glistening silver tray. I was barely able to move let alone sip, by reason of the constant barrage of people jostling me from every direction.

In the midst of a deftly executed half-pirouette around a man wearing a fez, my cell phone rang.

"Girlena!"

"Evie!" I stopped and shouted over the roar. "Where are you?!"

"Over here!" Craning my neck, I did a 360 on tippy-toes and spotted her at the food table (*quelle surprise!*), and waved. "Have you seen my parents anywhere?!" I asked.

"What?!" It was virtually impossible to hear over the din.

"Don't move!" I hollered into the receiver. "I'll be right there!"

I began moving in her direction, battling arms, feet, and the occasional stray elbow when a familiar throaty wail cut through the clamor.

"*Imoooogeeeeeeeeeene!*" A dense blue cloud of smoke, which could have been mistaken as the onset of a nor'easter, announced Spring's arrival. "Darling!" she cried, parting the crowd with grand swatting gestures. She was sporting a new "do" . . . and a new hunk. Open-shirted to reveal a major six-pack beneath hairless pecs, he wore skintight jeans, chains, and had curly, wild, shaggy hair. He oozed major rock-and-roll vibes, but he was clean, very, very clean. Mick, Malcolm, and Ian followed in her wake. "I've been looking everywhere for you!" she boomed, and stepped in front of a passing waiter. "And where do you think *you're* going?! There are people dying of thirst here!"

He rolled his eyes and lowered the tray.

"Oy, there are more male models here than at an Elton John barbeque," said Malcolm.

"You look like you just flew in from Paris," Mick smiled, handing me a glass of bubbly.

"Ditto," Ian added.

"Thanks," I blushed. The new me decided, if I couldn't go to France at least I could look like I'd been there. So here I was, in a very sweet, very borrowed from Evie, and, judging from the looks I got coming in, somewhat passé Anna Sui sundress—which I must admit, complemented my post fashion-rehab glow. It was last season's and I was proud of it because my new motto is: accessorize! I mean, just like French girls who wear the same clothes over and over and over again until they are absolutely filled with holes, but nobody cares because they have such great accessories. How chic! And how cheap! And how very French!

"Dahling, you out-poor the richest little poorest . . . poorest little rich . . . well, however it goes," Spring said flustered. "Anyway, you look fabulous. I just knew when I first saw you that shreds would be making a comeback. And speaking of Jock Lord, your coverage of the show was *absolutely fabulous*!" Spring beamed. "Everybody's talking about it. Do you know, three of our old clients have called us for appointments next week? And that's just the beginning."

"We're meeting with Jock Lord himself," Mick jumped in, "as soon as he gets back from his spa retreat in Abu Dhabi."

"I can't wait until you-know-who hears about it." Spring rubbed her hands together and chuckled.

"I'm *sure* Brooke will tell her," Malcolm said.

"Oh God! Don't mention that name!" Spring leaned backward as if to faint but lit a cigarette instead.

"What do you mean?" I asked.

"Didn't you hear, *maideleh*," Malcolm drawled. "Brooke's gone over to the dark side — not that she wasn't there already."

"She's working for Haute & About," Mick added, ". . . officially."

"Big surprise," Ian murmured.

"Imogene, dear, I simply *must* apologize for our little misunderstanding. That horrible"—Spring's eyes flashed as she struggled for words—"Brooke person was simply not to be trusted! I blame myself. If I had *only* worked harder with Madame Blatskovitch I would have known she was the traitor! I think the Kaiser was trying to tell me all along. He never liked her, you know."

"Well, anyway, we hope you can forgive us," Mick said.

"And, of course, you'll come back next summer!" Spring smiled her beautiful, big smile, looped her arm in Mick's, and stood there with Malcolm and Ian, happy and crazy—the most wonderful, wild people I've ever met.

"I can't wait," I said, suddenly feeling the urge to cry.

"What happened to you?!" Evie popped out of the crowd panting. "I didn't think I was going to make it over here. I was like, almost crushed to death!"

"Who is this strangely adorable creature?" Spring asked, eyeing Evie carefully. "And *what*, exactly, is she wearing?"

"Oh! Spring!" I jumped in. "This is my best friend, Evie. She's the new designer you featured in 'What's Haute.'"

"Of course you are!" Spring said extending a hand. "I thought I recognized that . . . uhm . . . what exactly do you call what you're wearing?" Well I had hoped Evie would actually wear something a bit more fashion pro, like a very grown-up Valentino ensemble, for the occasion. Unfortunately, or fortunately, depending how you look at it, she was completely coccooned in bubble wrap.

"It's from my latest collection." Evie leaned forward. "And if I can just give you a word of fashion-forecasting advice," she said confidently, as I intuited a fine print moment coming. "Imogene, are you listening?" Busted.

"Yes, Evie, I'm listening."

"By all means," Spring whispered as we both leaned toward her, waiting for the fine print moment.

"Plastics."

"Plastics?" Spring stared at her with rapt attention. "You mean . . . like TupperWare?"

"Evie, didn't you hear me? This is Spring Sommer . . . my boss." I nudged her, hoping she'd realize that she owed Spring a very big thank-you. Finally a spark of recognition ignited and she said, "Ohmigod, Spring! Spring Sommer! I can't thank you enough for putting me in your book. You and Mick, I mean. When my dad saw it, he finally agreed to let me be a designer!"

"When did this happen?!" I screamed.

"I just left him! Girlena, no more restaurant business for me!"

"Eeeeeeeeeeeeeeeee!" we shouted, jumping up and down, popping a few bubbles along the way.

"Listen, Evie, you have to help me find my dad," I said.

"Your father? Of course!" Spring bellowed. "I'm *dying* to meet him! I adore art you know. I once dated a gorgeous painter who *only* did nudes."

"Where is he?" Mick asked. I looked around, I knew he'd be wherever Mom was and vice versa.

"They should be right over there," I said, pointing to the camera lights and sure enough, Mom's head popped out of the crowd for a nanosecond. "There's Mom!" I said, motioning for everyone to follow. "Over by the camera crew."

"There's Nini!" Spring said waving.

"Good luck, girlena," Evie frowned.

"Don't be silly, ladies!" Spring took a determined puff and blew a pillar of smoke skyward like The Little Engine That Could. "C'mon!" she hollered, and plunged into the crowd. The going was slow but steady, and before you could say Francesco Scognamiglio three times fast, we reached a ring of onlookers surrounding the boom mike. At the center of it all stood my dad in front of one of his massive paintings, washed by the hot lights of a video camera, chatting easily with a reporter.

"Out of the way, dahlings!" Spring practically slugged an art critic from the *Village Voice*, pushing her way to the center.

"If you don't mind, I'm conducting an interview here," Missy Farthington said coolly.

"We don't mind at all," Spring laughed charitably. "In fact—"

"Are you ready for a surprise?" Nini asked Spring. "It involves you too Imogene. And your mother."

"Spring?" my mother, who had been standing off to the side chatting with Nini, stepped forward. "Spring Sommer?"

They stared at each other in disbelief.

"Isabelle?" Spring whispered.

"Well, I was hoping to do this reunion of Les Trois Coquettes a little differently," Nini said, wrapping her arm around my mom, "but since the cat's out of the bag . . ."

"That's who you've reminded me of all this time . . . ," Spring shrieked at me while making a mad dash toward Mom. "Isabelle!!"

My mom was the third Coquette? Okay, so I was totally blown away. I mean it couldn't be. My mother knew Spring

Sommer, who knew Nini, who knew my mother, who knew Spring. Confusing.

Well, everyone stood around looking at the three of them, wondering what a Trois Coquette was and in general waiting anxiously for something to happen. Finally, the three of them exploded with an ear-piercing "*Eeeeeeeeeeeeeee*!!" accompanied by a great deal of jumping up and down and simultaneous screeching chatter. I think at that moment they were 16 all over again.

It was cool. I mean the three of them hadn't been together for over . . . well, since like their GCA days. I guess I never mentioned Spring's name to my mom and dad.

Speaking of my dad, in the excitement I completely forgot about him and Missy Farthington, who was busy taking all this in—which is to say, checking out each one of us for celebrity status (just in case.) Her gaze abruptly stopped on Evie, then darted to me.

"You!" she hissed, "Both of you!"

"You know these two?" Dad asked in surprise.

"Know them! This one tried to impersonate me!" she pointed at *moi*, then at Evie. "And this one tried to pawn herself off as my producer!"

"Really?!" my dad said seriously, but I could tell he was enjoying himself.

"That's not the half of it," Missy huffed. "They masterminded the takeover of a McDonald's . . . in Greenwich!"

Suddenly, her voice fell away into abrupt silence. Music, talking, and clinking glasses, were replaced by hushed voices and muffled gasps that grew ever closer to our little group. Something had officially stopped everything and that something was heading our way.

A breathless murmur rose as the crowd parted and Caprice sauntered into the circle, her sparklingly beaded, nude colored, ultra-sexy, shredded JL couture gown accentuating her ample figure in discreet and tasteful glimpses. Men swooned.

"Hola, *chica*. Sorry I'm late," she said casually. "Not a day goes by during which I don't get hit on, flirted with, or blatantly checked out," Caprice complained. She averages at least three marriage proposals a week.

"Well no wonder," I said. "Don't you believe in bras?"

"They give me a headache."

"When are you leaving?" I asked, referring to her latest success. *Vogue* had booked her for a feature story. She'll be in Belize for a week.

"Tomorrow," she said squeezing my hand excitedly, "and when I get back, I start the Jock Lord cosmetics campaign, and then I'm shooting the ready-to-wear campaign for *next season*."

"This time, though, no sharks!" I said, hugging her tightly,

"Imogene, I can't thank you enough. It's all because of you . . . every bit of it!"

The silence was broken and from there, the party went into high gear.

"I want *all* these people, everything on tape," I overheard Missy whisper frantically to her crew. And she got it too.

After that, I mean everyone went crazy—at least that's what I heard on the late news. As for *moi*? I left early. I had a show to catch.

So there I was, standing outside the Glamonti show, invitation in hand, watching people go in. And why was I just standing there? Well, let's see, because maybe I was a tad nervous about seeing Paolo after publicly humiliating him. Oh yeah, and his sisters—I was sure they'd be overjoyed to see me again too.

To be perfectly honest, all I wanted to do was go back to the gallery and party. Unfortunately, there was this annoying new person inside of me, and this person wanted to jump out of my skin and scream the truth in my face. Deep down inside, I really had never believed Paolo did any of the stuff I accused him of doing. Then the annoying new person inside reminded me that kisses never lie.

I went inside.

The lights dimmed. I picked up the description card lying on my reserved front row seat just in time to read that the theme of the show was "Happy in Love." Ambient music gently wooed the crowd. Models appeared, as if conjured up out of blackness, and seemed to float down the runway in contemporary versions of classic couture. Stunning. But, after all, that was Glamonti's reputation—nothing trendy, just drop-dead, gorgeous style without any hype. It was a look that never grew old, only more refined year after year.

So there I sat, front row center, transfixed by one dazzling form after another for who knows how long.

The last group down the runway was the bridal party. The first bride was resplendent in a pure white fluffy confection so ethereal, it took my breath away. Its train was embroidered with flower garlands that circled the dress asymmetrically. Her veil was trimmed with pure white Chantilly lace. As the model got closer, I noticed that embroidered across the skirt, in exquisite, flaming deep crimson script, were the words *Amore' e' Imogene!* The model came to a full stop in front of me. I didn't know what to do. I just sat there blushing. The second bride followed suit, coming to a full stop directly in front of me. Her dress had slightly different words embroidered in large red script on an enormous white crème anglais meringue waterfall of a skirt. This time, the script read, and I quote, "Je t'aime, Imogene!" The third and final bride came down the runway. Her skirt read "Paolo Hearts Imogene." She was accompanied by Renzo Glamonti and the previously awestruck crowd went completely and inexorably . . . happy! Between shouts of "Bravo!" and "Bravissimo!" he disappeared, and in his place, out popped Paolo. He looked at me, placed his hand on his heart, and smiled the kind of smile that warms you in places you didn't know you had. Then he reached out his hand for me and, well, I stepped onto the runway and took it.

I put my lips to his ear and whispered, "It doesn't matter if you were a poor factory worker when I met you even if you weren't. . . ."

"Where did you ever get that idea, my sweet girl?"

"From you of course," and then, in midsentence, before I could say another word, he kissed me.

The last thing I remember after that is standing on stage surrounded by a galaxy of flashing cameras and the roar of applause, kissing Paolo for what seemed now, as before, an eternity.

Manifest Destiny

date: AUGUST 30TH

to: TOUT LE MONDE

from: MOI, IMOGENE

Affirmation: A coeur vaillant, rien d'impossible! (With a brave heart, nothing is impossible!)

Never let it be said that fate doesn't happen to a girl such as I. Okay, so maybe it takes a few unexpected twists here and there, and a smidge of emotional turmoil, but eventually you get there. As in, *Bonjour Paris!* Yes darlings, it's true. Evie and I are *absolument pas* in Greenwich anymore!

After I paid off my debt to Miss Stevens, I still had lots of cash left over—enough to go to Paris! So when Mom read the letter from Miss Stevens stating that my debt was paid off in full, how could she say no?

For the record, Paris is a veritable orgy of deliciousness right now and my CLW list has definitely reached critical mass. Evie and I have been busy shopping, eating, and getting invited to many, many *fêtes*. How? Well, it doesn't hurt to have a smidge of minor celebrity status. After all, there's nothing the French revere more than a kiss. Since so many photographers shot the Happy in Love kiss, Paolo's dad decided to use it for their fall fashion campaign. So now designers send me clothes — for free — which instantly solves any future credit card conundrums. I mean, I'm absolutely having kittens. I have more than a girl could possibly need, so now it's me that gives clothes to the GCA charity gift shop and my personal use-by date just got a tad shorter.

As for everyone else, Cinnamon has a whole new career ahead of her. After Dad's opening and the Glamonti show, everyone met up at the after party at Cinnamon's favorite karaoke restaurant. Caprice broke the ice with her rendition of "Material Girl" en español. Les Trois Coquettes did a Spice Girls medley, and Spring and Renzo crooned a rendition of "Just the Two of Us." But when it was Cinnamon's turn, the room settled down and without an ounce of stage fright, she belted out "Hero," and her voice was nothing short of phenomenal!

Yes, it's true. Evie's dad finally let go of his ancient ideas about what she's supposed to do with her life and has hired her to design the uniforms for all his restaurants, including the London McDonald's. Apparently the new Greenwich McDonald's was so successful that Evie's dad bought it. And the London franchise and the whole town is *raw-ther* abuzz with anticipation.

Dad's gallery show was an enormous success and he's committed to exhibits all over the planet for the next five years. Mom's garden was featured in *Greenwich Magazine* and word is that Martha Stewart will be dropping in for a peek. Mom, Nini, and Spring have pledged to have regular Coquette-fests to keep up their friendship. Paolo is back in Italy until school starts, after which he'll be back in New York. And with only 26 miles between us, we already have our next 52 weekends planned.

Well altogether, it's been the craziest summer of my life. Of all the things I learned, the most important is to follow your love no matter what the cost. For to be a true *jolie femme* is surely to love, and that is the most fashionable thing of all.

Heart,

Imogene!

Fade to black (which is the new black — really!)

Don't miss Imogene's next adventure!

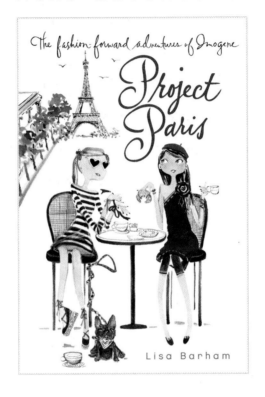